THE SCRAPER

Where Evil Meets the Road

Henry "Mouf peez" Williams

THE SCRAPER

IN LOVING MEMORY LEROY HACKETT
April 1, 1942 - October 6, 2010

SUMMARY THE SCRAPER
"Where Evil Meets the Road"
by
Henry "Mouf peez" Williams

Dorian Jackson is a young, inspiring athlete with dreams of riding a full scholarship. The doors are wide open to any university of his taking. Until he severely injures his knee, spiraling his dreams to the cold Vallejo, California streets where he finds a new, but reluctant passion. The criminal enterprise is Dorian Jackson's new game under the street name "Doe Getta," and hustling mhhhand getting money hand over fist is his agenda.

Dorian's high school sweetheart Deltrice Glaude, who is a Haitian immigrant, follows his triumphant rise and fall. She watches in horror as his promising career shatters like glass as the streets take hold over the Dorian she loved and knew.

Deltrice's feelings towards him went unnoticed until she casts a Haitian love spell on him, which has adverse effects. Dorian begins to love her unconditionally but money is Doe Getta's first love.

Caught up in a drug deal gone bad by jealous enemies who Deltrice personally knows, it would seem that Deltrice's love spell has paranormal consequences. Has Dorian's soul been avenging his own death, and by what means?

CONTENTS

PREFACE

It was May 18, 1986, and the streets of Port-au-Prince turned from desolate to chaotic in less than sixty seconds after Jean-Claude "Baby Doc" Duvalier was forced to resign from his seat as president. Corruption and repression crippled the poor nation of Haiti as wide scale emigration forced out its educated classes. Burning tires doused with gasoline cast an eerie demonic glow against the exotic Caribbean tropical weather.

Cars flipped with crushed windows; smoke billowed from melted plastic and scorched upholstery. A hostile crowd of looters with lead pipes, torches, and Molotov cocktails zig-zagged from one storefront to the next, smashing windows and quickly setting fire to them. A woman watching from a balcony, high above a cul-de-sac stepped inside and quickly closed the heavy glass doors, locking it and pulling the curtains.

"What's going on out there Mommy? I hear bad noises," said the young native girl in her native creole.

"It's just bad medicine from a bad doctor," responded the worried mother, referring to the ousted Haitian president. She glanced at the news on the large screen as it showed footage of the riots first-hand. "Hurry up Trice! Now be a big girl and put on your coat for Mommy okay? Today is your special day because you have a flight to the states," she said, grabbing her daughter's passport along with several pairs of clothes and an assortment of toys.

"You mean a real airplane?" Deltrice screeched with delight, clapping her small, soft hands. Her face suddenly grimaced in an impish way. "Mommy, you said it was my special day. Is it your special day too?" Trice asked, putting on her jacket and waiting for a response. Trice's mother quickly flipped over her wrist and looked at the time on her yellow diamond, presidential Rolex watch.

"We have twenty minutes," she said out loud. "No, honey it's only your special day. Mommy is not coming with you." Trice grimaced, her face turning instantly to terror as her mother gently picked her up, stroked her silky pigtails, and comforted her by pinching her cheeks. "It's okay Trice, somebody will always be with you."

"Are you, ar-r-r are you sure?" mumbled Trice.

"Of course I'm sure honey. You will be treated like the little princess that you are, and someone will meet you when your pretty little feet step off of the plane."

Loud shattering sounds came from the kitchen below. Fearful screams followed as the fire alarm and sprinkler system activated. Vera tucked the plane ticket into her purse and grabbed her daughter's luggage in one fluent motion. "Come on honey!" Vera began to walk quickly to the door, and then stopped dead in her tracks, listening like a wild animal does when an intruder breaches the perimeter. "Dem focken blud clot peasants. Dem in me house!" Vera screamed, dropping everything, and stared at the closet, sucking her gold-crowned teeth. She walked toward the closet, fumbled around the top and pulled out a polished chrome Russian-made AK-47. Vera released the extended black magazine with another magazine securely taped to it and inspected the ammo. Vera blew the dust out of it, tapped it on the butt of the rifle, and aggressively chambered a round.

All that training under Jean-Claude in the jungles should pay off, she thought. Another noise and then footsteps sounded. "Stay behind me Trice. Okay!" she demanded, picking up her purse and slinging it over her shoulder like a military medic bag.

"What about the big bag Mommy?"

"Leave it Trice, there is no time," she whispered, pulling the bedroom door open and pointing the heavy barrel in the direction they walked. Vera turned around tapping her finger to her lips, instructing Trice to be quiet. The hallway led to the stairs and into the living room. When the estate was originally built, a carport was positioned in the back of the kitchen so that the live-in chef could have easy access to the supplies. Now it was their only escape route if luck were with them. Vera slowed her breathing and loosened her grip on the trigger to avoid slip-ups.

The living room was ransacked as burn marks pelted the soggy new carpet. Drawers were opening and closing, and voices came from the kitchen as they approached. Vera stopped and pressed her back against the wall and peered in. She captured very detail as her eye quickly scanned the room. A machete was propped against the oven as a man stood near, making a sandwich. He had a .40 caliber pistol tucked in his waistband, at the small of his back. Two others were rummaging through the walk-in refrigerator. Her heart was beating like an angry drummer and she had a dry metallic taste in her mouth right before something violent was going to go down.

"How's the sandwich?" she asked, lowering the menacing rifle at center mass of his exposed, boney chest. The target looked up in total surprise as crumbs fell from his ashy lips. In desperation, he vainly reached for his gun as she lit his boney chest on fire. The sound of the assault rifle cackled to life like a pack of South African hyenas after tearing off a piece of fresh, bloody meat from a new kill. Like cardboard, the rounds tore through him instantly, shredding their way through the wall behind him. As the other intruders responded to the kitchen, she pulled the awaiting trigger and a spray of bullets wen about, dismembering human limbs and exploding skulls like overripe watermelons. Upon impact, bowels spewed across the floor towards the other two intruders as the body landed hard on it. Another intruder quickly grabbed a kitchen knife and threw it at her with lightning speed, missing her neck by inches as it splintered the wood next to her. She dropped to the floor in the prone position by trained reflex. She saw another intruder fumbling for the gun at his dismembered partner's waist. She aimed and squeezed off two rapid rounds in succession. One to this head and the other to his partner's ankle, which exploded upon impact.

"If yah bloody asses can't stand deh heat then stay deh fock out me kitchen!" she blurted venomously, switching the rifle to fully auto. And as she squeezed the trigger, the two bodies danced and jumped as they turned to two bloody pulps of mangled flesh. Smoke rose from the hot barrel as the smell of gunpowder permeated the large kitchen. Deltrice uncapped her ears and observed the destruction her mother caused. Her observation interrupted by an excited "come on!" as she felt a sudden pulling on her small arm. Vera slipped on the entrails, barely catching herself as she picked her daughter up and straddled her on the side of her shapely hip. Shards of shattered glass blanketed the nicely manicured grass as she stepped outside and ran down the white marble steps leading from the kitchen's exit to the carport.

Fumbling with her purse, she found the car keys and unlocked the padlock to the garage revealing a midnight blue Porsche 941 special edition. Vera quickly unlocked the door and Trice crawled in, sat in the passenger's seat, and buckled the awkward seat belt.

"You see honey, you're a big girl." The little girl smiled, showing her gums and a few pearly white teeth that were coming in. "That's my girl!" Vera said, leaning over and kissing her forehead.

Vera set her weapon in the back of the car and closed the door. The engine came to life as she pushed the clutch in and found first gear. As they peeled out, gravity wrapped them into the soft leather bucket seats. Before turning out the alley onto the main road from the estate, she turned on the radio for updates on the rioting.

"The United Nations has issued Martial Law in Port-au-Prince until order is restored. Anyone caught looting, or even loitering in the streets after the 10:00 pm curfew, will be shot."

Vera shook her head a the news brief and stomped on the gas, sending the powerful sports car into a wild fish-tail, just missing an overturned burning car by inches. Awkwardly, Vera looked at her watch to check the time.

"Baby, we still have time for you to catch your flight!"

CHAPTER ONE:

SPELL IT OUT

PURSUIT AND SEDUCTION ARE THE ESSENCE OF SEXUALITY. IT'S PART OF THE FIRE.

Deltrice sat at her desk in front of her flat screen monitor as she surfed the internet. She typed "Doe Getta" in the search engine's small field and within seconds, a page full of results appeared on the large screen. She proceeded to click the first one. A T.I. song came on, "You Can Have Whatever You Like." A looped video clip of Dorian bending a large stack of crisp $100 bills appeared; letting them fly at the camera like a magician's deck of playing cards. There was no audio from the clip, but she could read his lips as he chanted, "Doe Getta nigga!" After reading his biography, she then ran through hundreds of pictures in his photo gallery until she chose the one she wanted, highlighted it, and pressed print. The printer warmed up, clicked, buzzed, and pushed out an 8 x 11 colorful picture of Dorian standing next to a GMC Denali truck on custom 26' rims. He had fanned out a stack of hundreds underneath each shoe as he stood above them. The caption underneath read, "You got to have new feet!"

"He always has a gimmick," Deltrice mumbled to herself. She smiled and tenderly bit into her full lips, pulling the picture from the printer. Her firm hips swayed under her pink, silk nightgown as she walked towards the room that she prepared. It was dim except for a hint of candlelight. Positioned in the middle of the room was a square table with four large candles burning, each placed strategically at a corner, which represented the four elements: earth, wind, fire, and water. A small cast-iron bowl resembling a wok sat on top of a wooden stand directly in the middle of the table. Deltrice placed the photograph in it and picked up a velvet pouch from underneath the table. She reached in and pulled out a handful of wild red rose petals and tossed them into the bowl. Next, she took out a long stick pin and jabbed the tip of her left ring finger and watched as blood bubbled to the tip. Holding it over the bowl, she allowed it to drip. Putting her finger in her mouth, she sucked on it a few times to stop the bleeding. Next she threw freshly ground coffee beans and a piece of her thick pubic hair into the awaiting bowl, then lit each end of the picture with each candle. Chanting something in French, Deltrice circled the table three times as smoke billowed and spiraled to the ceiling.

There is one more ingredient that will make my love spell complete, she thought. She walked to her bedroom, pulled out a variety of sex toys and neatly laid them out on her bed as she stepped out of her gown. Laying back, she grabbed the nearest toy. Her back arched as one hand gripped the brass headboard. Gyrating her hips, she stared at the mirror on the ceiling as the studded tip of the toy massaged her pink, wet clit. "MMMMMMMMMHHHHHH!" she moaned, and her body shook uncontrollably as she curled her pedicured toes and her body writhed in pleasure. The intense heat within her affirmed that she had succeeded in producing the perfect orgasm. White cream oozed like sweet shipped cream from in between her soft inner thighs. She slowly pulled the toy from out of her and grabbed an empty cosmetic compact from under her pillow. Opening it, she scooped her love juices into it and closed it.

Dorian fumbled with the rental car keys as he sat waiting for his pill connect. He stared at the digital clock on the dashboard as he tapped on the steering wheel. "There he goes with his 2 Fast 2 Furious ass!" The exhaust was loud and ear splitting as Tran pulled into the pharmacy parking lot in a tricked out, custom blueberry 2007 Acura Integra. Dorian spotted him and slowly parked next to Tran and rolled down his window.

"What's good pimpin'?" Tran asked in a heavy Vietnamese accent.

"Supply and demand buddah, supply and fucking demand. Plus, I wanted to peep that new shit," Dorian said, showing a row of princess cut diamonds embedded in the upper and lower row of his ivory white teeth.

Tran had this distant look in his eyes, as if he'd seen a lot of death in his life. His ties reached as far as the Triads in central China, but the risky heroin trade was not lucrative to him yet. Once he got a work visa, which allowed him to enter the United States, he obtained his pharmacy technician degree and took street pharmacy to a whole new fucking level.

"Get in! Me got dat, them thangs, that smack, Doe! Dem hoes will be trying to rip dem denims trying to see what's in 'em," he said, as if he was trying to rhyme or something. He popped his driver's side door as Doe got out, walked around his rice rocket and noticed his personalized California license plate, which read "A.K.A. 47." Laughing and shaking his head, Doe gripped the door and got in.

"Damn Tran, what the fuck is that smell?" Doe said, looking around as if he could see the aroma.

"Opium-flavored car incense my niggah," Tran replied as he reached over to the glove compartment and opened it up. Scales of a tatted Black Mamba snake spiraled around his thick wrist and inched up his muscular forearm and disappeared under his light blue pharmacy smock. "Hm hm, here, here!"

Dorian grabbed the three shrink wrapped medicine bottles with a false label of what the contents were supposed to be. He scanned Tran's handiwork, opened the top and poured out several fluorescent green, round glossy pills which resembled small beads. A small, lowercase "i" was stamped on each one.

"Ok Tran, you Vietcong mothafucka, you. I mean they're cute and shit, but do they smack budda?" he asked, pouring the pills back into the bottle. Tran eyed him for a second before he spoke.

"Look Doe, some niggahs push this shit coz it a fad. Me is a chemist brah. Me won't eat if my food ain't cooked right, yah dig? Peep brah, I put a 1-3 ratio of cut MDMA per every milligram. Don't let size fool yah; no-no-no," he said, shaking his head confidently while his long Mongolian ponytail whipped around and hit him in his neck. "What yah hold one pill 100 milligram brah. That why me call 'em i-pod coz it small lot of punch!" Tran demonstrated a right cross as if he was sparring with an opponent. Dorian let his words hand in the air like potent cannibus. "I give you joog, good joog—"

"Look buddah, I'm game huh!" Dorian pulled out a wad of crisp hundreds from his sock and tossed them in his lap. "That's two racks brah. I'll take two of these," he said, tearing the other prescription bottle from the shrink wrap. "You said that there are 300 per each bottle, right?"

"Yah, yah, three-hun, three-hun. You joog ten for ten, or pill for pill you win!" he said as he put the money in a neat stack, folded it, and put it in his breast pocket. "We good?"

"Yeah, yeah, we good buddah fo' sho!" They bumped fists, clinking each other's diamond rings in the process.

"One more thing my niggah." He reached into his center console and pulled out a glossy 4x6 flyer which had a half-naked model cupping both of her plump breasts with thick white smoke covering her pussy, revealing her sensual curves. She had a green glow stick in her mouth like a cigar and at the bottom it read, "First Annual Feel Me Fest." Dorian smiled for the first time and bowed the flyer between his thumb and index finger.

"That's what's up!" he said under his breath.

"Investor throw rave. See how me product do. Large scale, feel me?"

"Yeah, yeah, I feel yah," Dorian said, flapping the flyer as if he was waving at someone and glancing at the San Francisco address.

"You tell bouncer Tran-Tran said you on guest list. He let you in. No search." Tran looked at his Blackberry phone. "Fuck, I got to clock in brah."

"Shit, all this bread you eating and you're worried about being late for a job?"

"You see I don't ruin rapport with company coz I plan on owning a chain of these stores brah. Train and employ own people from homeland. Create own work force, yah dig."

"Well you know what Mr. Fucking Jimmy Choo, just make sure you got a liquor aisle for a nigga." They both laughed and parted ways.

Deltrice dried her long, silky, brunette, curly locks with a large towel as she stepped out the walk-in shower and put on a soft, terry cloth Polo robe. *Let me call this nigga Dorian so I can see if he will meet a bitch. Plus, my homegirls have been trying to get something for his Frisco Feel Me whatever festival. They have been talking 'bout this for the last month.* She scrolled through her cell phone until she ran across the name "My Doe-Doe." *Look at me,* she thought to herself, *I'm already claiming what is rightfully mine.* Before she dialed the number, she quickly texted him "one half purp and ten i's.

Dorian scanned the text as the incoming call came in. He had his phone directly hooked up to the car's audio so he could talk through the speaker hands-free as he drove. "What's this square want?" he asked himself. "Hello, what's good Trice?" The sound system vibrated as she spoke.

"Sometimes me, but all the time you, Dorian." He cringed when people called him by his first name, especially a pill-head knock, but he knew her from his football days at De La Salle.

"You got it ma."

"No, you got it," she said jokingly in her French accent.

"Well, where you at?"

"Meet me at Starbucks, off of Sanoma in about hmmmmmm 10-15 minutes," she said, grabbing her keys and blue Fendi purse and adjusting the Bluetooth headset in her ear.

"Girl, you got doe?"

"Of course, I got you."

If only he knew, she thought to herself. Ten minutes turned into 30 minutes as she sat in the back of the busy coffee shop nursing a raspberry Frappuccino with whipped cream. She stalled time and picked up a *Vallejo Herald Times* and glanced at her horoscope. "Proper preparation progress plenty rewards but like any black widow, don't wrap your prey up too tight because they might just suffocate." *Ouch*, she thought, taking a long swallow from her hot drink as her eyes scanned the next horoscope. "Your pursuit of happiness will run like the rivers of your heart, but a dam will be without your knowing." *Okay horoscope, I don't like you today, okay.* She folded the newspaper and tossed it on the table. She scanned the parking lot and watched a jet-black Honda Accord turn wildly into the parking lot, missing another car by inches. The door opened and a billow of smoke and Young Jeezy poured out. Dorian smoothly stepped out with a black tank top, designer denim shorts, and Jordan slip-ons. A long, diamond cut, gold Cuban link chain hung loosely from his muscular neck. His hair was neatly parted and braided in a unique style as two 2-carat canary yellow diamonds hung like lemonhead candy drops from each earlobe.

"There he is, with his fine ass," she said to herself, waving her hand through the tinted glass.

Dorian turned around and pulled a brown paper bag out from under his seat and sl'mmed the car door. He heard a loud knock on the glass as he walked towards the building.

"Aight girl, I see your thick ass!" he said stepping through the door and quickly assessing his surroundings as he walked to the rear table where she was sitting. "You forgot your sandwich at the house honey," he said, dropping the folded bag on the table next to her before taking a seat.

"Ahh, babe you shouldn't have. Here, take a look at your horoscope while I order us some coffee." She slid the newspaper over to him as she stood up, and he couldn't keep his eyes off of her. Her almond-shaped eyes and high cheek bones radiated exotically. Her naked, plump ass bounced underneath her transparent, cream-colored capris and her hotness captivated.

Her matching waist-length coat rode above the small of her back where a large tattoo of a Haitian flag revealed itself. Dorian snapped out of his trance and opened up the newspaper, counted the money, and stuffed it in his front pocket.

"So did you read it?"

"Read what Trice?"

"You know, the horoscope."

She sat back down and set two tall Frappuccinos on the table.

"Trice now you know a nigga don't believe in that type of shit. I mean, it's just a way to get people to buy newspapers, square."

She rolled her eyes and took a sip of coffee.

"How long has it been since I've even seen you Trice, five, six years?"

"The last time I saw you was at our class graduation in 2000, at De La Salle High."

He took a long sip and smacked his lips. "Damn girl, this shit right here, man, I'll fuck with this!" People began to stare like prairie dogs. "You still hang with ahhh, ah what's her name? You know, the thick, short Cambodian chick—"

"Suam!"

"Yeah, yeah that's her name."

"Yeah, that's my homegirl. We're roommates."

"That's what's up."

"So what have you been doing these past years since graduation?" she asked, but she already knew the answer.

Dorian pursed his lips sarcastically. "Girl, come on, you know damn well what a nigga been doing after I tore my ACL and lost my scholarship—"

"Dorian, ok baby, I can tell you're emotional about it, but you don't have to take it out on me."

"Oh no-no-no baby girl, it's all good. It's just that I know you've heard my name ringing in the streets. You've seen me getting it and you know who I fuck with. It's no secret, you know. The streets be watching and talking, you feel me lil' mama? If that wasn't the case, you wouldn't have got your brown paper bag of goodies."

He smiled as he stared into her beautiful light brown eyes. She squirmed in her seat as if her vaginal lips were being opened and caressed. She shivered.

"You ok?"

"Oh I'm fine," she said, looking away embarrassed then back at him.

"So where's the party at?" he asked as he looked down at his cell phone checking an incoming text.

"Ahh what party?"

"Ahh what party?" he mimicked. "Trice, you're a terrible liar. I know you're not going to pop all those pills and burn a half to the face. So who is it for, your dude or something?"

"Ahhh Dorian, I don't have—"

"Yes you do. You got a dude. I know you do."

"Like I was saying before you rudely cut me off. No, I do not have a man okay? And for your information, this is for Suam and her friends. They're going to this First Annual Feel Fest in the city they have been talking about for months and—"

"Oh yeah, yeah, my folks told me about that. He shot me a flyer and shit."

"Are you going?"

"Well, I don't know yet. Depends, that club life shit ain't really for me. Niggas don't be knowing how to act. You know, getting hyphy, jumping on top of cars and if they jump on top of my scraper, I'm going to give them a fucking liquid diet."

"So what *is* for you?" she said smiling.

He stood up and stretched. "To get paper! I'll be right back. I got to take a piss."

That was Deltrice's chance. She watched him as he disappeared into the bathroom, took out the compact, opened it and scooped out the contents with his wooden stirrer in his coffee, then mixed it.

"Don't ladies usually powder their noses in the bathroom?"

Damn that nigga was fast, she thought. "Ahh, I thought there was something on my face." She put on her most convincing face. He sat down and drank the rest of his coffee and smacked his lips, describing it as creamy.

"It seems like it got sweeter at the bottom, but anyway, I was thinking I may just go to that festival. We'll see…you feel me?"

CHAPTER TWO:

YOU WET

THE CARES THAT INFEST THE DAY SHALL FOLD THEIR TENT, LIKE THE ARABS, AND AS SILENTLY STEAL AWAY.

Dorian ran his index finger across the touch screen of hi cell phone, scrolled down to a name and dialed it. "Dave Stringer my white folks," he said under his breath. Dorian's uncle "The Hoist" had did time with Strings upstate and connected him with Dorian. Dorian had been buying the highest grade of purple kush from Strings for the last five years. Strings operated from a secret compound on fifty acres of land that he owed up in Mendocino County. Dorian scoffed as he thought to himself, *He's on some straight Nazi shit though, but he doesn't bring that white power shit towards my way. He knows fucking better. Besides, it's all about business. For one, he needs a black buyer and for two, the only color he should be seeing is green.* The line picked up on the other end.

"SCHWUR HEY MENSCH DU GOT DAS WEINTRAUBE BEREIT VIER MICH?" (Strings, hey man do you go the grapes ready for me?)

"HERR GELD JUNGE. JA BRUDER ES GOTTEN. DEIN DEUTSHCE SCHON. DU BRING DAS KRAUT UND DS GRUN IS DEIN!" (Mister money boy. Yes brother, it's good. Your German is beautiful. You bring the cabbage and the greens is yours.)

"JA JA. WORT OBEN HERR GARTNER." (Word up Mr. Gardener.)

They're always pulling niggas over leaving Mendocino County, so Dorian left about 1 am to catch the California Highway Patrol during their shift change. The two-and-a-half hour trip wasn't shit, especially when the reward of getting paper was well fucking worth it. The gravel crackled like sizzling bacon underneath his car's tires as he drove on a secluded dirt road. It snaked through an orchard of apple trees. There was no light except for the car's headlights. A glint or a reflection of two glowing eyes floated in the distance.

"That must be Strings' Rottweiler, Strafe." He looked down at his glowing cell phone screen. "Fuck, no signal. I can't see how this cracker operates without no signal."

From a distance, headlights turned on and off twice, indicating two pounds. "Oh okay, he's on some paranoid threat level shit tonight. Someone must have been snooping around his property trying to fuck with his plants," Dorian mumbled under his breath as he clutched the .40 caliber he had in his waistband to reassure his safety.

He pulled up to a camouflage Jeep Wrangler. Strings sat in the driver's seat smoking a cigar, wearing crisp army fatigues with a long gray and black full beard. Dorian rolled down the window.

"What's up Fidel fucking Castro. What happened? The United Nations pissed you off about the Geneva Convention?"

Strings laughed as his cigar glowed in the darkness. "You got jokes my friend? Ahhh nawh, some intruders tripped one of my motion sensors around my perimeter. I was just having a looksey." Dorian saw the AR-15 strapped to his back. Strings whistled loudly. "Strafe come." There was rustling in the bushes and a huge muscular Rottweiler bolted out of nowhere with a bloody cotton tail rabbit in its jaws and jumped in the back of the jeep. "Ah Strafe, you shouldn't have. You brought dinner. Follow me!"

The compound was in the shape of an octagon. The structure was three stories but from the outside it looked like a one story, dilapidated, old red farm house. They both pulled up, got out, and greeted each other with a warm handshake.

"Man Strings, it looks like your fat ass is losing weight!"

He took off his hat and rubbed his bald head covered in tattoos of wicked looking demon horns, snake scales, and human entrails. "Well my bitch left me, so I have to cook for myself," he said pointing at the Rottweiler with the bloody rabbit in its jaws. Dorian shook his head.

"I can only imagine what else he's been eating," he said to himself as a chill ran up his spine.

"You ever tried rabbit?"

"Nawh man, never."

"Well son, it tastes just like chicken. You had chicken before haven't you?"

"Fuck you Strings. There you go with the race card jokes and shit."

Strings laughed as he grabbed a heavy chain out the dirt and pulled it. A large opening was revealed with steps leading down into it. "Come on. Strafe du wache." The muscular dog crept slowly over to the opening and stood guard like a mercenary soldier.

Dorian followed Strings into the hole as he stepped down. Motion light sensors came on and flooded the whole hallway with an eerie yellowish light. The aroma of potent high-grade cannabis intoxicated him as he followed.

"Smells like money son," Strings said. The floors and walls were solid cement and adequately ventilated. Turning a corner, there in front of them was a steel door to a walk-in refrigerator. "Hold up, let me take my jacket off because its' pretty humid in there."

He put his coat on a makeshift coat hanger. Under his army green tank top revealed a collage of swastikas, fl'mes, and cemeteries. On his back in bold letters read "HERRENVOLK." The door cracked opened and a rush of warm air permeated the room. As they both stepped in, another motion sensor light came on and there were plants growing farther than the eyes could see. At least two football fields of sheer white boy sophistication. Copper pipes ran through each base of the large, plastic, white buckets, which put a mixture of oxygen and nitrous oxide into the thick roots, like arteries in a human limb, and fed the roots with nutrients every hour.

"These will be ready for harvest pretty soon."

These plants look healthy and happier than a mothafucka, Dorian thought. "Shit Strings, these plants look like a happy crowd ready to start applauding."

"Well this might sound crazy but I talk to the plants. How are you doing my babies? You're going to be some good smoke, aren't you? I also play classical music over the surround system."

Dorian looked up and saw the expensive Bose system. *Ahh yeah, he's crazier than I don't know what, but he has the best purple kush in all of Northern California*, he thought. "Ok Strings, whatever."

"My curing room is over here. I got you some fresh shit you little fucker," he said, followed with an evil grin. He pulled back some heavy plastic hanging from an opening as Dorian followed him. Each wall was lined with thick buds in different stages of drying. He walked over to a countertop and opened a large plastic garbage can. It was full of hard-ball, sparkly, leafy buds with dense keefe crystals all around it. "This right here is my new strain called great-granddaddy purp. This has a very fucking high THC level bro. One puff and you will think God is personally talking to you. 'Behold, my dear child, is that purp that you're smoking?'"

They both started cracking up with laughter. "Man, you hot!" Dorian said as he watched him put on some gloves and grab several handfuls and set them on an oversized scale. Dorian pulled out two huge bundles of hundred dollar bills from both of his back pockets and began counting them.

"Nawh, you ain't got to do that son. I got a money counting machine over there by the shrink wrapper. But hold up, you said two right?"

"Yeah!" *As if we didn't discuss this shit already*, Dorian thought, *because I don't have no time for no bullshit.*

"I'm going to give you an extra pound for half price. I talked to Hoist earlier before you came and he said he wanted a sample of my new strain."

"Well what the fuck? I sure wish mothafuckas would of let a nigga know ahead of time. What if I didn't bring enough cash man?"

"Well how much cash yah got?"

"You didn't let me count it, asshole. 'I have a money counting machine,'" Dorian did his best Strings impersonation.

"Well how much do you think you have?"

"Shit, probably a little over six racks."

"Alright then, just give me five then we're good," Strings said as he separated all three pounds into neat nugget pyramids, then put each one in thick, large, sealable bags. He then closed the rectangular device over the openings. It extracted all of the air, sealing the bag to half size.

"When you see Hoist he will take care of you. Don't sweat it fucker because you know he will and I know you'll see him."

"Yeah, yeah man. Fuck, here." He counted out five thousand dollars with lightning speed, like a pit boss at a busy casino. Strings handed him the packages.

"Pleasure doing business with you."

"Ahh yeah Strings, fuck you. Oh yeah, you never told me how you got the name Strings man."

He gave Dorian a toothy grin. "Well it's not because of my last name. Put it this way, I am the reason why they don't distribute dental floss in prisons no more."

"Why is that?"

"One of our Aryan brothers had a unpaid debt so I came up behind him and strangled him with a strand of dental floss. I left him on the yard in a pool of his own piss and shit with green floss dangling from his fucking throat. The name Strings just kind of stuck with me ever since. Ask Hoist, he'll tell you."

A large crane picked up a storage container with the word "Mayflower" in big yellow letters. "The birds have fucking landed," Cl'mente "Hoist" Barboza said out loud as he sat in seclusion of the cab of the crane. One hundred kilos of pure cocaine just arrived from his native country, hidden in hollowed out furniture. Ever since getting out of the penitentiary from doing two dimes, one of Cl'mente's comrades had put him on as a crane operator at the Port of Oakland. Life was good, but not good enough for him.

Deep in the thick jungles of Central America, a cocaine plant operation was ran by wealthy Nicaraguan cartels who churned out pure, uncut, 100% cocaine. The coke then would be packaged and stamped with the cartel's symbol and trucked into the main business district of Panama on lumber trucks where it was then unloaded into the warehouse of Cl'mente's wife's export furniture business. Hired Panamanian locals labored for pennies on the dollar by separating the product, rolling the cocaine in cylinders, and concealing them in pre-hollowed out stools, rocking chairs, China cabinet sets, coffee tables, and anything else. From there it would be staged on pallets, shrink wrapped, labelled, and scanned before it was loaded onto fifty-five foot trailers and transported to the local docks where it was then placed on a cargo ship container and delivered to the land of the oaks in Oakland, California.

Cl'mente's muscular, tatted forearm wiped the beads of sweat which formed on his forehead. He had concentrated on loading and unloading, which wasn't easy. You could never take your eyes off of nothing. From two hundred feet up, the bay sparkled like rubies as it rippled in rapid succession. "Man I got to put a work order in on this damn air conditioner. They think this damn heat helps my concentration, shhhiiiittt they got me twisted," he said as he watched the container slowly lower. The diamond bezel on his presidential platinum Rolex blinged as he checked the time.

"Hey nephew, meet me in the parking lot. Don't trip about security at the front gate. I know he is new, but just tell him that you're here to see your uncle "H" and keep it pushing, ok?"

Dorian listened as he spoke. "I am here for Mr. Barboza," Dorian told the guard as he waited at the gate.

"Oh, The Hoist. Sure, no problem sir."

Workers with hard hats sat around covered eating areas and joked, smoked cigarettes, talked on cell phones, and ate their lunch. Dorian parked next to a black-on-black Benz 600 V-12 coupe sitting on 23-inch rims. Jazz music poured out the sunroof as the trunk popped open. He got out with a gym bag, walked over to it, and tossed it in. He then slowly closed it and it locked by itself.

"It's open nephew, get in."

"What's good Uncle?"

They both embraced each other for about a minute. Cl'mente had a salt and pepper crown of hair and a neatly trimmed goatee. At five-foot-nine, he was pure muscle, scars, and tattoos. His face stayed expressionless and his hazel eyes were penetrating and aggressive.

"I'll tell you what's not good." He opened the front page of the *Vallejo Herald Times* showing a picture of what appeared to be a Jamaican dude in a suit, wearing stunner shades and giving a mean thizz face. The article read, "Suspected bank robber makes off with an undisclosed amount of cash and disappears. A tree trimmer later finds a few bills and pieces of clothing in branches that may be connected to the crime. The case is still under investigation."

"You see, it's these type of niggas that put a black eye to the game." He paused for a minute and studied Dorian's stern face. "You want to know why?"

Ahhh shit, Dorian thought. *Here we go with one of his street political speeches.*

"Because it brings in the FEDS and they know niggas like him have habits, which drags niggas like us into the picture. So they target the pushers and squeeze them on who may have made large ass purchases of dope. Then these fuckers confiscate their cell phones, rip their numbers, and ping each call that comes in. They totally abuse the Patriot Act nephew, seriously. Shit, they're starting to classify niggas with dreads as terrorist cells which gives them the right to invade people's privacy and wiretap niggas' phones."

"Uncle, you're crazier than a Napa State patient on hot meds!"

"Yeah well, maybe nephew. Maybe I am but I'll tell you this: watch who you fuck with and pay very close attention to what you say on these jacks," he said waving his cell phone around in the air like an Olympic relay race baton.

"Look, aren't you suppose to be eating lunch?"

"Yeah, you're right. Grab those two lunch pails in the back."

"What, you packed me a lunch too?"

"Ahh this is a meal that you can't consume personally nephew, only your pockets can."

Having that in mind, Dorian opened up the lunch pail and counted out twelve ounces of tightly wrapped cocaine. He then picked up one clear plastic package and examined the sparkly white and yellow contents as if it was scales on a rare, exotic fish.

"You can tap dance on it if you want and triple your profit. That's on you—"

"Ahh Uncle you gave me a extra two and I'm only cashing you out for 10 zips."

"You said Strings gave that pound to you right?"

"Uhh he didn't just give me shit. I paid him a grand for it—"

"Okay, there you have it!" he cut in. "That's where the two extra zips come into play."

"Alright, alright Uncle," Dorian said closing the metal lunch box and handing him a wad of hundreds wrapped with a thick, yellow rubber band.

"Just toss it in here," he said, chewing on a sandwich and lifting up the center console. He eyed Dorian for a moment. "Boy, they call me the 'Hoist' for one simple reason nephew, and that is I lift worthy niggas up to their highest hustle potential. But if they even think about ever crossing me then I'll chain their worthless asses to a anchor, make a thousand small cuts on them, and drop them to the depths of the Pacific Ocean," he said, waving his finger like an angry communist dictator.

Well I'm glad we're family, Dorian thought to himself.

"Hey nephew, one more thing, because I have to finish my shift." Dorian watched him as he reached under his driver's seat and pulled out a military issued bulletproof vest. "Here, take this." He took it and tucked it under his arm and before he was able to say something, his uncle said, "Don't ask!" Dorian shook his head, looked around, and stepped out.

"Turn up the headphone D-Down!" Brick-B said as he spoke into the microphone, standing in the sound booth. Sweat beaded on his forehead as he wiped it off. Brick-B bobbed his head as he waited and listened. The bass line, high-hats, and snare snapped, popped, and beat. D-Down pointed through the soundproof window and gave him the cue to start as he sat in front of the sound boards like a black Captain Kirk on the U.S.S. Enterprise.

"Yo, yo I am blapping so hard from the thousand watt Zues/ I can feel it in my nerves like a dentist on a tooth/ Opened up the roof looking like Dr. Seuss/ Woke up the intersection trunk smacking on mute/ I like macking on two/ I like a challenge, don't you?/ Monster cables with the fuse/ I ride with no tent coz a nigga love the view/ Paint so wet I got to wear a life preserver/ Cookie cutter on the feet/ Turn the wheel don't cut her/ Slipping in my wake from the puddles of the butter/ No 'L's' or paperwork if I wrap it I'll buy another/ You see I keep it gutter/ A safe spot on the under/ Keep a bundle in a muffler/ And a thumper with my brother/ Stay in the rear view so they won't get near you/ Tweets in the ceiling/ Man I got that feeling/ That tonight's going to be a good night/ This product that I am dealing/ I'm bound to make a killing/ But I'm not going to be a spotlight/ Touch screen in the dash/ Ashtray full of cash/ Switch lanes from behind this I'me/ So I won't crack my glass/ Vacuum sealed bags, highs and mids on peek with up to date tags/ My nines under the seat while I'm floating through the fast track."

D-Down blended in the hook since this was the last verse. He then tapered off all the tracks. He leaned back in his engineer's chair and puffed on a blunt in a clear blunt wrap. "So what you think?" Manky asked while he was sitting on top of a computer tower in the corner of the studio sipping on a bottle of V.S.O.P.

"That shit right there slap folks. You know what I'm saying. But we shouldn't let that nigga Bricks know because he's going to want to have you burn him a copy and then he will let every nigga in the hood listen to it to get a second opinion. Besides, the shit is not even copyrighted or—"

Brick-B walked in. "What's good, what you niggas discussing? Ahh Manky, let me hit that yak my nigga." Grabbing the bottle, he took a few hard swigs and allowed the brown liquid to burn his young, nineteen-year-old chest. "What Manky?"

"What I was saying was that it's a hot track, but it needs to be mixed down and mastered, you dig?"

Brick-B shook his head silently as he put on his short sleeve, silk button-up shirt and adjusted his gold chain and pendant. He gave the bottle back to Manky and tied his long dread locs into a long ponytail. His face was smooth and jet-black with a thin pencil mustache above his lips. "Burn a nigga a copy." Manky and D-Down looked at each other and laughed while they both shook their heads. "What?!"

The paint shop was located in a secluded industrial area off of Sonoma Blvd. D-Down threw most of his money into the business since his profession was jacking. He robbed anything that had a safe in an unsafe place, and if you didn't get down when he said it the first time, then your brains would keep you company right next to you as you laid down. Originally from the shady 80's in East Oakland, California, he robbed the wrong mothafuckas and they wanted his head. D-Down resembled "Sticky Fingers" off of the old school rap group called "Onyx." Since banking institutions didn't put contracts out on niggas then, jacking was safer, which was D-Down's street philosophy: "Give 'em a note, get fourteen stacks, and walk out calm, cool, and collected in five minutes flat."

Manky was a grown "Baby Huey" type nigga that was fighting grown men at 15 years old. Now six years later at 21, he started hitting the bottle and then started hitting niggas with it in the club and running through their pockets. He liked the attention from women after he would knock their boyfriends out. They would say "Hey, why you looking at my broad" and before they could get the last word out, it was off with his head and KO'd on the hardwood dance floor next to the bar.

Brick-B would be one of the spectators and have his camera phone filming everything. He put a few clips of his footage on the internet and threw Manky's name in a few raps and behold, a star is born. It wwas funny how these niggas met. Manky pushed up on him and di som D-Bo shit to him coming out of the club. One of Manky's stripper bitches said the nigga that he knocked out was trying to press charges and was using footage off of the internet. Watching the whole thing unfold from a distance, I saw the broad E.T. finger Brick-B as the culprit and Manky walked over to him, cracking his ashy gorilla knuckles and clearing his throat.

"Ahh nigga, I seen that footage on your website. That was some funny shit how that nigga got knocked the fuck out."

Brick turned around from talking to a little shorty in the parking lot while she was getting in her car. When he did, he almost turned white like some Peruvian cocaine. I almost spilled my drink until I seen what happened next. I don't know what was said, but both of them niggas started laughing and giving each other pounds and hugs like they had knew each other for years. I scratched my head wondering what was this nigga telling him, so I pulled him to the side and asked him.

"Yo, my name's D-Down lil' brah. What you tell that nigga Manky to go from breaking your face to being best friends?"

Little dude looked me straight in the eyes and said, "Yo, I told him, dude you knocked out sent some goons after me to get that footage because I took it off before he could download that shit. I said, yo I got over 100,000 hits in less than twenty-four hours and a movie producer from Hollywood wanted to sign you a movie deal and he has the best criminal lawyer on his payroll for you. So I gave him the card and said call him."

"Then what?"

"Yo, the nigga starts laughing and said you're good brah. You aight?"

I thought to myself, this little nigga got game. Manky actually bought that shit. After that, I put him under my wing and put Manky on my payroll and retained him a lawyer for safekeeping.

The sound of a flatbed truck's hydraulics woke up Hatton Chase Banks out of a hard sleep. He rubbed his eyes and rolled out of the small bed in the plushed out trailer on the shop's grounds. He smashed some powder cocaine with a playing card, separated two pencil-sized lines, and snorted them with no quill or nothing. *I'm a beast*, he thought to himself. He put a clean, crispy black Dickies jumpsuit on, brushed his waves, put on his steel toe boots and looked in the mirror. Chase was a high yellow nigga. Almost albino. His features were close to Robin Thick but with a short, tapered haircut. Chase could chop a car in 1000 pieces with a blowtorch in less than an hour. He was a thief type dude. He would steal your keys to your whip and then help you look for them, then pull your car while you were asleep. He was a grimy nigga. He liked using meth when he worked. He said it opened his third eye. Yeah right; it opened his third pipe.

Chase ran some warm water between his fingers, snorted, and allowed the cocaine to drain through his nasal passages. Rinsing his mouth, he then stepped out into the early morning Vallejo air and spit a stream of water into the chalky dirt.

"What we got Jim?"

"What does it look like we got? It's money to be made that's what."

"Well good fucking morning to you too Jim."

"Sounds like you had a hearty breakfast and a strong fucking cup of coffee."

"Look Jim, money isn't everything bro, it's just the grease that keeps the machine functioning. If you disrespect me again and bite the hand that feeds you, then I'll pull your fucking contract cracker!" Chase said as he looked him in the eye for a few seconds.

"You're right, you're right."

He climbed out of the truck's cab with a huge beer belly. He was wearing a greasy baseball cap and a dingy khaki shirt. Chase circled the truck and surveyed the delivery as he made a phone call.

"Hello, D-Down? Yeah, they just arrived," Chase mumbled into his cellphone. "Mmmhmm, okay, yeah." Then he hung up.

He inspected a burgundy BMW 745i with front end damage, a Lexus GS with side damage and a Cadillac CTS that had slight damage to the rear quarter panel. All of them were of the newest models. Chase rubbed his ashy hands together like he was about to have a large gourmet meal with all the five courses. Jim unhooked the chains and positioned each car by the garage's opening and drove off. Minutes later, a candy, root beer brown Lexus SC 400 pulled up on chrome 22's. D-Down jumped out, stretched, took off his black Kango and rubbed his shiny bald head.

"What's good Chase?"

"Shit D, we already got buyers for all of this and all clean titles. We can ask for the full blue book value."

"What's the cost on parts?" D-Down asked as he opened the Beemer's driver side door and sat in the plush seats. It still had that new car smell.

"I would say around twelve to fifteen thousand."

D-Down nodded his head as if he was in deep thought. "What's the turnaround?"

"No more than a week. You know me, once I get started, I do a victory lap when I'm finished. But after everything is said and done, forty K profit easy, maybe more." He let the figure hang in the air like a Las Vegas slot machine that just hit the jackpot.

"I got to make some moves because I want this whip right here!" he said, slapping his palm on the hardwood grain steering wheel.

Chase sucked his stained teeth and glanced at the car D-Down was in. "What about the coupe my nigga?"

"Shit, dump it I guess. A nigga got to step his water whip game up sometime."

"You know brah… Do you… Look, all I know is that money fuels this machine."

D-Down knew exactly what he meant. Chase wanted his cut upfront plus labor and cash for parts so he could get started. D-Down wasn't thinking about touching his money in his safe or touching his jewels.

"Aight bet."

Right at that moment Chase's palms started to itch.

A pearl white stretch limousine pulled in front of the club that was hosting the "1st Annual Feel Me Festival." As the driver stepped out, Dorian scanned the large crowd. It snaked from the glass double doors, down the long city block. Dorian put out his blunt and glanced at his reflection in the door's window as the driver opened it. He stepped out, stretched his legs and looked around to see if he recognized anyone. *Just a bunch of Asian persuasion mommies chewing on glow sticks as if they were on something*, Dorian thought to himself. A stocky Samoan bouncer wearing an expensive black suit unhooked the velvet rope and allowed him to walk past everyone else.

"I am a guest of Tran-Tran. My name is Dorian J."

Without a word his stern face relaxed at the mention of Tran's name. He opened the large double doors allowing him to step in. After Dorian's eyes adjusted to the darkness, there was a sea of bodies dancing to a hypnotic-futuristic beat. The club was a renovated, ten thousand-square-foot building with a VIP section to the left and a large dance floor positioned in the center. A semi-circular, fully stocked bar of colorful bottles decorated the high shelves like abstract stained glass. Large black nets stretched across the circumference of the ceiling where beach balls and gold and silver confetti were held above the people. A DJ booth was by a stage as music pulsated though hundreds of hidden speakers. A short, thick Asian woman with blonde highlights and brown eyes, wearing a skimpy dress pulled Dorian's sleeve.

"What's good little mama?" he said, looking her up and down.

"Tran said to come up to the VIP and join him. There's some people he would like to introduce you to," she said in an Asian accented, womanly voice with a hint of alcohol on it.

Dorian instantly looked up at the VIP and saw Tran waving at him with a large open bottle in one hand and a tightly rolled, long blunt in the other.

"I see you, you Vietcong mothafucka you," he said, smiling.

The DJ mixed in every hot song perfectly as women grabbed their homegirls and ushered them to the dance floor while niggas followed them with drinks in their hands. Security stopped them and whispered a few things in their ear. They nodded in agreement and set their drinks on a nearby table, placing a napkin over them.

"Man, I couldn't do it," Dorian said out loud, eyeing people as they stepped off the dance floor and picked up the wrong drinks. Tran whispered in one of the security guard's ear and they instantly let Dorian in the VIP section.

"What's the business buddah?" They both bumped fists and nodded at each other at the same time.

Tran set the bottle back in the bucket of ice, took a pull from what appeared to be a blunt but it didn't smell anything close to trees. It had a sweet vanilla chemical smell to it. It reminded Dorian of Tran's opium car incense that hung from his rearview mirror. White smoke spiraled around his iced out jewelry on his fingers and accumulated underneath his blue Stetson brim hat.

"Have seat Doe, drink!"

An Asian and black girl in a skirt outfit leaned out of the shadows, grabbed a bottle, and poured him a drink. The bubbly fizzed like it had a chemical reaction once it touched the crystal flute.

"To history in the making," Tran toasted as they all clinked glasses and took long sips. "This is my business partner from my homeland, Sniper." They eyed each other for a few seconds and finally shook hands. "This here is Tripwire." Tripwire's dark eyes darted from left to right as they also shook hands.

They were both suited-and-booted and appeared to be in their late forties. Tripwire leaned forward and whispered something to Tran in his native tongue.

"Word is that you move alone on the streets. No crew. Why is that?"

Dorian had to think about that for a minute because he had never been asked that question before. "People have hidden agendas man. No loyalty. The only person that I can trust now-a-days is myself. No one else. Have you ever played chess?"

Tran translated for Tripwire.

"Yes of course—"

"Well, what is the most powerful piece on the board?"

"The queen!"

"No. Try again!"

Dorian wrinkled his nose while he was in deep thought searching for the right answer. The music continued to pulsate in the background. "The pawn!" Dorian quickly announced, snapping his fingers with certainty.

"Yes, the pawn. Their job is to solely move forward. The more pawns you have moving forward for you, the less vulnerable you are," Sniper spoke for the first time. "Object of game in streets is create empire, stack money, invest it, and get the fuck out," he said in a nasaled accented voice.

"True, true," Dorian agreed, taking a sip of the bubbly and allowing it to resonate on his dry palate.

"You bring granddaddy purp? Because I specifically told security not to search you."

Dorian responded by reaching in his waistband, pulled out two vacuum sealed packages and tossed them in his lap under the table. The keefe glowed like radioactive toxic waste under the neon lights in VIP. Tran took out a razor from his breast pocket and made a small opening. He pulled out two small, sparkly nuggets, inspected them and placed them in a brass hooka with six different braided hoses.

"Ahhh Tran, I think you're going to need more tree than that brah."

He reached in the bag, grabbed a handful of buds, stacked them on the hooka's bowl and lit it with a gold lighter in the shape of a dragon. Dorian picked up a hose like everyone else and inhaled the potent smoke.

Manky sat at the large rectangular bar as he had his eyes on an attractive redbone across from him nursing a drink. He noticed that she kept glancing in his direction, not knowing that VIP was directly behind him.

"Look at that nigga," Patricia "Peaches" Mitchell said to herself as she glanced at the VIP section. "Shit that nigga Dorian think he really doing, huh? Pulling up in stretch whips, trying to spank a bitch. If he only knew that he needs a solid bitch like me on his team." Peaches curled her full, glossy lips as she watched as Deltrice whispered something to one of the security guards at the VIP entrance.

Tran blew out light purple smoke and felt for his face as if it wasn't there. Sniper leaned over to Tran and nudged him in his ribs. "Visitor!"

"You know them?" Tran asked Dorian.

"Yeah, yeah, I know them. That's my homegirl Trice, her friend Suam and my dog from high school, Marcelos."

Tran nodded to security and they ushered them up the steps. Dorian watched as Deltrice's designer jeans clung to her curvaceous Haitian hips like latex gloves. Her hair was straightened and curled at the ends which fell around her shoulders and down her back. Suam stood at 5'5 showing off her shapely thighs and calves, yet she was not lacking in breast size. Suam's almond-shaped eyes, long hair, dimples, and bright smile always had niggas doing double takes. Marcelos resembled the R&B singer Genuwine. His platinum chain's white diamonds sparkled under the lights as he took the last few steps in butter Timberlands, baggy designer jeans and crisp black tee. Dorian stood up to greet all of them.

"Ahh y'all have a seat."

They all positioned themselves around the fluffy couches. Deltrice sat next to Dorian and they all locked eyes for a few seconds.

"Let me introduce you to someone. This is Tran-Tran and these other two gentlemen names is Tripwire and Sniper."

The ladies smiled and nodded their heads. Marcelos shook hands with each one of them and leaned back comfortably on the couch. He stared at the hooka, bucket of bubbly, and back at Dorian.

The bartender set a double shot of Patron next to Peaches as she sat at the crowded bar. "Thank you but I didn't order this love."

"Oh it's from that guy over there."

Manky held up his glass, smiled at Peaches, and slid off of his barstool. She sipped her mixed drink, bit the straw and watched as he approached her. "My name is Manky. I couldn't help but notice you nursing your drink, so I decided to give you twins.

"That's cute Manky. I appreciate that."

"What's your name cutie?" he asked, looking into her green eyes and high yellow, smooth complexion.

"My homegirls call me Peaches, but my real name is Patricia."

"Hmm I like Peaches better. A person always expects something seet and delicious when tasting a peach."

Brick-B weaved in and out of the crowed as he made his way towards the DJ booth. He had a crisp $50 bill in one hand and a folded $100 bill on top of a CD in the other. He ran his fingers through his dreadlocs and tugged his gold dog tag chain. A bouncer waited at the booth's entrance and scanned the crowd like he was babysitting a thousand mothafuckas on "E." Brick-B held up the clear CD sleeve case with the writing saying "Get Wet Volume 1." Dressed in all-black with bulging muscles, the bouncer fidgeted on his feet and took two steps towards him. Brick-B pointed at the DJ, catching his attention, so he pointed back. Brick-B then made an "O" with both hands and said CD.

"Hey young brah, we don't play unsolicited material and—"

Brick slid the fifty dollar bill as he shook his hand. "It's all good brah, look."

He glanced at the money then turned and saw the DJ waving him in. He shrugged and let him pass. He skipped up the few steps then noticed the view of the whole club. "What's wid it DJ," he said shaking his hand and giving him a shoulder hug, putting a hundred dollar bill in his hand. "Hey brah, I'm an up-and-coming rapper name Brick-B. I got a single called 'Get Wet.' I'm gassing on tracks like stupid brah."

He pocketed the money in his Coogi sweatsuit and snatched the CD in one fluent motion. He began to listen to the track before playing it. With a skeptical smirk on his face at first, he then relaxed and began bobbing his neck. "AAAAHHH this shit claps. OOHH-HHOO," he said, holding a closed tight fist to his mouth in excitement.

Brick-B watched in awe as the DJ went to work pushing buttons, scrolling through screens, and popping CD cases. Before he knew it, the music tapered off and his voice came in. "You feeling yourself?" The crowd responded in perfect unison, "Yeeaahh!"

Greenish glow sticks spotted the dancing crowd like a psychedelic Christmas tree. "I got a world premiere of a new artist name Brick-B, called 'Get Wet.'"

The sung blended perfectly as it pounded through the club's powerful sound system. Mesmerized by the crowd's reaction and rapping along with his song, Brick-B didn't notice the blunt in front of him being passed by the DJ. He grabbed it and pulled a long drag making the cherry glow red hot. When the hook came in the DJ pressed a button and hundreds upon hundreds of balloons, confetti, and glitter fell on the dancing crowd.

Peaches' attention was drawn from her and Manky's conversation as the crowd reacted to the falling balloons. At that split second, Manky squeezed four drops of liquid MDMA in her Patron and mixed it with her red stirrer.

"You wet?" Manky asked before sipping his drink. His pinky ring gave a radioactive sparkle under the neon lights.

"Not yet, but that song is hot though," she said, turning back around and sipping her fresh drink.

"That's my young nigga Bricks. Me and my folks is investing cheddar to put him on but that nigga don't have no patience though."

"Well he just knows he got a hot song and it's like a nigga who got money. It burns a hole in they pockets."

She sure is speaking like a boss bitch, Manky thought. "Yeah, I guess you right, but I got deep pockets and I go deep."

She smiled and licked her numb, full lips. "Ohh and how deep can you go?"

Manky looked at her thick thighs bulging through her True Religion jeans. His eyes followed the star design around her waist and round ass. "As deep as Reggie Bush baby."

Peaches tossed her head back in laughter, exposing a tattoo on her neck of a peach with a straight razor slicing through it. The pure ecstasy had her body numb and mellow.

"I got a hotel baby on big boy rims right out that door!" he said, pointing at the emergency exit in the cuts.

"You crazy but I like that." She slid off the stool and they both disappeared through the crowd as the door opened and closed.

Bubbly was being passed as people in VIP were laughing and having a good time. A purple cloud of smoke hovered above the VIP section like a comfortable blanket. Dorian leaned over to Deltrice. "Ahh shorty come on!" he said, pulling her arm. "Hey everyone, we're going to step out to get some fresh air."

Yeah right, Deltrice thought, *this nigga want to fuck. Straight up. Finally the spell is working*. Her clitoris quivered with delight as she imagined him pushing deep inside of her. They both stepped outside and the San Francisco air was cool to their skin. "So where is your limo driver hiding at?"

A car's lights flashed on and off as it was parked in an alley. "There he go!" he said as the pearl white stretch limousine quietly pulled out into the empty city street and parked directly in front of them. The driver got out, circled the vehicle, tipped his shiny cap and opened the door.

"Any particular destination sir?"

"Yeah, take us close to the bridge Mr. Driver."

Smiling, he knew they meant the Golden Gate. They climbed in and they pulled out slowly.

Manky's Chevy Suburban sitting on 24's was discreetly backed into a parking spot. A DVD porno flick played on all of the headrests behind the truck's dark tint as Manky and Peaches both sat in the roomy back seat of his truck. He gazed over the small of her back and watched the perfect "m" shape of Peaches' plump, naked ass as a reflection of Dorian's limousine passed by.

Dorian and Deltrice looked at each other for several minutes in silence as city lights blurred in the distance. "I don't know what it is but, but—"

Deltrice leaned forward and kissed him on his mouth, thrusting and probing her tongue in and out. He kissed her back passionately and began undressing her. She kicked her high heels off and allowed him to pull her jeans to her ankles. Kissing her every place, he pulled her wet panties down and played with her clit.

"MMMMMM!" she moaned as she bit her lip. He pulled her panties down the rest of the way and went down on her, licking and sucking. She focused on the parts between Dorian's braids as his head bobbed and weaved in slow motion between her soft thighs. She gripped the soft leather seats, arched her back, and curled her pedicured toes. After a few minutes, she couldn't hold back her orgasm. Shuddering, she gyrated her hips and bit hard on her bottom lip. He sat beside her with his chiseled physique, grabbed a bottle of Don Q cristal Puerto Rican rum from the built-in bar, and poured them both double shots as the limousine came to a stop. Taking it into her hand, she gazed in Dorian's brown eyes.

"To our relationship!" he toasted, and with bottle in hand, he opened the sunroof, stood on the seat, and grabbed her hand to follow him.

The Golden Gate Bridge stretched high and wide like pillars of glowing fire. The smell of sea water, splashing waved, and angry seagulls permeated their heightened senses. Dorian took a long swig from the bottle and wrapped his arm around her.

"What are you thinking about baby?"

Taking another swig and smacking his full lips, he hesitated before answering. "When a nigga builds something from the ground up, it has to withstand the hands of time, just like that bridge shorty!" he said slurring his speech, pointing the bottle, spilling a little on the roof. "As time transpires and hit happens, a nigga got to flex and conform to his surroundings. But whatever you build has to serve a purpose even if it's just getting from one point to another," he said as he pointed the neck of the bottle at one end of the bridge to the other, which disappeared behind dark, sinister clouds.

Manky slapped Peaches' ass hard and fast as he put his long, stubby index finger between her parted ass cheeks and stuck it in. With his other hand, he threw up the "W" at his camera phone, which he had placed in the rearview window, recording the episode without Peaches knowing. He then reached under her and pinched her large, brown nipples. She moaned and gagged at the same time as his pulsing manhood touched the back of her throat.

She gripped his thick shaft and slowly slurped her full lips to the top of his dick and ran her pink, long, wet tongue around the head. "OOOHHH bitch you're a fucking surgeon and I'm your loyal patient." Peaches' lips creased into a slight smile with dick in her mouth. She felt his manhood pulse so she slowed a bit. "Bitch, whatcha doing? You trying to give a nigga blue balls or something?" he said, grabbing a handful of her naturally curly bronze hair. She began to thrust up and down like a lubricated piston waiting for him to fire. "OOHH yeah, just like that, don't stop. UUGGHH!" Within that split second, Peaches leaned back and quickly stroked him as he skeeted a thick stream of cum on her plump breasts. "OOHH yeah, that's what's up. Rub that shit in like some expensive sunscreen bitch," Manky demanded. So she did what she was told, smoothing it over and rubbing it around each hard, taut nipple. *Man this girl is on*, Manky thought to himself, as he reached behind his back seat and grabbed a bottle of Patron silver.

"Come closer, let me give your sexy yellow ass a silver shower little momma." After Manky pulled out the tan cork with his teeth, Peaches pursed her full lips as he cascaded the tequila from her bottom lip, down her neck, between her cleavage and watched it formed a small, sparkly puddle in her pierced navel. Manky leaned forward, slurping and smacking his lips. "Yeah bitch, that's what I call a Manky body shot," he said putting the cork back on and then viciously thrusting the whole cork and neck of the large bottle inside of her as blood dripped down her thighs.

CHAPTER THREE:

GOTTA GET IT

THERE IS ENOUGH IN THE WORLD FOR EVERYONE'S NEEDS, BUT NOT ENOUGH FOR EVERYONE'S GREED.

"Baby, whatcha doing?" D-Down's girlfriend asked as she stepped into the large bedroom. She walked over to the computer desk where he was sitting and wrapped her soft hands around his back and rubbed the laced fabric of her designer bra against his skin.

"Searching for something on the net shorty."

She looked over his shoulder as he typed and clicked. "Baby if you're looking for some porn sites then we can have our own porn right here," she said as she began biting his ear and licking the side of his neck.

He stopped typing, swung his chair around and palmed both of her firm ass cheeks. "You need something to do, don't you?" She smiled, shook her head like a little school girl and looked down at his crotch. D-Down followed her eyes. "Nawh baby, not that yet. Business first." He pushed her off playfully, swung back around, grabbed a sharpie and a stickie note and began writing something. "Huh shorty, take this. I want you to write this exactly how I wrote it."

She snatched it and read it as he swung back around to tend to his business. "Baby is this some type of joke?"

"Nope, just write the shit and after I am done then you'll get all the dick you want."

SSSHHHIIIITTTT, she thought, *that was a fair exchange for her*.

He clicked on a Google Earth site which gave him a satellite aerial view of anywhere on Earth. He typed in the address he wanted then zoomed into the location. *Perfect*, he thought. *Right next to a freeway and there's a bike trail with plenty of tall pine trees a block away. That's what's up*. He deleted everything and closed out of the program before turning around in the comfortable computer chair, only to see her completely naked with one hand on her shapely hip and the other handing him the note.

"Yeah hello, Manky, what's good? Wait, wait, hold up; let me turn this music down. Aight. Yeah." His pearl white Chevy Suburban swerved into the next lane a little.

"I need a ride somewhere brah, and I'll probably need for you to swoop me up."

"Yeah, well when and where?"

"Corner of Main Street, next to the bike trail. Like in the next thirty minutes. Oh and ahh, don't trip. I'll cash you out something decent."

Manky glanced at his watch which read 11 am.

"Oh yeah, I'm at the hut."

"Aight!" Manky said, hanging up.

D-Down adjusted the dreadloc wig then examined himself in the bathroom mirror. The goatee mustache was the finishing touch to this disguise. He had on an olive green button-down shirt, matching silk tie and all-black Air Force Ones. He picked up his large chrome .45 and holstered it before he put his dress suit coat on. "Bumba clot. Me make ye famous," D-Down imitated in the mirror jokingly as he picked up his stunner shades off of the sink and grabbed a small leather attaché briefcase next to him. He heard the dual exhaust of Manky's Suburban pull up so he stepped out.

"Nigga who is you? Samuel Pulp Fiction Mothafucken Jackson?"

"It's called a disguise my nigga, and if mothafuckas want to say oh my god, the fucking nigger had a gun like the one Samuel Jackson had in *Pulp Fiction*, then so be it," D-Down said with his best white man impersonation. He then tapped his coat to say he was holding.

"You said Main Street right?"

D-Down walked past security who was standing outside of the Washington Mutual Bank and watched as he was giving an elderly lady directions. He stepped through the double glass doors and focused on all of the tellers. *HHMMMM who's going to be the lucky one,* he thought to himself. He glanced at the line of people and it was moving pretty fast. From the corner of his eye he noticed an attractive Hispanic female in her early 20's receive stacks of money from the manager, in order to replenish her cash drawer. *Bingo, you're 'it' baby girl,* he thought to himself as he snaked through the

42

velvet ropes. D-Down unbuttoned his suit coat as he casually walked up to her booth with a note in hand.

"How are you doing sir?" she asked smiling. "Just give me one moment."

He watched her count an endless supply of hundreds and fifties. "Sure Mariana, take your sweet time love." He set the briefcase on the counter and stood with his hands in front of him.

"Ok, sorry about that. How can I help you?"

"Sure I would like to make a large withdrawal out of my account please."

"Sure do you have an account number?"

D-Down handed her the note and as she began to read it her whole expression began to change from nice and bubbly to where all the blood rushed from her pretty face.

"AHHHHH can I please have my receipt back please?"

She gave him a look as if saying, are you serious. D-Down gave her the 'Mac Dre Thizz Face' like bitch, I ain't playing. As he opened his suit coat, she caught a glint of chrome and quickly began stacking fresh hundreds on the counter.

"Do you want 20's and 50's too?" she whispered.

"I want it all and I know there's more cash behind you in the reserve drawer too."

She stacked the rest on the counter as D-Down quickly stuffed it in his briefcase. She opened up the reserve drawer which displayed bundles of brand-new I00's in one thousand dollar increments. She also set all of them on the counter as he stuffed them in the briefcase. He smiled, turned around, and casually walked out. Mariana immediately hit the silent alarm as soon as D-Down stepped out the bank.

Right before getting around the block, he noticed security run into the bank and right at that point, he was running full speed. His heavy .45 bounced off of his ribs like a medicine ball. He hit the fence and could hear the police sirens in the distance. He jumped another fence and he was on the bike trail. D-Down looked both ways then climbed up a pine tree all the way to the top, which was about forty feet, giving him plenty of cover.

He quickly snatched the dreadloc wig and mustache completely off. He then quickly ripped off the clip-on tie and came out the slacks, suit coat and dress shirt in less than minutes. Underneath, D-Down had on a light gray Marc Ecko sweat suit. He put on a matching headband and grabbed all of the bundles of cash and stuffed them in both of his pants legs.

Manky's cell phone ranged twice before picking it up. "Damn my nigga that was fast," he answered.

"Come get me my nigga, same place you dropped me off. Oh and hurry the fuck up."

The line went dead. He climbed down the tree, stretched, and began jogging towards Main Street as Manky pulled up. D-Down quickly got in right before V.P.D. police bounced up the curb and drove wildly up the bike trail past them.

"So was it good?"

"Fo sho brah !" he said, re aching in his crotch and tossing him a thousand dollar bundle. "Now look nigga, don't be trying to buy the bar and shit. That right there is a nice little score for just thirty minutes of work."

"Well fuck, let me get some gas and a bottle then." Manky fingered the money then ran the palm of his hands across his smooth, healthy waves.

Crisp hundreds and fifties floated off the bed's Egyptian cotton sheets as D-Down was fucking his bottom bitch 'Sha wna' doggystyle. He pulverized her from the back as he slapped her firm ass cheeks. Shawna always wanted to role play like she was some type of high price escort. It was hard for her to stay in character when a price was trying to be negotiated.

"Ohh Daddy take this tight pussy. Mmmmmhhhhh !" she said in a low, plaintive sound, biting hard on her pink, full bottom lip. She cupped her breasts, frowned with pleasure to his entering and rapid exits. His shaft pulsed inside of her as she reached between her legs. While on her elbows and knees, she began playing with her clit to enhance her orgasm.

"You like this dick bitch, don't you? This town business bitch. You know what you're laying on huh, huh? You laying on fifty racks and up, just like I'm up in this pussy bitch—"

"Oh, oh, oh Daddy put it in my mouth so I can taste you."

He pulled out his pulsing manhood as she stroked it from behind. Turning around quickly, she took him into her mouth. He thrusted his hips, swelled in her throat, skeeting a continuous load into her empty stomach.

"Ohh bitch, swallow that protein like it's a fiv e-star meal bitch."

She closed her eyes and concentrated on pleasing her man by ingesting his hot fluid. They both locked on each other's gaze with only the look of lust and hedonism in their eyes. He pulled out of her mouth, got up, walked over to his glass dresser and picked up a loosely rolled blunt from a crystal ashtray. He lit it, inhaled deeply, held it in then, exhaled the pungent smoke. Shawna got up as he passed her the blunt.

"Look shorty, we going to wash up and count this gutta."

She reached between his legs and grabbed his shaft and gently squeezed it. "Baby you're still hard."

D-Down smiled at her statement. "Because you're getting this dope dick baby, live and direct."

"Baby I don't want you using that shit while you're fucking me—"

" Look, as long as your ass is satisfied, then that's all that really matters." She shivered from his spoken words as she passed the blunt back to him. "Seperate the money, grab the money counting machine from the top of the closet, and make ten thousand dollar bundles."

He walked into the master bedroom's spacious bathroom and turned on the shower. Shawna watched D-Down's muscular, sweaty body strut away.

"Ahh baby?" D-Down turned around as he puffed on the blunt.

"What!"

"You got a hundred stuck to your ass."

He turned around, looked and peeled the money off of him. "Now you see money chases me," he said as he handed it back to her.

A million different things ran through D-Down's mind as the scalding hot water hit his skin like needles. The contracts. The bones he made. The beef. Investing in this, investing in that, people who owed him, and finally making the biggest score of his thug life before the long arm of the law puts him in a vicious headlock. He could always hear his big homey Twiggy-B from the town say, "If yah black ass hit on some scrilla that's more than the average mothafucka make in a year. Then retain your ass the best criminal defense attorney there is in the area you in and also get your ass a bail bondsman that's with the business." D-Down turned off the shower, toweled off, wrapped it around his waist and walked back out to the bedroom.

"Next time, Daddy, don't barricade your sexy ass in the bathroom because a bitch want to wash her ass too," she said walking by him and throwing her silk, cream-colored Ralph Lauren robe over his head.

He pulled it off and playfully smacked her on her ass and watched it jiggle uncontrollably. He then made a rat tail and snapped it at her ass as she popped it and dropped it low for him. He turned his attention to the bed and saw seven neat stacks of money in yellow, thick rubber bands.

"Not bad, not fucking bad at all," he said to himself as he did the calculations in his head on how it would be spent.

D- Down saturated the clothes, wig and the rest of his disguise with lighter fluid in a large storage barrel, lit a match and tossed it in.

He watched it ignite as it burned furiously. The synthetic fabric of the clothes curled in an eerie dance early in the morning. As he squirted more fluid, the fingers of the fl'mes reached up like tentacles of a jellyfish. *No evidence, no case,* he thought to himself.

Chase flipped the dark visor to his welding helmet over his sweaty face, turned the knob on the side of his blowtorch and continued cutting metal. His cell phone silently vibrated on a wooden work bench that rattled the tool box next to it.

"This dude can't be asleep at this time of day," D-Down said out loud as he heard Chase's cellphone ring on the other end, then forward to voicemail. *At the tone please leave a message beeeep.* "Hey fool I'm coming through to the shop so be ready. We got some business to discuss."

Chase flipped his visor up, wiped the beads of sweat off of his forehead and noticed his cellphone lying face down on the shop's dirty floor. "I could of sworn I put the ringer on," he said as he pulled his heavy leather gloves off of each finger and reached to pick it up. "Missed call huh." He listened to the message, deleted it and tossed it back on the wooden work bench. "So be ready. Is this nigga serious? I stay ready so I don't have to get ready."

He opened up the toolbox and grabbed a glass pipe from the top compartment. He put it up to the light to inspect its contents and then picked up a Ziploc bag full of crystal shards. He snapped one in half, sprinkled the crumbs into the opening of the pipe, lit the bottom of the bowl and turned it side to side until the shards turned to liquid.

He took the fl'me away, watched it cool down and spider web around the bottom of the pipe. He put the stem into his chapped lips, lit it and inhaled the harsh chemical. He instantly felt the drug stimulate his senses and give him an extra boost of inhuman adrenaline. Chase then contorted his lower chin and exhaled a large cloud of smoke which exceeded anyone's lung capacity.

Taking a few more hits, he put it baek into his toolbox, then walked back to his project and continued working. The shop's closed-circuit monitor in the back office displayed a grainy image of D-Down pulling up in front and him walking in.

"Chase, my nigga, what's good?" he announced, tossing him a stack of tightly rolled hundreds.

Chase fumbled with the torch, took off his helmet and gloves in one fluent motion and caught it in both hands. He looked at the money, then at him, then back at the money again. "That's whats up. How much?"

"Twenty stacks nigga!"

Chase put the brand-new currency to his nostrils and inhaled. "Man I love the smell of new money—man what the... this money smells like sweaty ass and perfume my nigga!"

D-Down smiled and responded, "Let's just call it an ass baptism. Shawna sure in the hell wouldn't disagree." Then he walked past him to the rear office, straight to the safe.

CHAPTER FOUR:

THA OFFICE

AFTER A CERTAIN POINT MONEY IS MEANINGLESS.
IT CEASES TO BE THE GOAL.
THE GAME IS WHAT COUNTS.

A large Rottweiler carrying a leash in its massive jaws trotted through a makeshift doggy door, connecting from the backyard into Dorian's living room. He continued trotting up the spiraling, wooden staircase to the large master bedroom. He then stopped at the double doors, leaned on his hind legs and clawed at the knob until it opened. He padded in to the foot of the bed, rested his paws on the mattress, dropped the leash, growled and barked.

Dorian instantly reacted by reaching for his .40 caliber Glock mounted to the side of his nightstand. After he saw the leash at the foot of his bed and his dog, he fell back on his pillow, yawned, rubbed his head, and looked at the time. "Man I slept late. It's 11:36 am. Hey Schwartz, how you doing, boy?" Dorian said as he rubbed his dog's muscular head. Schwartz licked his master's hand with affection. "You want a walk huh? Well let me get up aight boy?"

"What does Schwartz mean baby?" Deltrice asked from under the silk sheets then pulled them down to her waist exposing her plump breast.

"Good morning Trice. I didn't even know that you was up girl."

"Well ahh babe, he he…"

"Yeah ahh, it means black in German."

"You know how to speak German?"

"JA WENIG DEUTSHE… I was a military brat. My pops was stationed in Germany for 7 years before he received orders to relocate to a base in Panama, which was closer to home for him since he was Panamanian."

"Are you and your dad close?"

"Well we were close… He died before we moved to the states."

"Well what happened?" Dorian paused for a minute. "It's ok you don't have to talk about it—"

" Cancer. He got diagnosed with cancer from being exposed to asbestos while patrolling the ships that came through the canal in Panama City. In the 80's Ronald Regan had this war on drugs campaign. Knowing America, we always want to police other countries and the military isn't designed for that, so my pops being a 'Master Sergeant' led these unnecessary searches of ships' cargo and engine rooms, exposing him to this shit.

"I'm—I'm…"

"Well, my pops didn't show no symptoms after he got reassigned, until he started developing large abnormal spots on his skin and experienced chest pains. When he finally decided to check into the V.A. hospital and have them run tests, it was too late. It already spread. It was stage four; you feel me shorty. It was like he had a fucking expiration date stamped on his chest. My dad was stubborn. No chemo. Nothin. His last words to me was 'take care of your mamy and if you start something always finish it son. It builds character in a man.' Those words stuck with me Trice."

"I'm sure itdid baby. I'm sure it did. And your mom——"

"She-she passed away. I believe it was from a broken heart."

" That's so sad—"

"Well, no one knew Trice. I just focused on my sports and my dad's brother treated me like his own. He raised me you know. With his help and my dad's pension and settlement, I was straight."

Dorian smiled showing his ivory teeth, got up, walked to the walk-in closet, and put on a Nike sweat suit and matching running shoes. "I'm going to take Schwartz for a walk around the block aight. Help yourself to whatever shorty," he said as he grabbed the dog's leash. Schwartz barked and wagged his tail in excitement as they left.

Trice stood up and stretched as she glanced around the spacious room. The glossy hardwood floors reflected the image of the fan above, attached to the vaulted ceilings. The sixty-inch plasma screen was mounted into the wall in front of the bed. All of his furniture was brushed silver metal and glass. African masks and spears crossed over the entrance of the room.

She studied all of his football memorabilia, team photos and trophies as she walked naked to the master bathroom and took a quick shower. When she stepped out, there was a brand-new outfit laid over the double set of marble sinks. She looked at the size, smiled, and put it on. *Perfect fit,* she thought as she turned off the light and walked down the flight of stairs leading to the kitchen.

Dorian was dressed in a short sleeve button-down, denim cargo shorts and Steve Martins, talking on his cellphone about where to meet. The counter top was set up with plates and silverware. He poured juice and then sat down.

"Damn baby I was only in the shower for a second."

He shook his head between bites as he looked at her outfit. "It obviously fits."

"Yeah, you're good."

"I know." His cell phone vibrated.

"You're busy aren't you?"

"Well I got to pay bills, yah know, supply and demand," they both said at the same time."

"Good, good, you're learning."

"Come on negro, I'm not slow and green. I'm a ripe, game tight bitch."

"HMMMMM is that right?"

"Yes Doe—"

"Well today is going to be bring yah game tight bitch to the office day."

"Office, what office?"

Dorian laughed. "You finished?"

"MMMHHMM !"

"Aight baby, let's push. You're driving," he said as he slid his laser cut keys across the counter towards her.

She followed him to the garage and opened the door. A black-on-black Chrysler 300 special edition was sitting on Asanti 22- inch rims.

She got in, started the car, then watched him as he leaned over the passenger side seat to push the trunk button and the garage door opener. From a distance down the street, an unmarked, white Crown

Victoria watched from behind smoked, tinted windows as the garage opened up, then he made a note of the residence activity.

Dorian kissed her before stepping out and walked back out to the trunk. " What is this negro doing," she mumbled to herself, sneaking a peek in the rearview mirror. Before she knew it he was back in the car with a Louis Vitton backpack.

As they were south on I-80 weaving through traffic, Deltrice cleared her throat. "So are you taking me to the office?"

He laughed. " This is the office," Dorian said waving his cellphone like a live grenade. He placed it in a small cradle and said, "Activate hands-free!" A computer voice responded. *Hands-free activated. You have an incoming call.*" Hey shorty, push that button on the steering wheel, Ms. Secretary." She cut her eyes at him as she pressed it.

" Doe Getta, this Young Tay."

"What's hood my nigga?"

"Shit, posted on the block. I need a zip of that soft. What it hitting fo?"

"Eight!"

"I got that, run that in."

"I'm on 80 so give me thirty before I touch, aight?" The line went dead. *Incoming call.* He looked at her and she pressed the button.

The Dunbarton Bridge rumbled underneath the car's tires like an aftershock from an earthquake. The smell of the Chevron oil refinery always let a nigga know that he was in Richman and there was always about to be some shit.

"Trice peep. When a nigga riding dirty, don't let mothafuckas ride your bumpers," Dorian said looking in his rearview mirror. " Drive offensively, you feel me. Like we trying to gain yardage, so speed the fuck up and weave around these cats." She pressed the gas and felt the powerful V-8 pull her as she smoothly switched lanes. He reached over and squeezed her thigh. " Alright now take this exit coming up ."

She looked in the distance and saw the freeway sign which read Pennsylvania Ave. "What part of Richmond is this?"

"The North--North Richmond baby." They drove past Rumel Street, Dubios Street, Third,and Market. "Make a left on Garameda at the next light."

She watched an old man with a matted beard, wearing dirty clothes, pushing a shopping cart full of cans. He stopped in the middle of the crosswalk and lit up a crack pipe.

"Damn, he couldn't at least wait until he got his black ass across the street? Man, no shame in his habit huh?"

"Welcome to the iron triangle baby," he said as they watched the old man take another long hit as he held up traffic, ignoring the honking. He then clowned by doing the old school electric slide while pushing the cart to the other side.

Incoming call!

Dorian reached over and pushed the call button. "I'm in your city my nigga."

"Aight I'm in the back," Tay said, then the line went dead.

Trice turned left and came upon a large, red, two-story housing project called Magnolia. The driveway was in the shape of a large horseshoe. "Turn here and drive over to young brah next to the Benz."

Tay was sitting on the trunk of a cherry red CL550 Benz sipping on a fifth of cognac Hennessey. No shirt, wearing red Coogi denim shorts with some throwback, coke white Nike Air Max's. Dorian jumped out with his backpack and greeted him with a hug, slipping him a package.

They talked for a few minutes but Trice couldn't make out exactly what they were saying. She waited in the car, studied the deep scars and bullet holes which plagued Tay's slinder, muscular body. *He looks no more than sixteen years old,* she thought as she saw him hand Dorian something. He walked back to the car and got in. "How old is he Dorian?"

" He old enough, don't let that baby face fool yah. He a straight killa."

"I'm surprised that he is still breathing from all of those wounds… Well babe, you got a missed call. It's a 415 number."

"Oh yeah, that reminds me; we got to take a trip to the city," he said dialing the number back.

"Holah amigo!"

"Hey Alexio—"

"Say where you at, in traffic?"

"Just leaving the Rich."

"Good, well I'm at my club."

"Oh yeah, which one?"

"The Pink Palace in South San Francisco. A few of my employees' clients want some of that excuse me while I kiss the sky." Dorian heard the music pulsate in the back ground as he remembered Jimi Hendricks' "Purple Haze" lyrics.

Deltrice took the same route to the freeway and tensed up when she saw two black and whites with their lights on blocking traffic. "Relax, they're just fucking with someone else."

They saw the old man from earlier handcuffed and sitting on the curb as they rifled through his shopping cart.

"Driving is really relaxing," she said as she merged on the freeway and rolled down the window, letting the cool air hit her face.

"Well shorty, you sure in the hell wasn't relaxed when you seen them police back there. I mean, you can't be doing the flashlight on the base head routine ma."

They both laughed and watched the passing scenery in silence. San Francisco was always alive with tourists, pimps, drug dealers, scam artists, prostitutes and jackers.

The bath water turned to a cloudy reddish color as Peaches stepped in, laid back and tried to relax. She grabbed her cellphone off the sink, dialed a number and waited for someone to answer.

"The Pink Palace," a woman's velvet voice announced on the other end of the line. "Hello,hello this is Tricia."

"Hey Tricia, how are you doing girl?"

"I am not doing so well."

"What's wrong?" she asked with a hint of concern in her voice.

"I'm, fine I'm fine." *If she only knew*, she thought to herself. "I am just going to be a little late starting my shift."

"Oh ok, well I'll let the other girls know then. Is that it?"

"Oh yeah, let Alexio know, because he gets all pissed off if a bitch don't tell him shit."

"Oh girl don't worry, I know how to handle his Mexican ass."

"Alright girl, thanks. I owe you one." The line went dead. Peaches cringed as she moved a little, when warm water lapped up between her thighs.

Manky pulled his Chevy Suburban into a car wash and jumped out as the deep bass pounded through his speakers. He dropped five dollars' worth of coins into the self- wash machine, grabbed the sprayer and began washing his truck. The beeping let him know that he had less than a minute to finish. He hung up the sprayer, got in and drove forward with the door open to the area with the vacuum. He reached behind him, grabbed a large towel, jumped out and began drying his rims.

He felt a cold, heavy steel to his neck and a deep voice say, "Nigga you remember me?!" Manky listened to the hammer cock back. He froze as he tried to recognize this mystery person's voice. His heart rate quickened as air drew from his lungs when seconds passed.

D-Down squatted down to Manky's eye level. "You got to be more on your toes my nigga," he said. Patting him on his back, he looked around and put his chrome .45 back into his waistband, covered it with the front of his shirt, then got up. "What's up?" they greeted each other.

"I knew it was you-"

"Yeah right nigga, how so?"

"I mean I had burners pulled on me before and you're the only nigga I know that cocks the hammer to a automatic."

"HHHMMM very fucking observant my nigga. I usualy cock the hammer to heighten the affect, you feel me. Kind of like a excl'mation point, but hey, I'm not going to be making a habit of putting tools to my nigga's necks. Anyhow, what's good?"

"Shit," Manky said as he finished drying and began vacuuming his back seat.

" How was that shit in the city? You come up on any work?"

"My nigga, did!" he said, handing him his cellphone.

D-Down grabbed it and looked at the grainy, dark footage for a minute or two. " Damn nigga,that bitch look like she is on like shit. AAHH man, not the Patron. Wow, she cool though. She got friends?"

"Every bitch got friends. I just gotta ask, to be honest."

"I think I seen her ass before but I am not sure were. I think a strip club in the city."

"Well she live in the city 'cause I dropped her off somewhere in Hunter's Point."

"Yeah-yeah that's where I know her from. She work at the strip club in South Frisco called the Palace. I had a yellow-bone Asian ripper that use to dance there," he said while handing the phone back. "She get it though and she will choose up."

"Yeah and the bitch forgot to grab her purse," Manky said, holding up a Burberry hand bag.

"Well you have a reason to call the broad now."

Mission Blvd. was busy with the afternoon rush as small mom and pop restaurants handled the foot traffic of customers. Vintage buildings with fire escapes from the seventeenth century clung to their exteriors and looked like overgrown vines. The marquee to the club read "The Pink Palace" in bright pink lettering surrounded by large clear bulbs.

"Turn in this alley right here." Deltrice pulled in and parked behind a maroon Maseratti Quattroporte. "Cool, Alexio is still here. Come on, I want you to meet this dude. He's good peoples-"

"Babe I'd rather-"

"Just come on!" Dorian said, grabbing his backpack and stepping out.

"Well aight."

As they both walked by the sports car, she studied each of their reflections as Dorian led the way. He banged on a rusted steel door and waited. A deep voice came from behind.

"Who the fuck is it?"

"It's Dorian J. Alexio is expecting me." Silence. The sound of heavy scraping metal and bolts echoed through the one-way alley as the door opened.

"Hey amigo come-come. Welcome to La Casa."

As they stepped in the club it smelled of incense, perfume and sex. The floors were carpeted and the walls were paneled with cedar wood. Strippers dressed in colorful floral bras and thongs walked in and out of beaded entrances as they followed Alexio up a wrought-iron spiraling staircase, leading above the club's bar and multiple stages. The club's second floor was a loft renovated into a large, spacious office. Alexio sat behind a dark stained oak desk. He leaned forward and made a steeple with his short, pudgy fingers.

"Have a seat."

They both sat down and glanced around the elegantly decorated office. Red velvet covered the walls with gold embroidered printed crowns. Hand carved wooden frames surrounded Dahlia surrealist paintings. Alexio started pulling money and began counting big faces. That was the cue for Dorian to come with the product. He reached in his backpack and fumbled around.

"So what did you want to spend?"

"Well amigo, I want a Q.P. of that mota and a zip of that cream."

Before he could finish his request Dorian tossed five tightly wrapped packages in front of Alexio and he went straight for the cocaine. Dorian stood up, walked over to his desk and picked up the neatly stacked money and handed it to Deltrice. "Baby, count this for me aight."

"Hey-hey come on amigo, you don't trust your compadre?" he said leaning back after taking a one-on-one. There was caked powder on his upper lip and both nostrils.

"There's twenty-four hundred here!" she whispered. He nodded.

"Are you going to introduce your lovely muneca?" Alexio asked.

"Oh yeah-yeah, this is my prospect accountantand main squeeze!" She frowned then smiled at Alexio.

"How are you Papi?"

"Bueno-bueno!"

"But now Alexio, I trust you or else I wouldn't be fucking with you in the first place. I just got to be accurate with my bread. You know what I'm saying. Besides, I don't have money to burn like you," he said waving his hand around the spacious room.

"Denaro tu calienta ptsss ! " he said as he took another long snort, inhaling the chalky substance. "MMHH bueno-bueno barely no drain," Alexio said with bloodshot eyes. "Man, I'm paying up the coolo for legal shit because one of my putas got caught up in a prostitution sting." He slicked back his dark, oily hair, frowned and rubbed his nose and continued to talk. "Well, VIP is not mic'd up with audio, just video surveillance you know. So there wasn't any record of the so-called proposition. District Attorney Anderson sent one of his undercover goons to fabricate charges on my establishment—"

"Wait-wait, you mean D.A. John Anderson with the Vallejo office? Come on, Frisco is not even his jurisdiction—"

"This I know but it was hard to prove until I started digging and digging. I did and you'll be surprised of how big a shovel money can buy, if you know what I mean." Dorian and Deltrice looked at each other from the corner of their eyes. " Well let's just say that I retained one of the best criminal defense attorneys in San Francisco County and struck gold from the digging, used a counter civil suit for leverage and they settled out of court. They dropped all charges as if this all didn't happen." He took another long snort, leaned back and slouched in his leather chair.

"Aight man, I'm about to shake—"

"Get at Hoist I-I-I want two keys of this shit right here," Alexio said tapping his quill in the pile of cocaine. "As a matter of fact, how is he doing? It's been a minute since I've—"

"He aight, just working and staying out the way. He's not in that line of work. Never has been Alexio."

"Sure-sure," he said smiling and stepping from around the desk, approaching him, slapping him on his back, squeezing his shoulder in a friendly way. "Look, just tell him I simply want to talk business," he reassured Dorian in a crafty way, pushing a glossy business card in Dorian's hand. "Besides, I may sell him this place and retire to my beachfront property in Costa Rica."

Sounds like he is running from something to me, Dorian thought to himself. He glanced at the card, bowed it between his thumb and index finger, took a picture of it with his camera phone and texted it to his uncle with the prefix "72-ZPS-ND2TLKINPERS."

"Lunch," was the response.

Pathump-pa thump was the sound underneath the car's tires as Deltrice switched lanes. *The call Dorian was on had to have been personal because he took it off the hands-free option*, she thought.

"Look Steve--Steve I've been dealing with you for a while man but I need the cash from the last deal and now this. You know what I'm saying. Look-look, I don't need no profiles. I don't need to clean up my credit. I don't need a loan approved because you put me in enough new whips already and I'm damn near ready to trade this mothafucka back in for something else," he said slapping on the dashboard.

"Baby don't trade this in—"

"SHHHHH," he said, putting his finger to his lips. "Hmm, listen Steve-Steve." *Click-click* "You hear that?" he said as he cocked his .40 caliber Heckler and Koch several times as unfired rounds flew out of the chamber. Thire was silence on the line.

On the other end, Steve swallowed hard, tugged his silk tie and shuffled through some car service papers of newly arrived vehicles on his lot. "Look Dorian, I'm-I'm sure something can be worked out. Just come by the Buick dealership tomorrow evening during closing."

Deltrice watched Dorian as he shook his head. "Aight, tomorrow," he said, then hung up.

"Who was that?"

Ignoring her, Dorian said, "You hungry? Because I know a nice restaurant at the pier overlooking the bay."

The waiter seated the placed their orders and took their menus. "The person that I was talking to, his name is Steve-Steve Fowler." he said matter-of-factly, smelling his red wine, sipping it and letting it resonate on his palate before he swallowed it. "He's a manager. A regionalmanager at a Buick car dealership and this dude been straddling the white horse for way too long. He needs to differentiate between owing a drug dealer and owing a creditor. You see, a creditor will simply just ruin your credit by dropping your credit score. A dealer will ruin your life and drop your body off somewhere."

Trice watched his full lips as they creased, puckered and relaxed as she hung on each word until the sizzling food that they ordered was brought to their table on several different skillets and large plates.

They walked Pier 39, putting money in the buckets and hats of performers doing side shows and entertainment for the passing tourist. They stopped and looked across the emerald green Pacific Ocean. "Look, you see that seaweed baby? It's called kelp. They harvest that stuff and use it as a mineral source or food. Imagine that."

"I'm glad that wasn't on our menu." There was a loud shriek from a large seal as it fought with several determined seagulls over a dead fish.

"AHHHHH and there we have in our midst the ever evolving food chain and look babe, look there in the distance. That's the bottom of our judicial food chain."

Ranch dressing dripped off of several crisp, seasoned curly fries onto a stack of napkins as Cl'menta "The Hoist" ate his lunch. "So this fool wants two pies huh?" he asked Dorian as he chewed on a mouth full of food, smacking.

"Yeah, that's what he wanted—"

"Yeah, well for that dude it's thirty a brick. Look nephew, it's about quality not quantity. You understand me? That fool needs to know that and after this first purchase, he is locked in a year contract fucking with me. Meaning that I want his ass to cop from us each month and increase his purchase every time."

Dorian listened intently as Cl'menta carefully studied his young face and continued. "You see nephew, this is a results orientated business. We move goods into the stream of commerce." Pointing at him, he said, "It's about repetition and staying consistent. You dig? But always watch these desperate mothafuckas because they're un-fucking-predictable. I mean, they're the type to compromise any given situation if they even have the slightest little hint that their coward, punk ass is going to get pinched."

"So do your homework, right?" Dorian said confidently.

"Not only that, but really-really study the material folks. That dude Alexio is a trick, who so happens to own a strip club. A profitable one at that. Don't get me wrong, he gets his money but he neglects his business and indulges too fucking much." He took a sip from his soda and looked across the parking lot in deep thought. "I remember that club from my early pimping days in the late 70's. Those deeds exchanged a lot of gangsters' greedy hands and came under different corrupt management, but they kept the name the same. Most of those hoes in there working are burning or running from the law because they can't work the blade."

"He wanted to sell you the club uncle—"

"Yeah right, I wouldn't invest in that shit. It's a liability, especially since one of his hoes got wrapped up. Then here comes me. A ex-con, a nigga. Shit nephew, if I did, I'd torch the place and cash out on the insurance."

"Like on some Sodom and Gomorrah type shit," Dorian said as they both laughed.

"Yeah, if his punk ass glances back he might just turn into a pillar of salt or even better, pure coke." He leaned down and pushed the trunk release button as he looked at his sparkly, diamond encrusted Rolex watch. "Shit look at that, lunch break is over. Ahhh nephew, it's in the trunk, aight."

He stepped out and walked to the rear of the Benz. *Man I got to cop me one of these Euro whips*, he thought to himself as he opened the trunk, grabbed a golf bag, which had a few titanium clubs in it, and closed it. "I'11 see you on the driving range. Oh and by the way, you get 10k off of each one. You already know what I want. Stomp on it if you want, but remember. Longevity!" he said, closing the sunroof and stepping out the car.

CHAPTER FIVE:

LAB

A HABIT IS NO DAMN PRIVATE HELL.
THERE'S NO SOLITARY CONFINEMENT JAIL.
A HABIT IS HELL FOR THOSE YOU LOVE.

"So you bought some new golf clubs huh?" Deltrice announced as she was fixing lunch in the kitchen. Dorian admired her coke bottle shape as she wore a sheer tunic and matching wedge sandals. "Hmmm taste this."

"What is it? It smells good," Dorian said, tasting the spicy food.

"It's called Curacao. It's Haitian; a Haitian dish of thinly sliced brisket, marinated in mango sauce over steamed brown rice."

"Alright Miss Rachel Ray!" Dorian said, pinching her firm ass and kissing her on the neck. "How did you enjoy your first day at the office?"

"Shhhiiittt, it sure is a hell of a lot of driving."

"I thought you said it relaxes you?" Dorian reminded her as he opened up cabinets and drawers.

"You relax me."

"Oh I do huh?"

"Yes."

"Well do you know what relaxes me baby?" Silence. "Money! I'm not trying to push you out of the equation, but when a person doesn't have money, this cold world that we live in tends to treat you like shit. Like you don't even exist. Don't get me wrong, love is a beautiful thing but let's keep it one hundred. It don't pay the bills baby."

She frowned but gradually respected his realness. She set a table for two and they ate. "So what is with the Pyrex jar, measuring cups and the box of Arm and Hammer? Baby if you wanted dessert then I would have baked us a cake."

He laughed as he got up and cleared the table. "This is what I call 'lab time.' I'm going to be giving you some hands-on training in whipping cocaine." She looked at him puzzled, still not getting it. "And you're telling me you're a game tight bitch. Here, put these on," he said, handing her a pair of blue latex gloves, and she put them on.

He walked over to the golf bag and pulled out a tightly wrapped, plastic, black package with a foreign looking symbol. It appeared dense when he tossed it on the granite countertop. He reached under it, pulling out a triple beam scale and small brass weights.

"First off, you got to understand the quality baby." He carefully peeled the package apart, layer by layer until the clear cellophane was exposed. "Look. You see how it's clumped together like this? If you look closer there's small, sparkly, light crystals," he said holding it up to the overhead fluorescent light.

"It-it-it looks sort of like a fish's scale baby. Like it's changing colors or something."

"Right-right, it's called fish scale. Yeah east coast niggas call it that when they holding some good blow." He set the package down, took out a straight razor and made an "X," cutting it open.

"My god, that smell!" Deltrice said pinching her nose. "It smells like lime and diesel fuel mixed together."

"That's what the laborers use to dry the coca leaves under heat l'mps and extract the cocaine. The smell gets less potent as it goes through different hands because niggas cut the drug to increase their profit. Some use all type of shit, like B-12 or some other shit called vitablin, but fiends don't like the taste of that shit on their pipe. So I stay Felix Mitchel 80's and keep it Arm and Hammer, you feel me?" Holding the baking soda box up as if he was filming a commercial, he said, "You got to know the ratio, which is a quarter of this for every ounce of that!" Dorian said pointing, "Hmmm take this." He handed her a paper mask. "I'm use to the smell," he said moving the slide on the triple beam scale in between 28 grams and 30 grams.

He set the small weights on the chrome, circular platter until it balanced, then scooped out a pile of pure cocaine and set it on the plate. It balanced perfectly. He scooped it into the Pyrex jar, reset the slide, adjusted theweight and did the same with the baking soda. He then opened some flavored bottle water and filled the jar up to a milliliter and mixed it.

"You sure that's enough?"

He just looked at her, smiled, turned around, put the jar in the microwave, and pressed one minute. He then took itout, stirred it with a glass ladle and repeated the process 4-5 times. Deltrice watched in amazement as it changed from a yellow mush substance to a solid, pineapple colored rock.

"Too bad there isn't a preset button on the microwave that says 'drugs' press 5 minutes."

He laughed. "Yeah you get jokes!"

She grabbed it out the Pyrex jar and inspected it like an archaeologist discovering a prehistoric fossil. "Now your turn!" he said, grabbing it and putting the dope into the freezer Ziploc bag.

Alexio leaned back in his leather chair behind his office desk and pulled aside Peaches' sky blue thong and entered her tight wetness. She held on to the chair as she straddled him, gyrating up and down. Then fast and slow on his pulsing hardness.

"You like Papi?" she said as she checked the condom with her fingertips. His pudgy hand gripped her sweaty, firm ass cheeks. Peaches' heavy breasts hung like gumdrops as he sucked on her excited nipples like a hungry, greedy infant.

"Benito ojo. Ohh un pinocha bueno-bueno!"

He better hurry up and cum so a bitch can leave, she thought to herself.

Alexio's cell phone vibrated in his shirt's front pocket, which he ignored. She felt him pulse inside of her vaginal lips as the condom caught his warm fluids. He gripped her and thrusted his hips inside of her.

"Ahh-Ahh Papi! You're not going to lay up in my cookies after you creamed in it." She lifted her redbone thighs over him and at the same time pinched the tip of the condom, pulled it off of his manhood, tied it and wrapped it in a napkin that she grabbed out his drawer. Noticing a shiny chrome .38, she closed it quickly.

Alexio watched with satisfaction in his eyes as Peaches' ass shook and bounced when she began walking to his office bathroom.

He stood up, buttoned his pants and fumbled for his cellphone. "Hmmm missed call," he mumbled **to** himself in Spanish. "Ahhh my amigo Dorian," he said as he pushed the call button.

Peaches flushed the toilet after ear hustling and walked back into the office. "Hey Momi. I got some business partners coming to La Casa so VIP treatment. Comprenda? Until then, we talk later. I got a important call so vamoose puta!"he said waving her off as Dorian answered on the other end.

"Hello-Alexio-Hello."

"Olah Amigo this me."

"Come on my friend. We can't do the phone tag thing. You got to pick up—"

"Okay-okay my friend."

"Listen Alexio, I got a line on those two brand-new Range Rovers you requested, zero miles, fully loaded, excellent condition and each one got 30-inch rims on them."

"Aight how much for both?"

"30 thousand each."

Alexio shook his head with understanding, then grimaced as he looked at his offices restroom. "Sounds aight, I got that."

"Aight then, meet me at the Buick car dealership off of Sonoma Blvd in Vallejo between 12:00am – 11:00am."

"Can you deliver the vehicles here?"

"Nawh amigo, you got to pick them up, and one more thing. Come alone man!"

"Ok,ok no problemo my friend. I be there. I be there." The line went dead. Alexio walked over to his restroom and stood in front of his urinal which had a sign that read "Out of order." He pulled on the porcelain tile and the urinal opened like a hidden door, revealing a steel, reinforced digital safe.

He punched in the codes then put his thumb print on a small touch screen so it could be scanned. It beeped twice from confirmation then opened. All of its contents were neatly sectioned and organized. Currency, bonds, jewelry and video CDCR disks. He grabbed a manilla envelope and stuffed it with six, 10-thousand dollar stacks, sealed it and closed the safe.

"Baby where are we going? I thought we were going to see the car guy at the dealership?" Trice asked as she merged onto I-80 going west bound and crossed over the Carquenez Bridge.

"I have a quick drop to make," he said looking at the tollbooth. "Take this exit in Rodeo and get back on the freeway going east bound back to Vallejo." She did as she was told and watched as he pulled out two bundles from a hidden compartment underneath the car's floor board. "Don't watch me bitch. Watch the road! The last thing a nigga need is to get broadsided with all this dope in the car.

"Alright baby!" She removed her hand from the wood grain steering wheel, gently touched his chin and merged onto the freeway. They crossed over the bridge and approached the tollbooth.

"Aight shorty, take the farthest booth to the left. Yeah-yeah that one over there."

They stopped in front of the booth and a frail old black man with peppered gray hair, wearing a uniform, smiled showing no front teeth and purple gums. His thick bifocals hung on the tip of his nose like dried tree sap as he held out his wrinkled, oily hand.

"Hmmm give 'em this," he instructed, handing her a crisp brown paper bag. She passed it to him quickly like it was about to self-destruct upon contact. "Hey old timer, don't eat all your lunch in one sitting because you might just get sick." In so many words, telling him not to overdose.

"Ahh youngs ta. I've been in the game for over 40 years and haven't fouled out yet," he said pointing to his heart. He put his back to the camera, reached under the cashier drawer and pulled out an envelope full of money. He then ripped a receipt to disguise their transaction. "Here you go youngster, don't forget yah receipt," he said, handing Deltrice the money. Then he gave them a military salute as they drove into the darkness.

"Who was that old man?"

"People in the hood call him Terry the toll man."

"He sort of feels like I've known him all of my life or something."

"Yeah you get that feeling also huh? Well one thing about me is that I treat my customers as people and not like fucking dope fiends. You feel me? They respect that shit."

She turned in the back of the Buick dealership and parked next to an imported, black-on-black Audi-RS. Steve Fowler leaned on the rear spoiler, trying to act all nonchalant, yet he was nervously tugging on his silk tie and checking his watch. He smiled and thrusted out his pale, cl'mmy hand towards Dorian as they both got out the shiny Chrysler 300."Hey Mr. Jackson—"

"Steve don't give me that salesman bullshit. You know me better than that fool!" Slapping his stretched hand out the way, he gave him a strong bear hug, lifting him inches off of the ground,then setting him back down on his feet.

"Doe getta my dude!" Steve said giving him a pound.

"So what suga mama did you slide up under and pull this fine European piece of machinery from?"

"Put it this way chap. Feast your eyes on the rewards of a anal-retentive, divorced, middle aged woman with a hot body, whose rich ex-husband didn't sign a prenuptial. I took it on a trade-in and I personally cashed her out. Oh, and I gave her a ride she will never forget. She is planning on repaying the favor later on tonight." They walked through the service area which seemed deserted. "I let everyone go home early if you're wondering. I didn't catch your girlfriend's name."

"Deltrice," she said seductively.

"Steve-Steve Fowler, nice to meet you. Beautiful name. I hear a hint of a French accent in your voice."

"Oh I'm from Haiti."

"Wonderful-wonderful," he said absently, looking at how her outfit hugged her sensual curves and figure.

"Focus-Steve focus." Dorian snapped his fingers several times as if bringing him out of a deep, hypnotic trance.

"Hey bro—I'm—"

"Look I'm meeting this club owner who's coming from the city to pick something up," Dorian said tapping on his leather Louis Vuitton backpack, then unzipping a small compartment and tossing him a thinly wrapped ounce of rock cocaine. "Disappear Steve, for like two hours fool!"

"Oh shit, no problem. I'll go David Blaine or Chris Angel on that ass. Hey if you need me, I'll be in my office."

Dorian scanned the huge lot and saw the fleet of SUVs. "Well there is a few things. I'll need the keys to that gold Cadillac Escalade over there," he said, pointing in the distance.

"Planning to test drive ah?"

"Na wh just a place to sit privately."

"Say no more." Walking to a wall of keys, he thumbed through them, pulling several of them off the hooks and handing them to Dorian.

"I said just the Cadillac—"

"No I insist, let your girlfriend take a look around."

Deltrice stepped forward and grabbed the pile of keys to Buicks, Oldsmobiles and luxury sedans. "Yes Dorian, he insists," she said winking at him.

"Yeah well stay away from the Benzs, Beemers and ah yeah you see that Aston Martin DBS. I think that's what that is over there. Yeah stay away from that shit too," he said answering his cellphone.

"Damn, you think a bitch going to break one of these big boy toys or something?"

"Nawh you're not going to break me before I spit any vows or before you spit out my junior."

"Boy you crazy!" She walked towards a row of new Buicks, stopped in front of new Buick La Crosse and began searching through the laser cut keys. She matched the year, make, and model, opened the sleek door, sat in the plush, leather bucket seats and started the powerful engine. *Now this is me,* she thought to herself closing the door.

"Amigo, I see your car but where are you?"

"Just park and walk around to the front." He waved at Alexio as he came into view. He saw Dorian standing next to a shiny gold Escalade on chrome stock rims.

"I thought they were 30-inches compadre?" he said jokingly, pointing at the tires and then shaking hands.

"The 30's is on here. Get in man." They both stepped into the spacious back seat and he tossed him the two kilos in two large freezer Ziploc bags. Alexio nodded his head, reached in his waistband and Dorian instantly grabbed his wrist.

"Whoa-whoa relax no-quta, no-quta, it's just the dinero."

He relaxed as he pulled out a bulky manila envelope full of money and tossed it on the seat. "Count it!"

He quickly did, shook hands and they parted ways. Steve watched the maroon Maserati in the surveillance monitor as it backed up and quickly drove away. "Nice-nice, wonderful taste," he said out loud then lit the tip of his glass water bong. The crackle of the cocaine sizzled in the small bowl attached to the stem as it bubbled and churned. He held in the smoke, blew it out, loosened his neck tie and took another long hit.

There was a tap on the windshield of the Buick and the door opened. Deltrice instantly woke up, quickly startled from the sound. "You ready, or you want me to pick you up in the morning?"

"Shut up negro!" She playfully pinched his arm and took the keys out the ignition.

"You must like this car huh?"

"Yeah it's nice, sporty."

"Looks like they changed this scraper's style," Dorian said as he looked at the design. "It has a big body and a beefier engine. A V-8 supercharger," he said as he looked at the small vents on the front quarter panels.

Cl'ment flipped a rack of seasoned baby back ribs with some tongs as he was bar-b-queing. The grill sizzled as he rotated lobster tails and potatoes wrapped in tin foil. Dorian pulled into the mansion's open four-car garage, got out with Deltrice close behind him and walked through the second story of the house towards the backyard.

As they walked down the hallway, above them there was clear ceiling revealing a narrow, crystal clear swimming pool with a see-through bottom. Glossy bamboo flooring spread throughout the elegant home which was decorated with expensive Indonesian style rugs, furniture, paintings and ancient artifacts.

"I'm back here nephew!"

Dorian slid open the patio door and stepped out onto the redwood deck surrounded by manicured lush green grass and shrubs. The enriched smell of his bar-b-que was satisfying and filling simply from the scent. Cl'menta's chiseled facial features and hazel eyes examined Dorian, relaxed, then smiled at Deltrice.

"Well-well-well, I finally have the opportunity to meet the first lady," he said, giving her a sarcastic bow.

"Nice to meet you Mr. Barboza."

"Please, please, please—we are like family so call me Uncle Hoist."

"Hoist?" She looked at Dorian.

"Long story of how I got the name."

"Ok," she said, caught off guard with the warm welcome.

"Make, yourselves comfortable," Hoist said, pointing his metal tongs at a glass patio table set with oriental style plates and chopsticks. Thick cushiony seats were positioned around it.

He took off his apron and brought over the steaming hot food on a platter and set it on the glass table, grabbed a bottle of wine and poured three glasses. "This is Bordeaux Pichon Lalande 1982," he pronounced fluently, putting the wine glass to his nostrils and smelling the well-aged grapes. "This is one of the most monumental wines of the last century."

He held the glass up, taking a few swallows. His guests did the same. "Taste like money Uncle," Dorian said smacking his lips. He set the glass down and began sampling the food in front of him.

"Well look at it as if we were sipping fifties at $650.00 a bottle."

"Well it's delicious and this is a lovely meal you prepared," Deltrice commented.

"Thank you. I like her already. So what do you do for a living Deltrice?" Cl'menta asked.

"I'm his personal driver!" she said jokingly. "No-no. I work at Kaiser Hospital as a medical transcriptionist. I am planning on enrolling in medical school and becoming a pediatrician."

"Sound like you got your shit together huh. That's what's up," he said while giving his nephew the evil eye. "My dad, who is his grandfather, use to always tell us to grab life by the throat and choke the shit out of it." Demonstrating with his hands, he flexed his thick forearms as if he was choking an imaginary throat.

"Yeah Uncle, ahh, you can't get nothing out of life if it's unconscious or near death."

"Yeah, well that's when you run through its pockets when no one's looking," he said darting his penetrating hazel eyes back and forth. "Come on, let's take a walk nephew. Excuse us." They both got up and walked around his large one acre backyard. "Ah how long have you been knowing little mama?"

"Hmmmmm I would say about six years off and on. We went to Del A Sal together."

"How well do you know her because she said she drives for you so she obviously knows what the fuck you do. I mean look at her, she's squarer than the storage containers I get paid to load onto ships."

"Unc-Unc relax—"

"Relax ssshhhiiitt, less is best man. The less a bitch knows about your business, your odds of her becoming a eye witness is very slim to none. There's some material nephew that's not worth studying you dig?" He glanced over his shoulder. "She do look like she got some cream though," he said sucking his gold-crowned teeth and meeting Dorian's gaze.

"By the way, how was your little golf trip?"

"Oh yeah-yeah it was straight. As of matter of fact, here!" He lifted up his shirt, reached in his waistband, pulled out a wrinkled manila envelope and he angrily snatched it.

"How much is this?"

"Sixty thousand."

"Why didn't you take your 20%?"

"Because I took it in dope, stepped on it, and doubled my profit in a week." He listened without saying a single word as he flipped through the stack of crisp one hundred dollar bills like a deck of playing cards.

"Is there something wrong?"

"Well this money sure in the hell looks awfully fucking new," he said, holding a bill up to the light.

"You think it's counterfeit?"

"Nawh, all of the security features seems to be there, but you never know. Thirsty niggas plus technology equals liability," he said, putting the bill back into the envelope.

"Its good nephew." Smiling, he patted him on his back and both of them walked back to the table were Deltrice was enjoying her wine.

"So Uncle Hoist"—she licked her lips—"am I approved to date your nephew?"

"Young lady he is a grown ass man but to answer your question, you good with me," he said staring at her.

"This is the Department of Justice currency division. Agent Rodriguez speaking," the woman's velvet accented voice spoke through the agency's phone.

"Hey cutie!"

"Ohh Cl'men ta how are you doing baby? Look I'm about to take my break so—"

"So call your cell, aight. I got a favor I wanted to ask you."

"Sure as long as it's legal 'big man' as long as it's--" The line went dead and seconds later her purse was ringing. She fumbled through it, answered the incoming call. "Pushy-pushy Señor Papi!"

"Ahh puta you sure don't be complaining when I'm pushing inside of you and you're digging your sharp ass nails in my back."

"Ok,ok Papi, what's the favor."

"Aight look. I already e-mailed you a list of serial numbers from about 20-to-30 one hundred dollar bills. I want you to run them through your database and see what comes up."

She looked around and whispered into her cellphone, "Does the currency look new or extremely worn baby?"

"New, too fucking new."

"This tells me that they haven't been in circulation for too long. Ok,ok well give me a few days and I'll call you. Oh and one more thing, don't call the agency's phone no more baby. They monitor all the calls very-very closely…"

CHAPTER SIX:

BETRAYAL

ANYONE WHO HASN'T EXPERIENCED THE ECSTASY OF BETRAYAL KNOWS NOTHING ABOUT ECSTASY AT ALL.

The setting sun hid behind the jagged Pacific mountain coastline, which set off brilliant colors of lavender, burgundy and canary yellows. A maroon Maserati zig-zagged through freeway traffic. The high performance exhaust rumbled with an angelic sound as Alexio hit the gas and took the exit to the Port of Oakland docks. The large parking lot was empty except for an unattended street sweeper in the far distance.

He circled a section of the huge compound and parked behind a warehouse, next to a Benz 600. Alexio stepped out holding a leather attaché briefcase, which contained his club's property deeds, financial records, licenses and certified appraisal of

the building. He felt the slight weight of the chrome .38 strapped around his right ankle. Adjusting his slacks, he wiped the dust off of his custom snakeskin boots and straightened his open collar.

He pulled the cargo elevator door closed and took it to the top floor. Cl'mente stood waiting with his hard hat in hand and wearing his Port of Oakland uniform.

"Hey, buenos tardes comrade," Alexio said greeting and embracing him, but at the same time checking to see if he was holding.

Cl'mente also did the same. "Bueno tardes comrade. Follow me to my office. I was just finishing up some paperwork and calculating payroll for my crew. Soooo 'Big Lex'...You're ready to hang up the velvet rope huh?"

"Huh, oh si,si."

"You know, get out the club business."

"Oh yeah, well it's sort of complicated," he said sitting down in an old fashion wooden straight back chair.

"Complicated—"

"Too much competition. But my friend, listen. If you hire the right marketing firm you can create a good brand—"

"Why haven't you? I mean you're trying to dump something without salvaging the goods first."

"Let's face it. I don't have the patience my friend. Look CI'menta, mira-mira." He set the briefcase on his lap, opened it and began pulling out colorful folders.

CI'menta studied Alexio while he kicked his feet up on his metal, narrow desk. Pieces of dried dirt fell off of his work boots as he fidgeted impatiently. "First off, Lex, how much are you actually asking for the business?"

"2.5 million."

After hearing that number he wanted to reach in his drawer, grab his Desert Eagle .50 caliber and execute him right in his office, yet he used all of his strength to resist. "Sure-sure Alexio, that's a logical asking price given it's a historical estate and its name, but this doesn't necessarily mean you'll get that fucking price."

"You'll double that in the first year and triple that in the second."

He flipped through the folders and studied the graphs as Alexio stared at the turning pages, transfixed by the stack. Dorian came out of the shadows from behind and tazed him. The snapping and popping from the powerful cattle prod enveloped the office as his body shook and grew rigid.

Small spit bubbles and foam formed at the corners of his mouth. "Alright-aight nephew." Dorian stopped tazing him and caught his unconscious body before it hit the floor. "Ah, I need him alive long enough to question his ass. Not cook him like a steak fajita!" CI'menta yelled, grabbing several plastic zip-ties. He secured his wrist to the arm rest and both ankles to the chair's legs.

"Well-well-well look what we have here," he said, pulling the chrome .38 out of Alexio's holster, opening the cylinder and spinning it.

"Hold up." He took out a round and inspected it carefully. "This fucker has nylon coated tip rounds."

"So."

"Sooooo! These rounds, nigga, can slip right through a Teflon or Kevlar vest," he said studying the metallic, midnight blue fibers. He put the round into his breast pocket, closed the cylinder, and dropped it in his side cargo pocket.

"This dude isn't no fucking gunsmith man. He working for somebody. I mean, what the fuck he need cop killer rounds for?"

Cl'menta reached in his breast pocket, pulled out a small glass vial of ammonia, opened it, and waved it under his snot filled nostrils, then slapped him. "Wake the fuck up bitch."

Alexio stirred, shook his head and came into focus. "What the fuck you-you what is this shit?" he said, assessing the situation in one breath.

"What does it look like? You're tied the fuck up to a chair."

"Why?"

"My answer is because I am going to ask your ass some simple questions. Who are you working for Lex?"

"Working for I-I work for no one mothafucka!" Dorian quickly tazed him. "AHHHHH fuck-fuck." His chest heaved. "Get-get your fucking goon off of me!" Cl'menta nodded to Dorian and he stopped tazing him.

"Look compadre, this goon you're referring to happens to be my nephew and it's the same person you gave sixty thousand dollars of marked bills for two bricks of 'my,' yes 'my' high-grade yola! Any fucking banking institution I would've deposited that hot bread into would've red-flagged it and contacted their channels and indicted my black ass on drug trafficking charges"

"Come the fuck on—"

"No-no you come the fuck on man. I got a connect that works for the Department of Justice and she ran the serial number prefixes and guess what? They distribute certain amounts to specific operations, for targeted counties, and ahhh my friend, they re-use this bread and inventory this shit, meaning they track it."

"If I tell you I am a dead man."

Cl'menta rubbed his neatly trimmed goatee, casually paced the floor, set the nylon coated .38 round on the desk and continued pacing. Silence. Cl'menta smiled. "Big-Big Lex. I haven't stayed alive this long without having some real solid people around me man. You dig?" he said, pointing at Dorian. Alexio looked at him and then back at the round on his desk. "Look-look I know you're hiding from the El Guiterez familia. They dipped their beaks too far into your business affairs, after they put you on. I mean you can't bite the supplier's hand that feeds you and now you're on top of their long list of contracts. I mean, you're in the way. You're literally a breathing fucking corpse."

"How-how in the-how did you know that?"

"Come on Big Lex!" he said grinning. "I'm Panamanian man. I negotiate with cartels from Managua, Nicaragua to Bogota, Columbia to Tegucigalpa, Honduras, and they're all the fucking same!" He eyed Alexio for a few seconds as sweat beaded on his wrinkled forehead.

"And ahh what-what is that?"

"Some have no morals. No loyalty," he said shaking his head in disgust. "They'll hacksaw their own blood madre's head off and upload the footage to YouTube, just to prove a sick ass point. Put it this way: There is this old Panamanian proverb. 'There is no rest for the wicked until they close their eyes for good.' So I'm going to ask you this one last time. Who in the fuck do you work—"

"Anderson--D.A. John Anderson," he said as his heart raced. "In place of protection from the Guiteraz Cartel. The Mexican government wanted to squeeze their Gosa Nostra's outlet into the United States and only I knew. Only me! They negotiated immunity with the district attorney's office out here in place of my testimony, yet Anderson's greedy ass wanted more. He-he wanted you man-you."

"So your coward ass gave me up!"

"He-he said if I could negotiate a drug deal with you then I'd be granted immunity and not be deported. Then he will have enough to indict you on and it would look good for his campaign."

"Wait-wait—Campaign? What fucking campaign?"

He swallowed. "Mayor-"

"Mayor? Isn't that about a bitch. He wants to disrupt a lucrative operation for his political motives. Then what the hell is this?" he said squeezing Alexio's face and holding the bullet in front of his eyes.

"They said that-that you had cartel ties and their ballistic technicians issued those to me."

"Oh yeah? Huh..." Cl'mente released his grip. "Is that fucking right? Huh…" he said, leaving the office.

Dorian couldn't believe what his ears were hearing. He watched as Cl'menta came back with a huge roll of heavy duty plastic and a plastic tub full of steaming water. He cleared the desk in one quick sweep, rolled out the plastic in one swift motion, and set a medieval 12-inch dagger on the table. He walked over to Alexio, tilted his chair back and positioned his feet into the tub.

"What-what!" He shoved a handkerchief in his mouth and taped it shut.

"Let me see that tazer because we're going deep sea fishing! This is fifty thousand volts. Including the hot water makes it circulate and enhances the voltage. Look!" He tazed him in the crotch for several minutes then checked his pulse on his neck. "You're not dead yet so wake the fuck up!" he yelled, slapping him hard on his fat chin.

Dorian cringed as his glossy eyes rolled back into his head. *Alexio is literally being electrocuted*, Dorian thought.

"I dont even expect to receive my dope back because it's probably sitting in a fucking evidence locker somewhere!" he yelled, tazing him between sentences. "What I want is your stash—the numbers to your safe—and I might just let your coward ass live."

"Hey Unc, Unc. I think he's trying to tell you something," Dorian said stepping closer.

"Oh ok. My nephew says you're trying to say something huh!"

He leaned closer to the chair onto the table. He set the tazer on the desk as they carried him to it, set him on it as if he was an astronaut ready to be launched. He gripped the knife, ripped open his shirt, baring his sweaty, pale chest. He made a deep cut across it. He ripped the duct tape off his mouth and yanked the wet handkerchief from his mouth, then he leaned closer.

Alexio mumbled something in Spanish and suddenly lurched forward biting his earlobe and taking his 4-carat chocolate diamond earring with it. He dropped the knife as a stream of blood snaked around his muscular neck. Alexio broke his hands loose from the plastic ties and groped for the knife on the desk. He tightly gripped it as if his life depended on it.

"My mothafucking ear. After I kill you, I'm going to make a necklace out your—"

Alexio slashed at him wildly cutting his palm and then his wrist on the second pass. Cl'menta tried to choke him but he couldn't get a solid grip around his neck and pry the knife out of his hands. "Doe shoot this desperate mothafucka man!!!"

Dorian looked around and saw the tazer on the floor. "Nigga don't even think about it. You'll taze my ass trying to taze him. Desk drawer!" he grunted.

Alexio bicycle kicked, spinning both of them, and they slid off the desk onto the floor. Dorian hurdled over the table like a track star and yanked all the drawers out until he saw the large .50 caliber Desert Eagle. Its triangular barrel looked mystical as he aimed it at Alexio's skull. He thrashed wildly on the office floor trying to avoid his fate.

"Get the fuck out the way!" Dorian yelled to Cl'mente.

He slipped on the thick plastic beneath him, diving out the way, as Dorian fired two ear splitting rounds. Orange fl'mes came out the barrel and recoiled. In rapid succession, both slugs separated Alexio's forearm from his elbow and exploded his skull, sending crimson blood and spongy brain tissue splattering across the clear plastic. The body's nerves jerked as a putrid stench filled the room from its bowels. A pool of blood formed around the body and inched its way to the corner of the plastic.

"Don't just stand there, that's what this plastic is for. Let's wrap this fajita piece of shit up man!" he said, quickly grabbing the corners before the blood dripped on the carpet.

They wrapped Alexio's body up and sealed the corners with duct tape. "Now what?"

"You're going to help me put him in his trunk and follow me to a cargo container, which I already got waiting to be loaded on a ship, ready to leave first thing early morning to Buenos Aires. They always lose shipments during rough seas all of the time nephew, and it's costly for the company to retrieve thosecontainers so the insurance writes it off."

"Tell me one fucking thing Uncle..." He looked him in the eye. "How in the fuck did you know all that shit about him?" he asked, pointing the barrel at the heap of plastic.

"Like I said, you got to not only do your homework on a mothafucka, but you really got to study the material," he said, grabbing his weapon from his hands...

CHAPTER SEVEN:

COCKTAIL MIX

SERIOUS GAME HAS NOTHING TO DO WITH FAIR PLAY.
IT IS BOUND UP WITH HATRED, JEALOUSY,
BOASTFULNESS,
AND DISREGARD OF ALL THE RULES.

Northern Cali's crisp morning air blew past a PG&E worker's neck as he was harnessed fifty feet above heavy traffic. A gunman sat in parked car below him loading nine millimeter rounds into a curved magazine. He inserted it into a Tech nine, pulled back the retractable cylinder, and put a round into the chamber. He positioned the sling around his shoulder and put on a quarter-length leather coat.

As he leaned back in the passenger seat, he watched from a block away as crowds of customers walked in and out of the busy liquor store to wire money or either cash their payroll checks. He knocked the dust out of his holey jeans and rubbed his nappy, full beard. He smoothly stepped out the car and headed up the block towards the liquor store. Each step seemed to be in slow motion as customers entered and exited, missing their demise by seconds.

The door beeped as he walked through the store's motion sensor. Loosening up his quarter-length coat, he put an Alka-Seltzer in his mouth and stepped past the long line to where there was a counter off to the side. He picked up a MoneyGram application and acted like he was filling it out. He then approached the counter that was encased with bulletproof glass.

"Sir I'm sorry but if you're trying to cash your check, you're going to have to wait in line," the teller said as he saw the MoneyGram application in his hand, smirked and pointed his thumb as if he was trying to catch a taxi.

The gunman gripped the counter, transfixed with foam dripping from the corners of his mouth onto the counter. His eyes rolled back into his head.

"Sir-sir are you alright?" The teller rushed from around the counter as the gunman staggered and fell in front of the door. A woman screamed as everyone watched in horror. When the heavy steel door opened up, he saw stacks of money and an open safe. He jerked his leg like a fish out of water and blocked the door from closing. "Sir-sir! Someone call 9-1-1!" The teller yelled, when suddenly he felt something pushed into his chest.

"Don't nobody fucking move or else all of you working class citizens will be witnesses to his fate." He stood up and pushed the cashier worker through the door. He then pulled out a black garbage bag from his crotch and handed it to the man. "Fill it up until I say when."

He grabbed it, snapped it open and quickly swept all of the exposed stacks of bills into it as the gunman aimed the Tech-9 at his sweaty back. "Aight lay face down and hug the carpet!" He did as he was told as the gunman ran out the back exit, hit a fence and doubled back up the block.

The gunman heard the sirens in the distance as he ran to the waiting car, but passed it up as his eyes met with the PG&E worker hoisted to a pole. *Fuck,* he thought to himself. His getaway driver slowly pulled out and made a U-turn, then sped past him up to the corner.

"My nigga come on get in!"

"HMMMMM take this!" he said, handing him the garbage bag full of cash. He quickly took off the quarter-length coat, stealthily wrapped the gun in it and dropped it in the back seat. "Meet me close by Cortola Parkway my nigga then snatch me there, they on me."

The car sped off as he continued northeast, hitting fence after fence. Dogs barkedand snapped at the intruder as he ran through the yard.

Crumbs from a bagel fell on Officer Rumsfield's uniform as he chewed and watched for the traffic light to change, listening to dispatch.

"We have a code-3, possible 211 in progress, 5th and Grant. Suspect fled on foot northeast. Black male, between 5-10 to 5-11, 180 pounds, wearing a gray leather coat and blue jeans."

"Oh fucking great, that just narrows it down to hmmm let's see, about three hundred thousand buffoons—"

"Look-look, however we look at the odds, we still have a job to do," his partner Staggs said.

"Yeah-yeah tell that to the detectives who take credit for us securing a crime scene."

Bushes moved in an alley as a man jumped over a fence. He then retrieved something from it and walked casually past the police cruiser.

"Hold it right there, you black fucker. Don't fucking move!" Staggs said unholstering his Sig Sauer .40 caliber. The man jumped over the hood, ducked and hit a fence. Officer Rumsfield circled the block as Staggs led the foot chase, pumping the heavy semi-automatic in his clenched fist like a curling bar. Veins in his thick neck pulsed with adrenaline and excitement as he stalked his prey.

"Stay in your homes. We're in pursuit of a suspect!" Officer Rumsfield yelled, pointing his weapon at the man as he ran across the street. The suspect threw up his hands in surrender but Rumsfield let off five rounds in rapid succession. Hot, empty shells dropped like chimes as one bullet missed his spine by inches.

"Why did you shoot a unarmed man?" the suspect asked. They ignored him, handcuffed him, and rolled him on his stomach so he could bleed out.

"Hey-hey cop. He-he's alive man. He needs medical attention."

"Ma'am-ma'am, we can arrest you for interfering with police business—"

"Fuck you, look at 'em—I am filming this shit," she insisted, pulling out her camera phone,

An angry crowd developed as people came out of their houses. Both officers looked at each other and nodded telepathically as if they were reading each other's mind. They went into action. One controlled the crowd as the other radioed for back up and an ambulance.

Staggs quickly walked to his trunk, opened it and grabbed a roll of yellow tape. He then unbuttoned his shirt, and stuffed a black .32 revolver in it. He taped off the perimeter and searched for the nearest bush with a flashlight in hand.

"Now you turn that off lady," Staggs said. As the officer stepped towards her, she backed up and disappeared into the crowd. That was all the time Officer Staggs needed to drop the revolver in the bushes and flash the light on it. He then yelled to his partner, picked up the weapon and set it on the cruiser's hood.

D-Down leaned out the Suburban's passenger side window and watched as a medical helicopter flew over the freeway, heading northwest. "Someone must of got aired out bruh." Manky brushed his healthy waves forward with the palm of his hand, took a sip from a chrome flask then capped it. "You got that bitch's number?"

"Yeah ahh Peaches. Let me call her and let her know a nigga coming." He scrolled through his numbers, tapped the screen and she answered on the second ring.

Peaches noticed the 7-0-7 area code, hesitated on sending the call to voicemail, then answered it. "Hello,hello who is this?" she asked, stepping back into the empty VIP section of the club where it was quiet.

"This Manky lil' mama. Ahh look, I got something that belongs to you--"

"Oh my purse." Her whole attitude changed once she recognized Manky's voice and remembered bits and pieces of that night. "How are you doing Daddy? You do have something that belongs to me. Look I'm at work so bring it by my job at The Pink Palace in the city. My shift just started, so ahh just call me and I'll come out front."

"Aight." The line went dead. Manky looked at D-Down in the passenger seat counting out stacks of hundreds in his lap as he was talking on his cellphone, then hung up. "Who was that?"

"This criminal defense attorney in Frisco named Pori. I'm p1anning on seeing him, probably retaining him and shit. He should be back in his office about time we get there," he said glancing at his watch. His office is off of Market Street."

"Shit, that's a block away from the hoe stroll."

"There you fucking go Manky. You is already thinking about tricking."

"Shit it isn't tricking if you got it my nigga," he said patting on his bulging pockets. "I support my habits my nigga!"

Vintage style buildings stretched like Roman pillars, which looked like they were holding up the clouds above. They both walked through the heavy automatic glass doors into the lobby then took the elevator to the floor where the lawyer's office was located. As they stepped in, a secretary who sat behind her desk looked down her nose over her reading glasses. She ripped her wiry glasses off of her face and stood up.

"How may I help you two gentlemen?"

"I am here to talk to Mr. Pori. I'm the person—"

"Oh you're his 2 o'clock appointment. He's been expecting you." She leaned down, pressed a button and spoke into the intercom. "Mr. Pori your 2 o'clock is here."

"Sure, bring him in."

The secretary nodded in agreement. Manky and D-Down both walked down the long hallway to his office and stepped in.

"You have thirty new messages." Deltrice listened with the phone cradled to her ear as she painted her nails. Suam's concerned voice came on as she listened.

"Hey girl. Where you at heffa? I mean I haven't seen your ass or even heard from you in a month it seems like. Let me know if you're aight girl, okay!" She set the phone down and put it on speaker as Dorian walked in.

"Who is that?"

"Suam!"

"Well call her back before they put a amber alert out on your sexy young ass."

She cut her eyes at him. "Yeah because you literally kidnapped a bitch!"

"Ha, come on shawty you entered this game willingly. I never put a Glock to your head and said 'bitch get in my limo.'"

"Yeah but you put your tongue in my pink limousine that night."

"Well your doors was wide open, so I couldn't help but get in." Dorian leaned down, hugged and kissed her neck. She could smell the chalky, metallic scent on his clothes.

"Babe you smell like gunpowder."

Suam adjusted her stethoscope and hospital ID pinned to her OR scrubs top. Her firm thighs filled out the uniform's material as she walked out the automatic glass doors of the massive building. Her brown and blonde highlights were pulled back into a tight ponytail as she wore dark Dolce & Gabbana sunglasses.

A reflection of a Chrysler 300 sitting on 22-inch chrome rims drove up slowly. The driver's side window rolled down. Suam lifted up her glasses and recognized the driver and the passenger.

"So you went Hollywood on us, all of the sudden. Huh bitch?" Deltrice said referring to her choice of shades.

"You know a bitch gotta shake the popparazis." They both gave each other girlish giggles and Suam leaned through the window to give her friend a hug and affectionate kiss on her cheek. "Dorian, ahh when are you going to un-handcuff my folks, huh?"

Dorian sucked his teeth and smiled at how attractive Suam was up close. "I got a big house and a big appetite for all flavors lil' mama."

Suam laughed, took off her glasses and licked her glossy full lips seductively. "I don't like being nobody's concubine in no king's castle. I like being the queen biioottcchh. Besides, you know what department I work at in here lil' daddy," she said waving her hand behind her.

"Girl don't tell him—"

"Vasectomy!"

"Alrighty," Deltrice said. "Does Marcellos know that he has a Lorena Bobbit on his hands?"

"Well personally, I don't have no problems out of my man—"

"Yeah after he got rid of all of the scalpels and chloroform," Deltrice said reaching in her purse and pulling out a thick envelope full of money and handing it to her.

"What's this Trice?" Suam asked, eyeing the envelope. Suam took it into her small hands, opened it, and began counting the bills.

"I guess that answers your question huh bitch?"

"Well love doesn't pay the bills but this right herrr does," she said in a fake southern accent as she rubbed the envelope across her cleavage and slid it in between her designer bra.

"Damn girl, don't have a fucking orgasm on my door. It's just rent money."

"Ithought a person was supposed to get benefits if they were fucking the landlord."

"Yes. Well lil' daddy that landlord happens to be my man and yes he owns the building, but who says I pay anything?"

"Point taken. But ahh where is Marcellos' black ass at any way?"

She looked at her watch. "Hmmmm, he should be showing a potential buyer a house right about now."

"A house!"

"He's a real estate agent baby," Deltrice explained.

Dressed in a cream-colored dress suit and dark burgundy silk tie, Marcello's matching Stacey Adams gators clicked across the estate's spacious marble floor as he escorted the visitors out of the house that he was selling. His Blackberry vibrated. He plucked it off of his belt loop, loosened up his tie, took off his coat and answered it. "Mr. Mitchell speaking!"

"Any luck with La Casa?" Dorian asked matter-of-factly.

"Hey bruh, what's good?"

"How are you Cellos?" Trice and Suam said in perfect unison.

"Hey—you must got me on speaker or something. What's up y'all."

"What is it my nigga?" Dorian announced. "You, me and these lovely, beautiful ladies who need a week end getaway to 'Sin mothafucken City.' On me!"

"On you?"

"On me pimping. Besides, selling houses in this fucked up economy, my nigga, you need a break." Deltrice and Suam looked at each other with surprised, quizzical looks.

"When you talking brah?"

"Depends."

"Ahh Dorian, it depends on what?" Trice asked while she slowly zipped her purse.

"It depends on how fast you can pack."

The attorney swiveled around in his leather chair, threw his feet off of his desk and stood up in one fluent motion as Manky and D-Down stepped into his large office. Law books stacked in glossy wooden book shelves decorated the background.

"Attorney at Law Thomas A. Pori, certified criminal law specialist," he said thrusting his hand out like an upscale European import car salesman. Manky made eye contact and shook the man's hand as well as D-Down.

"Have a seat gentlemen; sit-sit." His suspenders went slack as he also sat and folded his hands with intensity. D-Down rubbed his shaved head and cleared his throat.

"I was referred to you by a close friend of mine."

"Ohh, who?" he asked, leaning forward on his elbows.

"He goes by the name Twig. Twiggy-B."

"Ahh yes, Mr. Bolton. I remember Mr. Bolton. I went to bat for him. Got the feds and ATF off of his ass and his felony gun possession dropped. He paid his counsel handsomely," he said, pointing to himself. "What's your story my friend?"

D-Down leaned forward, plucked a business card out of his gold-plated case that was on his desk and bowed it in between his fingers. "Well you see, I'm originally fromthe 'town'—"

"Oh yeah, what part of Oakland?"

"84th and Bancroft."

"Ahh ok—"

"Well that's not important," D-Down explained. "The point is that with the type of business I'm in and the spontaneous lifestyle I live, I need that security, that insurance. You feel me? You know, just in case my crew gets pinched."

The attorney nodded his head slowly in agreement. "I totally understand. I respect a man that's prepared and values his freedom." He stood up, ran his veiny, oily, pale hands through his thick, wavy, salt and pepper locks of hair, and adjusted his Ernest Hemingway olive shell glasses. He thrusted his hands into his pockets.

"Gentlemen, as you may already know, I've been in this business for over thirty years. I've represented every type of defendant, every case from first-degree murder, capital cases, drug trafficking by cartel families and bank robberies. You fucking name it. I also went up against the most aggressive, dirtiest playing district fucking attorneys from northern to southern Cali—"

Mr. Pori stopped in mid-sentence as he observed D-Down reach under his black t-shirt and pull out two thick, brand-new stacks of neatly folded hundreds and casually toss them on his desk. The attorney also saw the other man reach in his back pocket, but instead of pulling out money, he saw the man with a chrome flask unscrew the top and take a long swig.

"Is ten racks good enough for a retainer fee?"

He took a gold pen from his breast pocket. "Let me see that card." He wrote something down on it and handed it back to him. Then he leaned forward, pressed the intercom and cleared his_throat.

"Yes Mr. Pori?"

"Write Mr. D-Down a receipt for ten thousand dollars. We just brought on our newest client."

"Ahh what number is this?" D-Down asked.

"My personal cellphone number. Your direct line to your new counsel on record. I don't give that number out to just anybody, but hey as we say, 'let's keep it one hunned,'" he said as he picked up the two heavy stacks. "You definitely paid for it."

Black exhaust and dust spiraled from beneath the private jet's tires as it landed on the air strip's tarmac, taxied and stopped next to an olive green, candy stretch Lincoln Continental limo. The passengers gazed out the plane's oval windows as the sea of lights sparkled off of the blanket of casinos.

Dorians's 22-karat Pave' ScaraB ring twinkled and glistened off of his pinky as he filled everyone's glasses with bubbly. He set the bottle down and held up his glass.

"Let's all enjoy ourselves and leave three times wealthier than we came." They all clincked their crystal flutes, took long sips, licked and smacked their lips.

"Sir-sir your driver's waiting to take your guests to your hotel."

"Aight, y'all ready?"

Everyone stood up and strolled through the plane's fuselage and walked out onto the tarmac. The evening air was humid and warm as Dorian, Deltrice, Marcellos and Suam got into the cool, leathery confines of the luxury limo. As they quietly pulled away, Marcellos reached into his inside Burberry blazer's pocket, pulled out a blunt of northern lights, lit it and inhaled deeply.

The bass and high-hats from the strip club's speakers mounted high above, pounded and vibrated. Peaches arched her smooth back, extended her firm legs, bounced, shook and made her ass cheeks clap, while she held on to the brass pole in front of her. She craned her neck to look behind her to see the reactions of customers as they covered the stage with money. Biting her lip with excitement, she wrapped her calves around the brass pole, spiraled upward to the ceiling and dropped straight down to the floor doing the splits. Her pierced, pink pearl tongue, kissed the glossy hardwood stage's floor.

She stood up, blew a kiss to the crowd and scooped the pile of money up, before disappearing behind heavy velvet curtains.

"Hey girl, you have a few missed calls," another dancer said handing Peaches her cellphone.

"Thanks girl." Taking the phone, she looked at the area code and instantly pressed re-dial.

A Suburban pulled up to the curb and stopped in front of The Pink Palace strip club as a stalky bouncer suspiciously eyed the tinted SUV Manky looked at the incoming call. "Here go that bitch," he said answering the phone.

D-Down rolled down the window halfway as the curious bouncer stepped towards them. "Ahh, we're just waiting to drop off something to one of yah co-workers folks!" He nodded in agreement and stepped back.

"Don't you need your purse for you to put all that bread in lil' mama?" Manky asked as he was breaking down a fluffy bud of some purple kush and began rolling a blunt.

"You're right on time Daddy. I just finished my shift. Where are you at?"

"Out front, yeah me and my folks."

"Give me a minute and I'll be right out." The line went dead.

Peaches' turquoise, silk quarter-length robe clung to her shapely body as she walked in matching six-inch stilletos. She stood outside looking left and right as if waiting.

"Peaches."

She turned her attention to who called her name and walked towards the car.

"We don't bite lil' mama. Come here. This here is D-Down and as you already know, I'm Manky."

She smiled and held out her hand. He took it into his hands and gently shook it. She tightened the waist belt on her robe. "Nice to meet you. Now ahh, do y'all mind if I get in?"

Manky hit the unlock button as she stepped in and closed the car door. "So how is business?"

She shook her head and smiled. "It's just another day at the office," she said glancing at her purse sitting next to her. She opened it and threw it over her shoulder like it was an ammunition pack. "Look, I really appreciate you bringing this here to a sista 'cause—"

"It's good lil' mama. I might be a grimy nigga, but I'm not starving. There's certain rules and principles that I abide by and lifting a bitch's purse isn't one of them."

"Hmmm."

He handed her a lit blunt and she stared at it like a stick of dynamite as thick smoke rose from its cherry. She took a long pull, held it in and slowly exhaled, and began hacking and coughing.

"Baby you got some virgin lungs," D-Down said smiling, plucking the blunt from her fingers. They spent a few minutes passing it around. "So what do you do when you're not here?"

She blew out a cloud of smoke and wiped the corner of her mouth. "I'm slowing down enough so money will be able to catch me."

"I like that answer. Money chases you?"

"Yeah something like that."

"Well look baby, my company is throwing a private album release party for one of our artists name Brick-Band. I would like to invite you and a few of your sexy ass potnas," D-Down said.

Manky looked at her in his rearview mirror. "Have you done any video work lil' mama?" Manky nudged him.

Well I've been in a few projects here and there. Some photo shoots or whatever. I mean, I didn't have no agent. Plus I was independent. Business was kind of slow, but wait-wait nigga. Are you like trying to book me for something, or is this—"

"It will be worth your time. So relax lil' mama, besides I just want to get to know you. You know, let your hair down and shit, you feel me?" Manky reassured her.

"Well look, you got my number so let me know when, and ahh I'll holla at few of my homegirls," she said as she scooted across the leather seat towards the door.

"By the way Peaches, have you seen that fool Alexio lately?"

Peaches' heart skipped a beat when she heard that name. "How-how you know Lex?"

"How do you know Lex?" D-Down playfully mocked her. "Come on now." He turned around in his seat and smiled, showing a mouth full of platinum diamond cut fronts. "We both know he got the cut sewed up in the city."

"Well ahh, to be real, I haven't seen him for a while. Nobody has, but there's some serious players looking for him though," she revealed, then left to go back to the club.

D-Down and Manky glanced at each other with suspicion, then looked back at Peaches as her see-through robe showed her cream, lace thong disappear between her ass cheeks. "My nigga, I gotta see that footage of her on your phone one more 'gain." Manky smiled and tossed it into D-Down's lap before pulling away from the curb.

"I haven't seen Señor Alexio at all El Gatillo. Either he is El espiritu santo or he made it across the border, plus these cerdo got 24 hour surveillance on this place," he said scanning the foot traffic on the busy city street.

"Well I personally wouldn't step foot into his place of ocupacion because I'll be targeted, tailed and eventually it will lead to La Familia."

"Si,si mi amigo. I trust your judgement as mi Capitanear. So we may have to redirect our atencion. Check our inside fuente de vi. These cerdo putos can turn over a rock and find his rata anidar." He exhaled a long breath.

"Bein El Gatillo." The line went dead as he snapped the cellphone closed and pulled the black-on-black luxury Range Rover slowly into heavy traffic.

At 4:00 am Chase stood in his trailer next to the shop, examining his intricate lab of tubes, beakers, flasks and portable electrical stove which was boiling purple-colored toxic ingredients at a regulated, controlled temperature. He adjusted the mask on his face so he wouldn't inhale the potent, toxic chemicals. He kicked several dozen empty Sudafed bottles and threw away crushed up containers of Drano as he walked down the hall. He stepped outside to inspect the chemicals which were being absorbed from the flask.

"Good, no obstructions or blockage."

He followed the hose through the opened window to a huge plastic bucket full of cat litter, with a rigid tube inserted in it. It absorbed the chemical nicely with no problem. *I should have another four hours of cook time and another two hours of cooling and yield about 1.8 pounds,* he thought to himself.

The ring tone of the song "The Server" by E-40 played through his cellphone. He didn't recognize the 702 area code but he still answered it. "Yeah hello!"

"Chase, what's cracking? This is Dorian. Dorian Jackson."

"Yo bruh. Man it's been a hella long ass time since De La Sal man. What the fuck have you been up to man?"

"Shit man. You know, staying out the way and capitalizing at its best. I heard you got your own shop now."

"Well not exactly man. I got a business partner I went in with but, I'm here most of the time conducting business."

"Well ahh that's whats up. But ahh look, I got a Buick Lacrosse that I want sprayed, some beat, TVs in the head rest and ahh, I need a safe spot in the whip somewhere."

Chase rubbed his short growth of hair on his chin and calculated everything. "Any idea of a color you want?"

He thought for a moment. "I want that shit that be changing colors."

"Yeah-yeah, I know what you're talking about. Well they got this new paint on the market call Chameleonic candy paint. It's a two stage with three coats of clear. You'll put Crayola out of business and be shitting on niggas."

"So I'll be wet?"

"You'11 be slipping in the wakes from the puddles of the butta mane." Dorian smiled from the slick Bay Area gift of gab. "I'11 joog you on the 2 quarts of paint and labor. I got a connect, so toss me 4,300 and if you can, have the car delivered today or tomorrow morning so I can get started."

"That's what's up man. Look I'm out of town, but I'm going to have a driver from a Buick dealership deliver the whip tonight, with cash; and everything you'll need will be in the trunk."

"Shit, I like the way you do business my nigga."

A crowd gathered around an elaborate crap table as Deltrice shook the polished dice. She blew on them and watched as gamblers place their bets on colorful, saloon style numbers printed on the long oval table. A crystal chandelier was suspended high above the vaulted Roman-style ceilings.

"Seven!" the pit boss grunted. The dealer moved the long, curved stick back and forth as if he was cooking the dice on a large heated wok, then pushed them back to the shooter. More bets were placed as others let theirs ride. The dice bounced off of the green cushioned sides of the table and spun as one landed on six and the other on five.

There were a few empty seats at a single deck Blackjack table with a hundred dollar minimum. Dorian grabbed Deltrice's wrist and guided her onto a cushioned stool. The other players' somber faces lit up from the new enthusiastic players. Dorian set his two drinks on coasters and stacked his chips in front of him like a medieval fortress. The dealer, dressed in a shiny gold and white button-up and bow tie, smiled, nodded and motioned for them to place their bets. Deltrice unknowingly pushed a stack of chips forward. Dorian shook his head with disapproval, but it was too late. The dealer already began to lay out the cards. Dorian smirked at him but he smiled back. *You sure in the fuck ain't getting a tip,* he thought. He lifted his card and saw the seven-of-hearts.

"Let me see your cards baby girl." She bent the corner and showed him. *Queen of clubs,* he thought.

The other players took sips and sucked on their cigarettes as they glared at the dealer's hand. He flipped over a three of spades. Dorian scraped the table with his card for a hit. Jack of diamonds. *Seventeen,* he thought. He dropped his card and waved his hand. Deltrice looked at the dealer so he dealt her card face up. King of spades. Dorian looked at the large pile of chips in front of her that she betted and shook his head with satisfaction.

"Double down Mr. Dealer." She flipped over her other card and slid an equal amount of chips for an additional bet.

"Whoa-whoa-whoa dealer, hold up. Deltrice do you know what you're doing?"

"Sure I do baby, I use to play this online."

The other player doubled over with laughter.

"Baby ahh, this isn't virtual cash bonita. No do overs."

She waved him off with confidence. "Run dat in!" she said, aiming her hand at the dealer.

"We have another winner for the lovely lady."The stick man pushed several stacks of black chips towards them.

Dorian leaned forward and whispered, "That's the rewards of betting and hitting on a 32-1 shot baby girl. When you bet big, you win big." He put a small stack of chips on the come line before she tossed the dice again.

"Your point is four." The cheers at the table tapered off as the dice rolled and spun. It took seven rolls before she hit her point, before passing the dice.

Marcello took off his designer shades, cleaned the lenses and winked at Deltrice before putting them back on. Suam scooped up all of the markers, balanced them against her breast and headed towards the cage. The sounds of slot machines, foot traffic, laughter and the sweet smell of expensive Cuban cigars filled the cool, air-conditioned casino which set the atmosphere.

"You know I want my cut bitch," Deltrice said while she playfully pinched Suam's ass. She turned around, smiled and blew her a kiss before setting the chips on the counter to get cashed out. Deltrice watched the large disc spin at the roulette table. The white marble bounced around and finally came to a stop. A man in a cowboy hat, accompanied by two blonde beauties hung off of his arm like trophies, pumped his fist with excitement from his good fortune.

Dorian leaned forward and whispered, "Baby he's excited because the mothafucka broke even. That game is pure luck and no strategy."

The cowboy downed his drink, threw down his cowboy hat and started doing the funky chicken around it. He shrugged and flipped over a six of clubs then a four of spades.

"Hit me!"

He then flipped over an ace-of-hearts. "Ten."

"Hit me!"

The dealer laid down a nine.

"Hit me!"

The dealer fidgeted when he laid down a two-of-hearts.

"Twenty-one baby!"

She grabbed him by the neck and kissed his cheek as the other players got their cards and busted as well as the dealer.

"I don't believe it!!" one of the other players said as the dealer picked up the cards. He got out of his seat and walked over to the couple. Dorian could smell the alcohol on his breath as he came between them both. He caressed Deltrice's back and cleared his throat.

"Darling this here must be a special occasion coz er uh, thee only time I'd have my here arms around a pretty looking black girl like yourself iswhen I'm either choking 'em or holding their black asses for dem there police!!" He leaned in and snatched her drink, downed the potent dark liquid, sl'mmed down the glass, smacked his lips and wiped his mouth on the sleeve.

Dorian chopped him in his throat before he could say another insulting word, instantly crushing his larynx. He stumbled back holding his neck, gasping for air. "You trying to say something masa?" Dorian gripped his collar and pulled him closer, nose-to-nose, and slapped him viciously several times, blooding and bruising his nose. "You sees iza field nigga masa! Yes iza am," he said, pushing him off.

Dorian jumped up and quickly roundhouse kicked him in his eye socket, sending him straight to the fancy carpet. "Fuck this casino. Y'all got enough of my money for one mothafucken night. Come on let's go," he said, grabbing Deltrice's arm and stepping over the man's body.

She scooped her winnings with the other free hand as Dorian grabbed his other drink off the table and splashed it on the unconscious man's face. Trice made a running start and kicked the man square in the nuts. Spectators winced from the scene and others payed no attention.

The sun peaked over the Las Vegas Red Rock Mountains in the distance as Dorian stood at the ceiling-to-floor window of their presidential suite in the hotel. A blunt dangled from his fingers as he replayed all of the past days' events. He took a deep hit, exhaled, and watched the desert sand sparkle in the distance like rose gold and bronze. He tugged on one of his loosened braids, stretched and looked at the Prada, Gucci, Channel D&G and other high-end apparel stuffed in crisp bags, scattered around the spacious room. Empty champagne bottles, pill bottles, room service carts, ripped open condom packages and metallic confetti was strewn across the floor. Dorian took another pull from his blunt and took everything in all at once.

Deltrice moved underneath the covers in the huge octagon-shaped bed and he pulled the silk covers back exposing her naked, shapely body as she laid on her stomach. Putting the blunt out on an ashtray, he noticed two lines of powder cocaine and a rolled hundred dollar bill. He leaned over, took a snort and felt the chalky numbness wake up his chest. He ran his finger between her ass cheeks and played with her clit from behind until it was warm, excited and wet.

She arched her back and rocked on his fingers as he gradually inserted four of them. She turned over, blinked and smiled. "I guess no room service for you!" She tightened her muscles then loosened them on his fingers. "Don't stop baby, oooohhh yes." She reached over and grabbed the glass plate next to her and did a one-on-one in each nostril.

Seconds later Dorian felt her muscles pulse and contract, so he slowly removed his fingers and she gushed a thick stream of cum on his waist, soaking his boxers. "You on like shit!" He pulled them off, opened her up like some scissors, put one of her thighs over his shoulder and entered her.

She accepted, biting her lip and pushing her breast together. "Take this Haitian mami pussy Daddy, uhhh take it," she cried in a pleasured pain tone.

He thrusted and gyrated in her in a rhythmic, stylistic way that excited her. She curled her toes as they both locked eyes like a lioness and lion. Beads of sweat rolled down his forehead and accumulated on the tip of his nose. It dripped in her open mouth like a tropical pitcher plant. She could taste his sex in his DNA as she smacked her lips. Deltrice smiled then felt him pulse and stiffen inside of her.

He closed his eyes and long stroked her, viciously thrusting his hips deep inside of her. "AH-AH-AH."

She grinded her hips against him and gyrated until he finished and fell on top of her.

Suam and Marcellos stood in front of the double doors of the presidential suite, as she swiped the card key and walked in.

"Come on Cell. I want to see what's up with them because they haven't been picking up their phones."

"Daaaaammmmmnnnn what the—y'all must have been doing y'all mothafucken thang."

"Have y'all even left the room for the last week or what?" Suam asked, looking at the confetti and empty bottles of Moet, Cristal and Miloan 1860. "Hello,hello Deltrice."

"Hey I'm back here." She stepped out of the side dressing room fitted in a silver halter evening dress by BCBG and matching open toe ostrich skin pumps. She adjusted a 4-karat black diamond earring then hugged both of them.

"Where is Dorian?"

"I'm out here bruh, taking a call. I'll be there in one minute," he said closing the drapes, and began pacing on the balcony.

"So how's Sin City?" Steve asked as if it was his natural element.

"Well I see why they call this place lost wages man, because you come here on vacation and fuck around and leave on probation."

"Oh shit bro, ahh what did you do?"

"You don't want to know man. Believe me. But ah look, I want to buy that new Buick Lacrosse on your lot and have it delivered to a paint shop call the 'Wet Shop' off of Sonoma. I already made arrangements so ahh, I need the deluxe pack. TV's in the head rest, custom beat, rims and all the accessories. I'll situate the installments. He will contact you after it's done and I would like for it to be delivered to a private airport in Sacramento called Allendale Avionics."

"Ahhh is that it?"

"Ahh yeah, by the way, put a red bow on it."

"Will do."

"I got to go. I have a dinner date with the dutchess." He stepped into the suite draped in a Chinchilla overcoat, stripped silk button-up, linen pants and Gucci slip-ons.

"Damn nigga you went from Steven Seagal to Don mothafucken Jaun Bishop."

"Yeah ahh, your temper almost killed that guy Dorian. Luckily the paramedics got to his ass in time to resuscitate him. They performed a tracheotomy on his ass before he fucking flat lined," Suam said dressed in a Ralph Lauren cream one-piece, and puther hand on her hip with a finger in Dorian's face.

"Ahh-na-aah bitch, don't be trying to say it was my man's fault bitch."

"You-you don't even know the real."

"Whoa, hold up, hold up." Marcellos and Dorian got in between them, to keep them both from moving furniture.

"Look, dude was drunk and he put his hands on her, period point mothafucken blank. Then to add salt to the wound, he made a racial ass remark, then downed her drink so I downed his ass." Dorian paused for a moment. "Man look, he was hating because of her beginner's luck," he explained pointing at her.

They both laughed for several minutes. "Giiiirrrlll. I seen you get a running start and field goal that man's package. Oooohh you sooo wrong," Suam said laughing with Deltrice.

"I think that's what resuscitated his racist ass."

"Ahh I don't mean to interrupt y'all precious moment, but my stomach is applauding my back," he said tapping his watch. They all walked out the hotel suite into the hallway and took the private elevator to the casino's exclusive five-star restaurant.

Manky swerved in and out of traffic on Cap Street, turned up Mission Blvd and passed 16th street. D-Down watched a machine of prostitutes on both sides of the street get in and out of different cars servicing tricks.

"You see that hoe right there bruh?" Manky said pointing at the corner of 19th and Mission.

"Yeah-yeah I see that hoe."

A Punjabi woman with coffee brown skin and a shapely body, knelt down and wiped her wedged high heels off with a dirty, lipstick stained napkin. Her skirt raised up a little.

"Ohh my nigga she's caking," D-Down said as he admired her long, jet-black wavy hair cascading around her smooth shoulders.

"At least she got on the right uniform. No panties."

"Pull up next to this hoe mane and if she tries to break a heel, I'm on her." Manky knew what that meant, a runner.

She stood up adjusted her shirt and scanned the busy street. She saw a pearl-colored Chevy Suburban on rims pull up next to her so she approached it and smiled. D-Down jumped in the back seat, tucked his platinum link chain and put his chrome .45 in the middle of his back.

"Follow my role my nigga," D-Down said confidently as he rolled down the rear window. "Ahh you, yes you, beautiful. You remind me of a queen in me homeland. Ehh Saudi Arabian queen."

She got her one, she thought as she listened to the heavy accented African man in the back seat. "Queen huh! And where are you from Papi?"

"Abuja Nigeria Af—"

She stopped him in mid-sentence by putting her small manicured hand up. "Papi,papi, I know where it is but there's one thing you got to know lil' daddy. I am not Arabian. I'm Pakistani."

Like that makes a fucking difference, D-Down thought. She took the bait, jumped in the back seat and closed the door. Manky locked it and punched the gas.

She studied his face for a few seconds and sensed something wasn't right. The driver kept glancing in the rearview at her. "So do you want to pay for this mocha and take a sip?" she asked pulling up her skirt, opening her legs, showing a thinly trimmed bush and plump protruding lips. She stuck her fingers in between her lips and played with her wet, pink clitoris. He touched her thigh and she closed her legs like a tropical cI'm irritated by a curious, hungry fish. She put her fingers in her mouth and savored her own juices. "To taste my mocha daddy it's going to be $1,500 all night."

"Bitch! You're in the presence of a pimp.You just officially got pimp-napped bitch." D-Down pulled out his chrome .45 from his back and set it on his lap. "You see, you're on the right court but you was on the wrong team bitch. I need all that paper, eevvrryytthhaanngg!" he said turning up his lip.

"You must got no pimp do you,do you?" She shook her head no. "Yeah because then you both would of been out of mothafucken pocket. Then I would have had to serve his non-pimping ass papers for you choosing—"

"I don't need no pimp!"

"Iz yah serious? Nawh I'm going to ignore that comment." She looked away, then back at him. "Bitch don't look stupid. You know the rules of the mothafucken game bitch." She glanced at the gun on his lap. "Don't trip bitch, guns don't kill people. People do bitch." He gripped the handle and shoved the cold steel barrel into her ribs. "Open up!" She opened her mouth. "Nawh bitch, your legs bitch, your legs!" She slowly opened her thick thighs and D-Down rubbed the tip of the barrel between her wet, pink lips. "You see bitch, if you had a pimp then another pimp wouldn't be doing this to you."

"Look out there bitch.Look!" She kept her eyes straight forward in fear. "This is my block and ahh, these grimy, thirsty ass niggas who work for me will bust your pretty head like popping a tag on a pair of new Jay Jonas bitch, so you better thank the Mack god bitch. Thank em! Bitch I'm not playing, say it!" He pulled the hammer back on the heavy Colt .45.

"Ok,ok thank you Mack god, thank you Mack god."

D-Down smirked then uncocked the hammer and stuck itback into his waistband, as he watched a tear run down her scared face.

Manky's Suburban slid across the loose gravel and stopped in front of the paint shop as his music pounded to perfection. D-Down jumped out of the passenger side, holding a creased fifty dollar bill with powder cocaine in it. He took a few snorts, folded it up and dropped it on the passenger's seat. Chase was in the five thousand-square-foot warehouse equipped with state of the art hydraulic lifts, paint booths, sprayers, welders and equipment for forging and bending metal. Chase was underneath the Buick as it was lifted and stabilized on jack stands. The hood, trunk and all of the doors were wide open as Brick-B had all of the seats taken out and set next to it.

He went to work laying speaker wire under the carpet connecting amps, woofers, tweets, mids and crossovers. The plush leather seats already had the high definition flat screen installed in the head rest, ready to be mounted to the floor boards as loose wires hung from them like fish hooks. The florescent lamps above gave the car's fresh candy paint a nauseating effect as Manky and D-Down walked in.

"Thisis my victory lap," Chase said as he rolled from underneath the car. He pulled up his dark welding goggles and wiped the beads of sweat from his forehead.

"You done with the other job?"

Chase pointed the welder's blue pilot flame towards three covered cars parked in the rear of the warehouse. Chase then rolled back underneath the car.

D-Down walked over to one of the cars and snatched one of the covers off. *He did his thing,* he thought to himself. He ran his palm across the front end where the damage used to be present then stepped back and looked at the 7451 BMW emblem.

Chase pulled out a voltmeter to test the connection for the car's safe spot then stood up and leaned into the seatless passenger side. He flipped down the ashtray, opened the arm rest compartment, pulled out the cigarette lighter, pressed a small black button and watched as the bottom of the compartment quickly opened exposing a deep hollow tube leading to the base of the car. He then pressed the button and it slowly closed, locked and vacuum sealed itself. "Perfect," he said snapping his fingers, then he put everything back in place. "Aight Bricks, let's wrap this shit up bruh!"

Twirling the BMW keys on his finger, D-Down walked around the Buick and looked at the dealership plates. "This whip is fresh off the lot huh?"

"Yeah the dealership driver should be here to pick it up."

"Wait-wait, is there something ya not telling me?"

"What do you mean is there something I'm not telling you?"

D-Down looked deep into Chase's eyes for any sign of betrayal, but there was none. "Soyou landed a mothafucken contract with a Buick dealership and didn't pull my coattail about--"

"First off nawh, I didn't land no extravagant mothafucken contract. Second, we never mentioned in our verbal contract, when investing in this establishment, that side jobs was prohibited, folks," he explained, waving his leather gloves around him and taking the goggles off of his charcoal smeared face.

"Well whose scraper is this?"

"This dude I went to high school with. He heard about this shop. Hit me up then had this car delivered and paid a nigga in full."

"In full?"

"Yeah my nigga, cashed me out," he said pointing to his chest.

"So what's this lottery winning nigga's name?"

"Doe Getta."

"Doe Getta!" D-Down let the name sit on his mind for a moment before responding. "Dorian."

"You know him?"

"Nawh but I know of him. My cousin who played for Skyline sweated it out on the field many seasons against Del La Sal. Yeah dude had scouts commissioning the NFL to draft him straight out of high school. Dude was that good until his career got ended. After that, nobody heard nothing about him. It's like he fell off or something. But ahh, I know his big uncle hasn't fell off though."

"Well Dorian really never talked about his uncle too much."

"Yeah, well his name is 'The Hoist.' Word is he got that cartel money. His shit be coming from Central America some mothafucken where. He put a lot a niggas on and a lot a niggas came up missing and haven't been found 'til this day."

A G-6 private jet landed, taxied and pulled to a stop as Dorian and his entourage waited with carry-on luggage next to them. Airport personnel drove a portable staircase up to the jet and the door of the plane opened.

"Y'all ready to get back to the land?"

They all walked up the metal staircase, stepped into the plane and took their seats. Dorian reached into his bag, pulled out a pill bottle and opened it.

"Baby you ain't never been air sick before," Deltrice protested as she put her bag into the overhead compartment."

"This will have you on air, aight!"

"Hmmm, hold out your hand." She examined the small fluorescent pill with a lowercase "i" stamped on it and watched Dorian as he quickly popped one.

"They're called i-pods baby."

"You mean ecstasy"? He nodded his head.

"That's a cute name. Let's take one daddy and be on one for this flight," Suam said, reaching over as Dorian poured two of them into her hand and handed one to Marcellos. They opened their mouths and fed each other their pills. Suam stood up, walked over to a small fridge, opened it, and took out a bottle of Moet and four champagne glasses from the top.

"Damn girl, you don't waste no time do you?" Deltrice said popping her pill, buckling up and grabbing her glass full of bubbly.

A blanket of clouds stretched beneath the G-6 as it ascended high above and leveled off. Deltrice unbuckled her seat belt and reclined back in her seat. Dorian touched her arm and refilled her champagne glass. His touch radiated through her body like static electric.

"You aight?"

"I'm fine baby," she said leaning over and passionately tongue kissing him.

He looked over and saw Suam straddling Marcellos, kissing and rubbing him. Her dress was off as she had on a canary yellow floral bra and matching thong. Marcellos squezzed her thick, firm tattooed ass.

Dorian kissed Deltrice's neck and felt her body shudder. He put his hand up her skirt, pulled her panties aside and felt how wet she was. She ripped her silk blouse off and buttons flew everywhere.

"Hey Trice-Trice," Suam called in between kisses.

"What bitch?"

"I-I got two racks that I can make my man cum faster before yours."

"Well put your money on the wood bitch!" Deltrice challenged, slapping her hand on the table next to her.

"Pttttsss it's nothing to a boss bitch," Suam said reaching into her bra, pulling out a folded stack of hundreds neatly wrapped in a silver butterfly money clip, and tossed it on the table.

This girl is serious, Deltrice thought, pulling out her wad and also tossing it on the table.

This is going to be good, Dorian thought as he looked at Marcellos who was thinking the same thing.

"It's a bet then." Suam slid down between Marcellos' legs, unbuttoned his pants, grasped his thick shaft and gently squeezed it. "I know a ancient Cambodian sex secret."

"Oh yeah, what?"

"Bitch if I told you then it wouldn't be a secret," Suam told Deltrice as if she was on stage talking into a mic.

Marcellos leaned forward and whispered in her ear, "What ancient secret?"

"Don'ttrip daddy. I don't have no K-Y jelly any way."

"And what were you planning on doing with that?"

She demonstrated by putting her finger through her closed thumb and index finger. Deltrice read between the lines, started laughing then got between Dorian's legs. She unzipped him and took him into her mouth.

"Hey I didn't tell you to start-"

Marcellos shoved his shaft in Suam's mouth while she was in mid-sentence. He slapped her ass and played with her tight, wet clit. She moaned in between slurps and smacks while he tied her curly locs into a bun so his juices wouldn't ruin them, and leaned back.

She slid down to the base of his manhood, gagged then slowly spiraled her way to the tip. They both locked on each other's hedonistic gaze as she bobbed and bounced like an experienced gymnast on a trampoline. Suam looked from the corner of her eye as she slurped then stroked Marcellos as her small, taut lips stretched around his throbbing shaft.

Deltrice caught her looking, pulled Dorian's shaft out of her mouth, stroked him several times, slapped it on the side of her face like a stiff, black rubber hose then devoured it.

"Cello you feeling yourself?"

"My nigga am I. Those i-pods smack huh baby?"

"Ah huh."

Dorian laughed as he watched Suam concentrate. Deltrice slightly bit down to get his attention, then pointed at her eyes. "Ok, ok I see you and I'm having a party in your mouth."

She squeezed his nut sack harder and sucked faster. He threw his back against the seat, gripped the back of her head with one hand and pulled her breast with the other. Trice felt him swell and stiffen. *I can't swallow because then she wouldn't know*, she thought to herself. She pulled back and stroked him quickly.

Suam did the same but had Marcellos' nuts in her mouth. *Damn bitch you working way too hard for two racks*, she thought. Suam's face sweated as she continued to work.

"Ohh if it don't get all over the place, it don't belong in your face," Dorian announced as thick, milky cum squirted all over Deltrice's face for several seconds and ran down in between her cleavage.

She began to rub it in like expensive skin cream, then she continued sucking so she could taste him. Marcellos watched Deltrice then looked back at Suam and came in her throat. Suam and Deltrice both stood up, grabbed their shower bags out of their luggage and ran to the G-6 cabin shower.

CHAPTER EIGHT:

THE ARRIVAL

*THE MORE LAWS AND ORDERS ARE MADE PROMINENT,
THE MORE GANGSTERS AND KILLERS THERE WILL BE.*

Dorian looked at his watch as the G-6 landed and taxied on the runway. He scanned the private airport's small parking lot. "There it is," he said under his breath. When the jet came to a stop, he grabbed his luggage and stepped out the plane onto the tarmac, then walked to the gate leading to the parking lot. Marcellos and Suam followed close behind them. Dorian turned around.

"Aight my nigg, I had fun bruh," he said as he shook his hand and hugged him. He then hugged Suam. "You keep him in line lil' mama."

Deltrice hugged them both and they walked off. "Come on. I got a surprise for you Trice," he said, grabbing her wrist as they walked through rows of cars.

She shrieked with delight and broke away from him. The Buick was sitting on chrome 24's and wrapped in brand-new Perrelli tires. The contours of the car's big body and candy paint made it sparkle like a tropical flavored now or later candy.

"Ohh I'm wet baby,"she said walking around it and admiring the chrome pipes. She looked at the red bow, pulled the end, opened the driver's side door and got in.

"Pop the trunk so I can put this luggage up." She frowned, found the trunk release button and pushed it.

"Where's the keys baby?"

"Check the ashtray!" he said closing the trunk, then walked around the car and got in.

Deltrice snatched the laser cut keys out of the ashtray and started the car. She ran her fingertips over the Buick emblem in the middle of the glossy, woodgrain steering wheel while listening to the V-8 supercharged engine quietly purrrr. She revved the engine, listened to the dual exhaust bark then put it in reverse.

"So how does she handle, baby girl?" Dorian asked as he glanced at her, then out of the window, as miles of fields and orchards passed by them. Cows in the distance grazed on dry grass and bounced to an unheard rhythm as they trotted to another patch of foliage.

"This rides like an import baby. It hugs the road when I switch the lanes. It's smooth."She put her hand on his and briefly stared into his *eyes.* "I love it," she said, issing him quickly on his lips and putting two bands back on the steering wheel.

"Well I'm glad you like it but ahh, technically this is a import."

"Huh?"

"They don't build these joints in the U.S. no mo!" he said, slapping the dashboard. "China!" Dorian said as he ran through a song list on the car's touchscreen and played "Sheymago" by J-Diggs and Macdre. Dorian nodded his head, admiring the job Chase had done. Every instrument peaked but didn't clip. It was ear candy as the bass, high-hats, mids and tweets clapped as if they were in a sound booth.

Deltrice slowed down as they entered Solano County and saw lit flares being dropped onto the ground by C.H.P. officers, motioning traffic to merge into one lane. "Must of been a accident baby."

A car was flipped over in a ditch as E.M.T. worked quickly to release them from the wreckage. Glass, twisted metal and shredded pieces of tires decorated a wide strip of freeway, then traffic began to move again.

Dorian's cellphone began to vibrate then chirp a custom ringtone. He saw Chase's number which he had programmed as a'$.' "What up mane, I just got back."

"You sound like you're in traffic."

"Yeah-yeah I am. Shorty is driving the whip. She feeling the attention. I might have to upgrade on my arsenal of weapons to keep these haters from pecking at her."

"I peck back and I clip beaks," Deltrice said making a trigger finger as if she was busting a tool.

"Hey pimping, look, did you figure out where tha safe spot was at?" Chase said looking over his shoulder before continuing, not knowing that Manky was leaned back in one of the covered luxury cars, unnoticed.

"Nawh m-mh where is it?"

"Well lift up the center console. Aight, then move yah arm real quick." Chase listened in the background as Dorian took Deltrice's designer purse out and set it in the back seat.

"Now what?"

"Open the ashtray, take out the lighter and press that button."

The carpeted bottom slowly opened releasing a tight vacuum seal and revealing a reinforced steel tube. "You Michael Weston *Burn Notice* ass nigga. That's the business," he said closing the compartment and putting the lighter back in the ashtray. "I got some niggas that may want other work done like this."

"I-I really don't do shit like this for everyone, because it's just a matter of time a nigga is gonna slip, the police will stumble across it and put it in their punk ass, mothafucken play book. You feel me?" Dorian rubbed his chin and thought about it. "Well it's not about the money when it comes to this. It's about preserving the craft my nigga."

"That's what it is man."

"Look I got to go. I got work to do. Oh yeah by the way, you know a nigga a chemist," Chase mentioned glancing at his locked tool box.

"What's the shelf life?"

"Two to three days, tops."

"What's the turn around?"

"Twenty-four hours. The longer the method, the more potent."

"What's your take?"

"Eight to 11 per zone, 1.8 per batch."

Dorian rubbed the bridge of his nose in deep thought as Deltrice focused on driving and trying to figure out what type of code he was talking in. He quickly calculated the figures.

"Aight Chase, give me 24 hours man and ahh, let a nigga make some calls."

"Aight my nigg." Chase looked at his watch then the line went dead.

Dorian looked at the digital dashboard speedometer. "Baby if you're going to speed, at least slow down when you get to the overpasses." He felt her decrease her speed.

Officer Staggs sat in his police cruiser, listening to the dispatcher's squabbles and static as he watched footage of the officer involved shooting on his iPhone. "Technology is a damn curse!" He watched the person filming get a panoramic view of the crime scene and the reaction of the crowd after the shots. Also a few frames as Officer Rumsfield put something in between his vest. He then distracted the crowd as he walked to some bushes.

"Fuck Rumsfield. Not good man. Not fucking good at all. I feel the wagons circling chief and every attorney, activist and Internal Affairs investigator is going to be shooting their poison-dipped arrows at our asses." His eyes followed a flashy, newer model sedan on shiny big rims pass by after exiting the freeway. He pulled behind it and followed it for a few blocks before lighting it up.

Deltrice looked in the rearview mirror and saw the black and white following them. "Don't panic baby he's probably just checking us out since he can't run the plates. If he pulls us over we're legit. Everything's in the glove compartment." She felt at ease but held her breath when she saw the red and blue lights. "Just pull over some place safe."

She pulled into an empty parking lot and cut the engine. Officer Staggs notified dispatch then stepped out of his police cruiser, adjusted his Sig Sauer forty caliber and pulled out a long, black flashlight. He walked past the car towards the driver side window and tapped it twice.

"Can you crack your window please ma'am?"

Trice smiled. "Sorry officer."

"Can I see your license and registration please?"

"Sure." Dorian quietly handed her the papers as she reached behind her, grabbed her purse and pulled out her license.

Officer Staggs studied the documents for a few minutes, as he flashed his light across the ID's hologram and called it into dispatch. "Ms. Glaude ahh, where are your California plates ma'am?"

"We just bought the—"

"Ahh sir I'm talking to the lady, not you sir!"

Deltrice looked at Dorian as he shook his head in frustration. "Well ahh, Officer Staggs," she said, looking at his embroidered name tag, "wepurchased this car and recently got it painted and added the accessories but we will definitely have this car registered first thing Monday morning." She smiled and he couldn't help but smile back at her stunning beauty.

"That doesn't answer our question officer."

"Ohhh yeah smart guy, and what might that be?" he asked angrily.

"What was the real reason why you pulled us over?"

Staggs looked over his shoulder at their car. "Oh yeah you guys have a broken taillight."

They both looked at each other, then watched him walk to the rear of the car, smash their right rear taillight then walk back to the window. He then dropped a fix it ticket with her ID on her lap.

"Are you fucking serious cop!"

Dorian snatched the ticket, balled it up and threw it at him. He spoke into his radio attached to his shoulder and another cruiser pulled up minutes later. A female officer got out with a sullen look on her face as she approached. "Sir are there any drugs or weapons in your car that we may need to know about?"

"Man n!"

"Well do you mind if we search your vehicle?"

"Fuck yeah, I min!"

"Good then, could you please step out the vehicle please?" she said, obviously ignoring Dorian protest.

"I don't think you heard me clearly cop. I said that I do mind if you search my car." Officer Staggs eyed him, sucked his teeth and stepped back. He nodded at the female officer and they both drew their weapons. "Sir put your hands on the dash board and the driver, keep one hand on the steering wheel, pull the keys out of the ignition and toss them out the window." Deltrice pulled the keys out and dropped them out the window.

"Driver, step out the car with your hands up and back up towards us." Dorian shook his head in disgust from the blatant harassment and abuse of authority. He looked in the rearview mirror as Deltrice was frisked by the female cop, handcuffed and put into the back seat of the police cruiser.

"Passenger, step out of the car with your hands up, and slowly walk back towards me." He aimed at his target's head and waited for any sudden moves. Dorian stepped out with his hands up and walked backwards. He could feel the heat of the spotlight on his back as Officer Staggs holstered his weapon, quickly frisked him, took out his personal effects, tossed them on his hood, handcuffed him and put him in the other cruiser.

"Man I don't believe this shit," Dorian yelled out loud. He watched as both officers rifled through the car and worked their way to the trunk then the engine.

Deltrice noticed the officer reach under the passenger seat and pull out a tightly wrapped baggy. "What the fuck bitch? I just seen you put that shit there! Baby, baby." Dorian looked in front of him as Deltrice tried to use her elbow to point. "What's up? They're trying to plant something."

"What, set us up?" He watched the officer pull out a glass vial, add solution and shake it up. Then he pulled them out of each police car.

"Sir we found two grams of heroin, which tested positive of the controlled substance." Dorian and Deltrice looked at each other with surprised looks, then back at the officer.

"You can't be fucking serious. Your partner planted that shit and you know it." He leaned forward to make a mental note of the officer's badge number. "You crooked fucking cop. Who put you up to this shit man?"

"You have the right to remain silent. Anything you say can and will be used against you in the court of law." Dorian listened to his rights being read and refused to make any statements, as well as Deltrice.

"Baby you'll probably be OR'ed."

"OR'ed? What does that mean?"

"Own recognizance. I may have to post bai." He turned to the cop. "Look cop, I read about that shooting man and yeah man, shit happens man. But you can't be pullingevery black man over with a fresh whip. I mean look, I know people." The officer didn't respond. "Ifyou don't have nothing to say then look, call a tow truck and at least let me see that our car is safely secured because I know that you're not going to let me have someone pick it up."

He sucked his teeth and eyed Dorian for a few seconds, nodded his head and guided him to the back seat of the police cruiser. Dorian watched as Deltrice was transported off. They both sat until a tow truck arrived, secured the car, lifted it and drove off.

"Now with the fun and games," Dorian said to himself.

Officer Staggs looked at Dorian in the rearview mirror before pulling off into traffic. He drove through a large, steel garage door at the entrance of the county jail. He waited as it closed before stepping out, then opened the door. Dorian maneuvered out the backseat and stood up. He gripped his hands which were handcuffed and guided him through a thick, bulletproof glass sliding door.

They walked past holding cells and into central booking. Uniformed and plain clothes officers stopped what they were doing and glanced at Officer Staggs.

He opened a metal door to a holding cell that had a phone and list of transparent numbers of bail bondsmen taped to the window. He then took the handcuffs off and closed the door behind him. The stench from the toilet caught Dorian's nose by surprise. "Damn, hell nawh. Hey-hey don't mothafuckas know what cleaning is!" He stared at the list of names, fancy logos and crazy catch phrases to persuade stressed out detainees to call them.

Marcellos picked up on the first ring and accepted the collect call. "Hello,hello."

"Ahh bruh, Cello-"

"What the fuck happened man? Why are you in jail?"

"Look before I get into all of that, I'm going to need two things before they book a nigga and start trying to question me. I need for you to deliver some money to a bail bondsman at Aladdin. Once I find out my bond and Trice's bond—"

"They arrested Trice too?"

"Listen, call my lawyer and tell him that a Vallejo police officer by the name of Officer Staggs planted drugs in my car after pulling us over for a broken taillight, which he smashed. I got my suspicions man and ah, I just got to sit tight bruh. But ahh, as far as Deltrice, I don't know how she's holding up, but I'm sure she is keeping it solid. Visiting hours is probably tomorrow, so try to see her and let her know not to talk to anyone about the case. Give her my lawyer's name and that we're arranging bail as we speak."

The line went dead and Dorian quickly punched in the numbers to the bailbonds and it dialed straight through. "Aladdin bail bondsman," the young woman's southernvoice said over the line.

"How are you doing? Look I'm in a bind and need to arrange bail payment for me and my—"

"What are your charges? What is your full name, birthdate and what are the last four digits of your social security number?" He quickly gave it to her and also Deltrice's information. "Well as you may already know, you havent been booked so you're not in the system yet, but Deltrice Glaude has been."

Dorian listened to the silence, except for the rapid sound of fingers hitting plastic keys. "Ms. Glaude is being charged with drug possession of a controlled substance, driving on a suspended license and resisting arrest. Bail for all of these charges is set at seventy-five thousand dollars."

I know these charges are trumped up, Dorian thought to himself as the bail bondsman called Marcellos three-way to arrange payment.

"Why haven't you been booked yet bruh?" Marcellos asked.

There was a tap on the window as a stalky, white, burly looking guard dressed in a faded black uniform stood there cracking his knuckles. "Mr. Jackson, let's go!"

"Look, they are about to process me, so ahh I got to go." He hung up and followed the guard out into the pen area of inmates sitting in cushioned chairs, going through metal detectors and drunks being fingerprinted. "Am I being booked or what?"

The guard said nothing, walked down several hallways then stood by an open door of a large investigation room. "Hey Mr. Jackson, we have been expecting you."

He stepped in, sat down, looked at the digital recorder on the table, a note pad and manila folder. "We?"

"Oh my partner is getting some coffee. He will be back in a few minutes."

His gray blazer, yellow button-up and polyester blue and gray striped tie matched his mood. The deep creases in his leathery face, puffy eyes, gray hair and five o'clock shadow spelled out veteran detective.

"My name is Detective Melville, homicide." He unclipped his sparkly badge, flashed it and put it back into his inside coat pocket. "This is my gopher or uuummmhhh, I mean Officer Godfrey. He will just be observing." He silently nodded at Dorian, set the steaming coffee on the table and sat down. Dorian folded his arms and stared at each one of them.

"Look Mr. Jackson, I'm going to cut to the chase. We know that you and your girlfriend had something to do with Mr. Alexio Guliteras' disappearance."

"Whoa-whoa, I don't know no damn Alexio or whoever, and personally I don't have to answer none of your mothafucken questions." He watched the detective quickly flip open the folder and lay out a colored 8x12 glossy photo. *This is a picture of my house*, he thought. He looked closer, saw himself in the passenger seat of his car and Deltrice in the driver's

seat. He flipped over two other photos of him going into Alexio's club through the side entrance and leaving from the same entrance.

Dorian leaned back, stretched and smiled. "Look Melville ahh, that is yah name right?" His face was expressionless. "Well, there isn't a crime in going to see some ass and titts!" The younger officer laughed slightly then coughed to cover it up after Melville cut his eyes at him. "Personally, I never met the owner and ahh, I hope you'll find the man—"

Melville tossed another photo on the table like a large tarot card. It seemed to float and stop in front of him. It showed him with a Louis Vuitton backpack inone hand and Alexio shaking hands with him standing next to a Cadillac Escalade at a Buick dealership. *These mothafuckas got me under straight surveillance and the D.A. got his goons on me. They still don't know shit,* he thought to himself.

"If you don't know Alexio then why are you meeting with him at a Buick dealership after hours?" Silence. "Mr. Jackson come on man. This is not my first rodeo. I know how you get down. But unfortunately you unknowingly got your ass and Ms. Glaude involved in an ongoing investigation."

"Well look, you just keep on investigating sir and ahhh how about you give me your business card and my lawyer-"

Melville slammed his hand on the table. "You listen here fucker. All we have to do is subpoena Alexio's phone records and his surveillance footage from the club--"

"I don't give a shit cop, either charge me or let me the fuck go because you got nothing, period, zip! Get a court order or what-"

"Oh we're going to charge your ass alright and your little girlfriend has a first-class ticket back to Haiti."

Dorian waited for a few seconds after standing up and heading towards the door. He ignored the last statement, but it was in the back of his mind as he was led to booking, fingerprinted, inventoried his property and signed his property sheet. He then walked in the dress out room which smelled of stale ass and feet. The property officer set a bed roll on the counter and slid it through the window.

"Glaude you have a visi!" a voice announced through an intercom. She got out of the lower bunk, wiped the sleep out of her eyes, washed her face, brushed her teeth and got dressed. Her cell door buzzed open as he pushed it open and walked out into the day room. A tv behind plexi glass was mounted to a wall in one corner surrounded by metal tables and phones. An officer behind tinted glass pushed a button.

Deltrice walked up a cement staircase and glanced atother female inmates on a small exercise yard pacing. Through the glass she saw Marcellos and Suam walk into thevisiting room on the other side. After being buzzed in, she quickly sat down, grabbed the phone, wiped it and put it to her ear.

"Hey girl, you look well rested. How is the food?"

"Ihaven't touched this Alpo dog food shit girl, but I eat the fruit."

Marcellos pulled the phone from her. "Deltrice listen, I paid Dorian's and your bail so don't get comfortable in there because you're going to be up out of there okay?" She nodded in agreement and zoned out at the scratched up and graffitied metal surrounding the thick window. "I recommend that you don't speak to no one about your case, no one. No other inmates, no cops, no detainees. No one!"

He eyed her for a few seconds before writing something down, then put it up against the glass. She read the lawyer's name to herself and memorized the number. He folded it up after she was done.

"Now ahh, he should be visiting you sometime this morning."

"Okay I'll be expecting--"

An older man in a charcoal gray, shiny pin stripe suit, matching silk tie and a peach-colored button-up walked in. His black leather attaché briefcase complimented his Italian taste of shoe wear.

"Is that him?"

They both turned around and made eye contact with him. "Are you here to see a Ms. Glaude? A Deltrice Glaude?"

"Yes-yes actually I am."

"Well she's right here." She stood up smiled and waved at him.

"I don't want to interrupt your guys' personal visit."

"No-NO. I insist sir. This is way more important."

He walked in a side room for lawyers and their clients to talk privately. He poked his head out then gestured her to enter on the other side.

"Aight y'all. You know I love you guys and pray that God will find a way--"

"You'll be okay, just go on!" Suam blew a kiss as they both got up and left.

"How are you doing Ms. Glaude? Please have a seat. My name is Mr. Pori, attorney at law." He pulled out a folder, set it on the counter and flipped through it. He adjusted his glasses and cleared his throat. "Luckily I got here as soon as I did because the vultures are circling." He knew that she didn't have a clue of what he was talking about. "Put it this way, there were two homicide detectives eager to question you. Apparently, you and Mr. Jackson are under surveillance."

"Surviellance? For what?!"

"Well as this was put to me, you two unknowingly got yourselves involved in an ongoing investigation."

"Unknowingly?"

He took off his glasses and looked her straight in the eye. "The D.A. lost one of their informants."

"Well fuck them. They should of had a tighter choke leash on their rat. You think?" He laughed at her candidness. "Look sir, we have been in Las Vegas for like hmm, the last two weeks. We fly in, my boyfriend surprises me with a new car, then we get pulled over. Our car gets vandalized by this deranged ass cop and he plants dope in it."

He was in deep thought for a few seconds before he spoke. "I am going to subpoena their department's dispatch records and also get the dash cam footage that every police cruiser has. We basically need leverage so that the D.A. takes two steps back. I know that these charges are trumped up, but what is this resisting arrest thing all about?"

"Never happened. I mean come on. Look at me," she said standing up. "What do I look like resisting? There's no evidence of bruises or anything on me." She showed him her wrist. He glanced at her and scribbled some notes.

"Well look, I'm going to request an OR or a bail reduction at your arraignment this afternoon. You won't have to say a word. I'11 do all of the talking okay? I found out that the officer's partner was involved in an officer involved shooting and this could play a factor in our defense because he was looking for reprisal. Look, in the meantime here goes my card. Call the office collect if anything comes up." She took it as he slid it through the slot and she put it in her breast pocket.

Dressed in a faded, wrinkled blue jail jump suit and plastic sandals, Deltrice was led out into a courtroom in handcuffs by a bailiff and brought in front of a wooden podium for her arraignment. Marcellos and Suam smiled and waved from the audience amongst strangers waiting for their loved ones to face the same judge.

The attorney stood by her, next to the podium, and smiled. "How are you?" he said warmly, squeezing her shoulder.

"The honorable Judge Collins presiding," the bailiff announced as a short, aged white man resembling Danny Devito walked in, wearing a black robe two sizes too big. His balding head was covered with a few strands of hair.

"You may be seated." He grabbed a folder from next to him, opened it then tensed his bottom lip. "Case number A-72970, People V. Glaude. Your charges are felony possession of a controlled substance, driving on a suspended license and resisting arrest. Counsel, how does your client plead?"

"Not guilty your honor."

"Okay, a preliminary hearing will be set a month from today."

"Your honor, I would like to request my client to be OR'ed."

"Denied!"

"Your honor, can I move the courts for a bail reduction for my client?"

He paused for a moment and shuffled some papers. "Itappears here that your client is gainfully employed and her bail is currently set at seventy-five thousand, but hold on here." The clerk next to the judge looked at him as she paused. "Ms. Glaude, are you familiar that you have an immigration hold?"

Deltrice's lawyer leaned over to her. "Are you aware of this?"

"No, of course not."

"Hold on your honor, can I view those documents?"

The judge handed them over to the bailiff and she walked them over and handed them to the lawyer. He scanned the U.S. Customs and Border Patrol logo and flipped a few pages.

"Your honor, for the record my client is here on a student visa and upon completion--"

"Counsel this is not my jurisdiction nor can I address this matter in my court. Next case."

"I'm-I'm being deported?!" Tears started running down her cheeks in surprise and regret.

"I will take care of this so don't worry?" She wiped her face and was led back to her holding cell.

"Your client doesn't want to cooperate counsel. Yes we may be fishing but it's about what type of bait we use and where we actually cast our lines."

"Oh, and it so happens that you're gunning for a conviction right at the time you're running for mayor."

"Are you implying that this is a publicity stunt for political gain?"

"I'm implying that the spoiled bait you're using is causing more repulsion then attraction Mr. Anderson," he said as he opened up a laptop computer, pressed a button and turned the screen towards him so he could see. The grainy footage showed a female Vallejo police officer stealthily pull out a small, tightly wrapped sandwich bag of what appeared to be heroin, and drop it on the driver's side floor board while searching a vehicle.

"Where did you get this?"

"Not where, but the question is how Mr. Anderson. How!"

The district attorney slowly sat back down behind his desk, folded his arms and showed a slight smile. "So what do you want Mr. Pori, off the record?"

"Well for starters Mr. Anderson, my client has deep pockets and now he has sufficient evidence to sue the department for entrapment, false arrest, harassment and punitive damages."

"So I'm going to clarify this again Mr. Pori. What does your client-

"All charges dropped at the discretion of the court. I'm sure Judge Collins won't oppose it, especially if you're in agreement. And besides"—the lawyer stood up, closed his laptop, put it into his briefcase and snapped it shut— "your confidential informant probably just doesn't want to be found."

CHAPTER NINE:

SET UP

A WOMAN WATCHES HER BODY UNEASILY,
AS THOUGH IT WERE AN UNRELIABLE ALLY IN THE BATTLE
FOR LOVE.

Peaches did a handstand, balanced herself, opened her legs into a "T" and popped her ass cheeks several times. The other strippers danced around her in a tight circle. Guests held up their colorful drinks like lit torches and grinded as Brick-B's vocals blared over an eerie bass line with a catchy guitar riff.

Manky passed a half full bottle of Vodka beefeater to D-Down as one of the strippers unzipped his Pelle Pelle sweat suit jacket and began rubbing on his chest. Brick-B satin the spacious soundproof with a plate of crushed tar heroin, mixed with cocaine. He watched the crowd through the thick plexi glass, dancing in the production room. A sexy Latin stripper stepped in wearing a red lace two-piece bikini.

"Can I join you mi amor?"

He met her eyes with a glazed look, pulled back his dreads, smiled, scooped another pile of his balushi mix on to his gold diamond encrusted medallion and took a deep snort. He wiped the chocolate milk colored powder from his nostrils as she gently grabbed the plate from his hands and set it on the sheet music stand in front of the microphone then straddled him. Her long, straight, black hair smelled of kiwi and strawberries as she pushed her firm breasts against him. He gripped her small waist and ran his calloused fingers across her thick ass cheeks.

"Didn't think Latinas had it like this huh?" He smiled from her comment, looked into her hypnotizing light brown eyes and admired her high, angelic, exotic cheek bones. He felt her smooth hands as she rubbed on his manhood. "I want to make some musica pap!" she demanded in a heavy accent.

He waved his hand around the spacious soundproof room. "We in the right place to lay something down."

She pulled down her left bra strap from her shoulder, showing her golden brown, taut nipple.

El Capitone sat in his black Range Rover across the street from a recording studio. A neon sign hung over the entrance as strippers came and went. Benzes and several old school drop Mustangs were double parked on the street, as some of them stood on their hoods, dancing with bottles in their hands. Behind the tinted glass, he answered his cellphone on the first ring.

"Ahh El Capitone."

"El Gatillo. How are you?"

"Bueno-bueno."

"No sign of the rata huh?"

"No!"

"Well my sources told me that they had two people in custody. They were only able to question one of them before the lawyer beat the wolves off, before they could take a bite off of the carcass. They have no criminal record but I think the woman is a illegal and they both were last seen with Alexio."

He watched from across the street as a couple came out of the entrance and joined the block party. "The one that was questioned, what did he say?"

"Well not too much. He was smart. He let the wolves put their paws in their own mouth. He set a trap and they sprung it."

He laughed for a few seconds, drew in a few breaths, and looked across the vast vegetation of jungle. The beautiful rivers and waterfalls were the back drop of his Tegucigalpa estates. Clouds hung over the jagged mountain range in the distance, like peeled cotton. The sounds from the different species of insects, birds and monkeys blended together like chanting demons praising their master. A horse he was mounted on snorted and flung its tail to ward off the hungry insects. He repositioned himself on the saddle and loosened the strap which secured his military issued camouflage rocket propelled grenade launcher.

"El Capitone. I think someone or something did our job for us. I don't like taking losses but we may need to lick our wounds."

"All due respect Señor Gatillo, since I'm out here, I might as well make a handsome withdrawal for our services," he said matter-of-factly while glancing at a loaded Mac 11 on the passenger seat.

"Ahh of course, of course. Time is money Captain. Time is money."

"What is your name mami?" Brick-B asked between kisses.

"What, chu want that girlfriend experience or something?"

He smiled and lightly smacked her firm ass. "Nawh mami, it's just while I'm fucking you, I at least want to call out the right name."

"You can call me whatever chu want papi."

"Aight bitch!"

She smiled. "You see, that wasn't that hard," she said pushing her panties to the side. She stroked his manhood and quickly slid a condom on him in one fluent motion. He probed her, then entered her tight, wet folds. After a few minutes of thrusting inside of her, he abruptly stopped and fell on top of her.

"Hey-hey!" She shook him a few times but there was no response, then she checked his pulse. "Uh, oh my God, somebody, anybody help!"

Strings of yellow spit hung from the corners of his mouth as his eyes stared blankly at the ceiling. Manky glanced in the sound booth, tapped on the window with a bottle to get her attention then stepped in. "What is wrong with my nigga? The pussy couldn't of been that--" He got closer. "Re's od'ing bitch, get out the way. As a matter of fact, get me a bucket of ice bitch!" She stood there as if she was someplace else.

"Hey bitch, listen. If my homeboy dies bitch, I'll put this on everything. You'll be pole dancing in a wheelchair bitch." She then ran out of the sound booth. He lifted him out of the chair, laid him on the ground, ripped open his shirt, spread his arms out and began pounding his chest with both fists.

She ran back in and slightly tripped, sending a few cubes of ice across the hardwood floor. "Bitch get up out of here and take this shit!" he said, handing her the plate of dope. "Flush that shit!" He turned back to Brick-B, picked up the bucket of ice, poured it all over him and began pounding on his chest with all of his strength.

His body jumped from each hit and after a minute he checked his pulse. "Nothing!"

El Capitone put on some leather gloves, grabbed the Mac 11, screwed on a silencer and put one round in the chamber. He tucked it in the inside of his dress coat and opened up the armored, reinforced door of his truck. Sirens blared close by as cars pulled over to the side of the street. He quickly stepped back in, closed the door and watched through the limo tint as an ambulance screeched to a stop and got to work.

The rear doors flew open and two E.M.T. workers jumped out with equipment and rushed in the building. Everyone ran through the rear emergency exit after hearing the sirens and seeing the paramedics come in. They stepped in and saw a stocky, muscular black man knelt over a body, pounding his chest in a pool of half melted ice.

Manky looked over his shoulder with anxiety and beads of sweat on his face. He stood up and stepped aside. They checked his pulse then opened up all of their equipment. "Clear!" His body jerked as they shocked his heart with the powerful defibrillator. "I got a pulse but it's weak," the technician said measuring his blood pressure and looking at his watch. "Are you guys his family?"

They both looked at each other then back at the E.M.T. as one of them extracted a solution into a syringe, flicked it and injected it into Brick-B's arm. "I-I'm like his brother."

"Well ah 'I'm like his brother.' What type of drug did this guy here overdose on?"

"Man I-I don't know!" The E.M.T. looked around for any signs of drugs then opened Brick-B's eyelids and flashed a pen light in them. "Well he was snorting something."

"Well that tells us a lot man."

"Hey-hey, look man, you two are the trained fucking professionals. Not us!" Manky announced while wiping his face.

An E.M.T. left and came back with a gurney, picked him up, strapped him in, wheeled him out and Manky followed them.

"What the fuck happened to Bricks?" D-Down asked while watching them lift him up into the open ambulance doors. They quickly put a, IV in him, closed the doors and drove off.

"He overdosed."

"He what? The nigga od'ed, you serious?"

"Hell yeah I'm serious. He almost popped his heart from that bulushi mix. Little nigga flatlined and then they brought his black ass back."

Peaches started to shed a few tears after hearing the details of what happened. "We-we need to go make sure he's okay."

Manky and D-Down looked at each other and they knew that emergency rooms were rest havens for detectives. "Yeah aight come on, we will take my car."

"Where's the party at?" Chase asked as he pulled up in a burnt orange Dodge Magnum, revving his engine a few times.

"The party's over."

"What?"

"The party's over folks. That nigga Bricks is in the hospital. He overdosed."

"Wow!" He lifted up his sunglasses and rested them on his forehead, lit a Newport and exhaled. "Y'all going to go see him?"

"Yeah we're on our way."

"Well I'll follow."

"Man this is some ill shit my nigga. I step out the studio to get bossed up and then all of the sudden it's mash 4077 in the mothafucken sound booth. I thought I lost my investment, fucking with this dopefiend ass nigga."

"I mean niggas need to know their mothafucken limits."

"Limits? Ppsshhtt, man that little nigga don't have no limits."

136

"Then why did he—"

"Pure shit!" Mank and D-Down looked at Peaches. She wiped her running mascara with a napkin. "Sometimes I'd see your friend Bricks come to the Palace just to see this one Asian girl. She would get quarters from Lex and have her deliver them to dude at the bar. He kept talking about somebody called 'The Hoist,' and he got the cream."

D-Down remembered that name, then put two and two together. "Dorian," he said under his breath.

"You know him?"

"Who Dorian? Nawh-nawh. I heard of him and his uncle you just mentioned. But he knows him," he said pointing behind him at the Dodge Charger following him. D-Down split a blunt with his pinky nail, dumped out the tobacco in the ashtray and crumbled a sparkly, pungent bud into it and rolled it.

"Well I heard Alexio telling one of the other girls that he coped two keys from him."

D-Down lit the blunt and coughed. "What? You mean Dorian?"

"Yeah, I seen him and that bitch Deltrice at the club weeks ago."

"Well he did just cash my mechanic out five racks for a paint job, music—"

"And a safe spot on his bitch's car," Manky interrupted.

"Ahh I don't believe this. That nigga bought that hoe a whip."

"Shit lil' mama, look, if a nigga got it, then a nigga can feed them to keep them. He took a long hit before continuing. "But now what happens when you put too much torque on a screw?"

"It gets stripped."

They all said at once, "You mothafucken right."

CHAPTER TEN:

SCOOPED UP

THE SPACE YOU LEAVE BEHIND,
IS AS IMPORTANT AS THE SPACE YOU FILL

Dorian waited for De1trice in front of the county jail as his Chrysler 300 idled. Dressed in a sky blue Akademics sweat suit, he glanced at his Cartier diamond encrusted watch as Deltrice stepped out of a metal door. He tapped the horn, smiled and waved to get her attention. She blocked the sun as she scanned the parking lot. He pulled up in front of her. "You need a ride?"

She quickly got in, hugged and kissed him. "Girl I got something for you." He reached in the back seat and pulled out a dozen roses of hundred dollar bills made into a bouquet.

"How lovely baby." She sniffed the flowers. "It smells like money."

He leaned towards her and sniffed her neck. "Baby you smell like jail lil' mama, but ahh I'm about to pamper you."

"Pamper me, pamper me for what?"

"For keeping it solid!"

D-Down sat in the passenger seat of his BMW 745i and watched the entrance of the hospital. Medical personnel dressed in white lab coats and OR scrubs, scrambled during their shift change.

"Isthat her?" Manky asked pointing his flask and taking another sip from it.

D-Down watched Suam stop after walking out of the revolving glass doors. She dug into her designer purse, put on her sunglasses and fished out her keys before heading across the huge parking lot.

Manky scrolled through his digital pictures on his camera phone until he came across Suam. "Yeah that's her," D-Down said

tightening his pants drawstring on his black OR scrubs. He tucked his .45 in his waistband and covered it with his shirt.

He flipped down the visor mirror to look at himself then adjusted his black du-rag and gold wire-rim tinted shades.

"What is the laptop for?"

D-Down opened it and showed Manky the cracked screen. "You will find out bruh just follow me when I drive off." He stepped out and ducked next to a dark blue Nissan Altima, then double backed around to were Suam was just about to get into her car. When D-Down saw her lean down out of sight, he crouched and ran full speed to the car parked next to her.

Manky laughed and took another swig as he watched him. "This dude is on some covert mission, operation type shit."

As Suam started backing up. She heard a loud bang and felt her car shake. She then put it in park and quickly got out. "Oh my God, sir are you okay?"

A black man who appeared to be an employee was laid out unconscious on the ground. His laptop was smashed and their was a small dent in her fender. She leaned down to check his pulse and D-Down grabbed her wrist.

She felt something pushed hard into her rib cage. "Look bitch, I'll take that!"He grabbed her cellphone before she could call anybody. "If you so much as breathe bitch, I'll have you staring at your bloody kidneys right where I'm at. You understand?"

She nervously nodded in agreement. "Aight, grab my laptop, put it in your trunk and ahh, keep it company." He slowly got up, concealed his chrome .45 and watched her pick up the laptop, close it, pop the trunk and awkwardly climb in. D-Down slammed the trunk, glanced around, walked to the driver's side, got in, backed up and drove off.

Dorian weaved in and out of heavy west bound traffic on the I-80 freeway. Black exhaust came out the smoke stacks of a bus in front of them as they began to drive beside it. "I'll be damned. A county jail bus. They got to be coming back from court or something."

"Well I'm glad it's them and not us baby," Deltrice said while studying the criss-cross metal bars mounted over the tinted, spider webbed, cracked windows. Dorian glanced at her and licked his lips.

"Give them lonely ass niggas a taste of what they missing baby."

"That's what you want?" Dorian put his hand on her thigh, pushed up her skirt, pulled her panties aside and began playing with her clit. She pulled her panties down to her ankles, rolled the window down halfway and watched the bus swerve in their lane then straighten out. "I think the transportation guard caught a glimpse of us."

"You think?" She smiled, took off her panties and put one leg on the dashboard to let him gain more access inside of her. She then pushed up her skirt to her waist, turned towards Dorian on all fours, pulled down his sweats and tried to devour his swollen shaft. "Ahh-gack!"

"You aight lil' mama? Don't choke." She pulled him out of her throat and stroked him a few times.

"Just a natural reflex. I'm going too fast."

Yeah right, you just underestimated the dick, Dorian thought. "Well ahh slow down then baby."

She spiraled her tongue to his base and gently touched her teeth on the way up, smacking and licking as she went.

"Ohh I like that," he said looking down her arched, smooth back, admiring her shapely, round ass. He rubbed his hand over her Haitian flag tattoo, then ran his finger through her tight, moist folds and played with her g-spot.

"Ohhh Daddy I need to get tightened up. I need that."

Pulling his sweats back up and sitting back, she grabbed her panties then slingshot them at the bus. They wedged in between one of the bars and fluttered like a flag in the wind. "What are the odds of that?"

Seconds turned into minutes and minutes seemed to turn into several hours as Suam lay in the fetal position anticipating whether she was going to live or die. Sweat dripped from her face, more from the lack of fresh air than fear. The noise from the outside was drowned out from the car's loud bass played by the kidnapper but it couldn't disguise the ride. *It went from smooth to tough as if in a rural area*, she thought. Dirt, gravel or maybe sand. "Fuck I dont know!" she screamed and began kicking the inside of the trunk. She felt the car stop. So she stopped kicking, but the music still played.

D-Down pulled into the shop's paint booth, parked, stepped out and cut off the overhead heat lamps. He opened the overhead vents in the ceiling to let in a hint of light. He put on a surgical mask and pulled out his chrome .45 before opening up the trunk.

"Hold up bruh—"

"What you mean hold up?" D-Down asked.

"What's the purpose of the mask? The bitch already done seen your face." Manky asked while walking through the thick hanging plastic leading into the paint booth.

"Yeah you got a point, but this right here," he said waving the large chrome .45, "seems to make people lose their memory when they're on the opposite end of it."

Manky shook his head and took a swig from his flask. *Niggas*, he thought as he watched him pop the trunk.

Suam instantly jumped out and ran blindly into the darkness, but got knocked out cold. Manky caught her by the collar with the same hand before she fell on the dirty, chalky cement. "We can't damage the goods. Yah know what I'm talking about?"He took another swig, leaned the unconscious woman closer to his face and squinted.

A little stream of blood trickled down her lip. "Didn't mean to knock your little sexy ass out," he said looking at her smooth yellow skin and busty cleavage. He easily picked her up and put her over his stocky shoulder.

"Put her in this," D-Down said, kicking over an office chair on wheels. "Here. Zip-tie her ankles and wrists." He handed Manky four plastic ties. Her head leaned forward and bobbed from left to right. D-Down set the heavy gun in her lap, reached in his breast pocket, cracked open an ammonia vial under her nose and expected her to instantly wake up.

"Damn my nigga. What did you do? Kill the bitch?" He said checking her pulse.

"I barely tapped her."

"Well fortunately she's alive." He pulled back her long hair and viciously slapped her hard across her face twice. She flung her hair back with a look of sheer terror written on her face.

"Don't kill me. Don't kill me—"

"Calm down, calm down Ms. Suam Xio Lee," he said, reading her name off of her California ID then putting it back in his breast pocket.

She felt that there was someone else in the room but she couldn't see in the darkness. The light above only shined on the chrome gun in her lap. Suam bit her lip and squirmed.

"Listen, I'm going to say this one time and one time only. That in your lap will help your memory. I want you to call Dorian, tell him you got a sale for him and it's for one of your co-workers. They want to spend ten racks on a quarter brick of that cream and a quarter pound of that hydro."

D-Down walked over to her purse, opened it and set a crisp stack of neatly wrapped one hundreds on top. He set the camera feature on her cellphone, took a picture and saved it. "Text them this," he said, showing her the picture. "Tell him you're working extra hours to cover someone's shift and you'll meet him at 11:30 pm at the pier," he said dropping the phone in her breast pocket and picking up the heavy double action .45.

"If you tip this nigga that it's a set-up, I'll personally make sure your pretty face is on a silk screen t-shirt bitch!"

She watched the unknown man in the surgical mask cock the weapon, then cut one of the zip-ties loose.

Deltrice stepped out of the shower drying her hair. Her quarter-length Ralph Lauren terry cloth bath robe rode up her thighs. "You got a missed call baby," she said, holding up Dorian's phone. "You ah also got a picture in your inbox too."

Dorian sat at the end of the bed and stared down into his open safe mounted into the floor of his master bedroom. He fell back on his bed, grabbed the phone from her and stared at the vaulted ceilings.

"Its Suam. She left a message about… She just said it's important and call her back."

"Hold up." He touched his screen, scrolled through his inbox and opened it. "Money!" Dorian said under his breath.

Suam answered on the first ring. "Dorian, hey cutie. I'm on my break and ahh I'm covering for someone. Look ahh, did you get—"

"Yeah I got it."

Suam cleared her throat and watched the man with the surgical mask fold his arms with impatience. "My co-worker wanted to spend ten grand for a quarter key and a quarter pound of hydro. I get off at 11:00 pm so meet me at the pier around 11:30 if that's alright with you?"

"If that's alright with you?" Dorian playfully mocked her. "You high on something? Because you don't sound like the Suam that I know."

"Hey girl—"

"Shh." Dorian waved Deltrice off. "First off lil' mama, as far as the cream, hard or soft?"

"Hard or soft," Suam repeated in a monotone voice. D-Down made a squeezing gesture. "Soft of course."

"Soft of course," Dorian playfully mocked her again. "Wit' your square ass-"

"Look Dorian, I don't have time for games. I'm serious. I'm playing with money that's not mine."

"Aight-aight, well ah I got a little less than a pound left of high-grade blueberry kush. A lot of dense accumulation of keefe. I'll throw in a extra zone--"

"Aight Dorian, so 11:30 at pier."

"Yeah-yeah it's good and ahh, one more thing, come alone." The line went dead.

Dorian pulled his .40 caliber Glock from a hidden holster mounted to the side of his nightstand. He released the magazine, examined the shiny, hollow point bullets, inserted it and loaded a round in the chamber. "You remember how I showed you the chef skills?"

"Yeah, of course baby. How could I forget?" He gave her a raised eyebrow look. "What!"

Dorian shook his head. "Well you're not whipping nothing Ms. Wolfgang Puc. Just measuring and sealing," he said reaching in his safe and tossing her two wrapped, plastic, football sized packages of pure cocaine and dense cannabis. She put the package of the sparkly bud to her nose.

"Smells like team spirit baby."

"Well ahh this team is going fishing." He walked to his walk-in closet, grabbed a fishing cap, coveralls and tackle box. "I need you to weigh out nine ounces of that," he said, pointing to the cocaine, "and five zones of that."

"Aight daddy," she said holding the two packages like new born twins. "Ahhh baby what are you planning on using as bait?"

Dorian closed the safe, locked it and changed into the coveralls. "You're holding the bait."

Deltrice smiled, spun on her heels, walked through the double doors and headed down the stairs to the kitchen.

Deltrice flipped down the ashtray, pulled out the cigarette lighter and pressed the button. She opened the center arm rest and pushed the two pre-wrapped packages into it. "Dorian you're not really going to go fishing are you?"

He pulled down his fisherman cap, put on his stunner shades and slid his .40 caliber Glock in his cargo pants pocket. "Even though our charges got dropped baby girl, as far as we are concerned lil' mama, we're still suspects. So ahh we got to make things appear what we want others to see."

"Well ahh in that case, where's my fishing pole?"

Dorian lifted up his shades and glanced at his crotch. "Oh I got a pole for you!"

She shook her head, started the Buick, let the dual exhaust bark then drove off.

The pier was deserted except for a few cars in the distance. An army of angry seagulls battled over rotten trash. The wooden boardwalk stretched for miles, like brown piano keys, as empty wrappers danced and spiraled in the wind. Deltrice parked and leaned the seat back.

"Don't get too comfortable," Dorian said, grabbing the two packages.

"No baby, just leave them in there."

He paused for a moment then stared at her. "Aight, yeah you right baby." He grabbed the tackle box out of the back seat, stepped out and walked to the dock. The digital clock on the GPS screen read 11:20 pm. "Were is this hoe at?" Dorian asked himself, looking over his shoulder at the huge parking lot full of cars across the street, in front of a condominium complex.

Deltrice followed his gaze then put her seat into the upright position.

"I think they see us. Let me call them," Suam said reaching for her cellphone on D-Down's lap.

"Whoa. Hold up, hold up. Your ass isn't calling no mothafucken one yet!" he said snatching it from her reach. He looked at his watch then met Manky's cold eyes. "You ready to strip this nigga?"

"Yeah let's peel this nigga." Cocking the modified black and chrome Mossberg pistol grip twelve-gauge shot gun, he pulled his black ski mask over his face, then laid on the back floor of the spacious Chevy Suburban. D-Down also laid flat on the leather seat and pushed the barrel of his gun to the back of the driver's seat.

"Hit the block one time, call Dorian then pull up beside them."

He answered on the first ring. "Where you at?" he asked scanning the area, watching a few cars drive by.

"I'm pulling in right now."

He watched a tinted, pearl white Chevy Suburban on chrome 24's pull in. "Where's your car?" The line went dead.

Suam drove the length of the pier and turned into a parking space next to them. Heart beating wildly, she managed to smile at Deltrice as she rolled down the window. Dorian walked to the window, blocking Deltrice's view.

"You catch anything?" she asked, looking at his fishing gear next to the railing.

"Nawh I haven't yet." He looked around the interior of the SUV which screamed 'block mobile.' "So ahh, before you hung up I was trying to ask you whose whip this was." He eyed her suspiciously.

"Oh ahh, I'm borrowing this from my co-worker so I can ahh grab this from you. You know. Do this deal."

"Hmmmm," he murmured, staring at her designer purse in the empty passenger seat. "You got the chedda?"

"Yeah." She leaned over to grab her purse and directly behind her, he was staring down a barrel of a chrome .45 with a determined jacker in a surgical mask holding it.

"Keep yah hands on the window seal nigga and ahh, where's the shit?"

Dorain gave Suam a look of death. *Bitch, you set me up*, he thought. He gazed upon the man with the gun. "Don't shoot man."

D-Down cocked back the hammer. "Wheres the shit nigga? You think I'm playing?" He looked over his shoulder at the tackle box, then back at him. Hey bruh, grab that and I'll cover this nigga."

Manky climbed over the seat, got out and trotted around to the front of the truck with the gauge visible but close to his denim jeans. He quickly kicked the tackle box in between both the cars.

"Open it!"

"Nawh nigga, tell his bitch to open it." Manky swung the gauge at point blank range at the passenger window. Deltrice couldn't believe what was unfolding in front of her eyes. He tapped the short barrel on the tinted window. "Get out on my side."

She crawled over the middle console and stepped out.

"Open it."

She knelt down, unsnapped the tackle box and opened it. Manky rammed the butt of 12-gauge pump in Dorian's mid-section, and he doubled over. He grabbed the handle and put his finger on the trigger of his .40 caliber Glock, hidden in his cargo pants pocket.

"Aight, aight-"

"Look I know you got a safe spot in yah scraper nigga." Dorian looked at Deltrice and nodded.

"She got you, she got you!"

Deltrice climbed back in the passenger seat, opened up the center console and pulled out the two packages. As soon as Manky lowered the weapon to reach for it. Two shots rang from Dorian's cargo pants pocket, like exploding bubbles, splintering Manky's shin with the hollow point tip rounds. Blood sprayed across the passenger seat as he clutched it. He wildly fired a round, ricocheting buck shots off the ground, sending pieces of asphalt everywhere like shrapnel.

Flames spewed out of D-Down's .45 as he fired two shots, shattering their front headlight and decorating their right fender with bullet holes. Suam slapped the gun upward sending another shot through the roof. He pistol whipped her one time and swung the heavy gun back out the window.

Dorian rolled under the Buick, stood up on their side and fired three rapid shots in the door of the SUV, grazing D-Down.

"Mothafucka!" He felt his skin burning, then he switched hands and fired back, shattering both windows. Deltrice took cover as pieces of broken glass showered on her.

D-Down crept out with his gun drawn as Manky hobbled around the car to the driver's side of the Buick. He stepped over Dorian's lifeless body, knelt down and felt around his pockets. He took off his diamond rings, platinum necklace and matching platinum tennis bracelet.

D-Down yanked the passenger side door open. "Get out!" D-Down demanded looking nervously around him in the distance as lights came on and curtains opened and closed across the street.

"Fuck this shit man, this bitch is playing," he said grabbing Deltrice by her hair and pulling her like a rag doll through the shattered driver's side window.

"Ahhh-ahh nigga you're hurting me!" she yelled, kicking and scratching him. It was like razors to her flesh as she began to bleed.

He let go as he grabbed the two packages, got in the Suburban, backed up and began to drive away. Manky set the gauge next to him and started the Buick. He put it in reverse and punched the gas, engulfing them in a plume of smoke, then peeled off. She pried the Glock .40 from Dorian's right hand, kissed the cold, black steel and began firing shots. She ran out the cover of the smoke like an assassin.

In rapid succession, she fired rounds at the driver, shattering the left rear window and putting bullet holes in the fender. She steadied her aim at the driver side door, held her breath and squeezed off five more shots. The last round exploded the rear window as Manky fishtailed and disappeared in the street.

Deltrice instantly ran over to Dorian's bullet riddled body, knelt down next to him, supported his neck and rested the emptied gun on his bloodied chest. A pool of crimson blood surrounded him like a puddle of fresh motor oil.

"Baby don't die on me. Please, please don't die on me!" Tears ran down her cheeks as she stared up into the night sky. He blinked and lifted his blood soaked hand towards her. She looked back down at him and quickly grabbed it. "Ohbaby I'll try to stop the bleeding. What-what are you trying to say?" She leaned forward and pressed her ear to his full lips.

"Our-our love is eternal baby, don't-don't never forget that."

He coughed up a clot of blood, closed his eyes, loosened his grip and his body went limp as squad cars screeched to a halt with guns drawn.

CHAPTER ELEVEN:

AFTERMATH

THE HOUR WHICH GIVES US LIFE,
BEGINS TO TAKE IT AWAY.

"We got to clean this shit up bruh," D-Down said as he looked at the damage to both the cars. Manky winced from his gunshot wound as he grabbed the Mossberg 12-gauge and stepped out of the driver's side seat. He knocked shards of glass onto the chalky floor of the paint shop as D-Down saw the dried blood on Manky's shin.

"Hospitals are out the question--"

"Yeah,yeah I know and ahh, letting cup-o-noodle go is out the question too my nigga," he said pointing the barrel of his weapon at his Suburban, where Suam laid motionless on the floor board. "We got to split her seasoning pack folks. If we let her go, you know the bitch is going to march her yellow ass straight to the police station and say she was forced against her will to become a accomplice in a murder robbery."

He paused for a few seconds. "Special circumstances nigga!" Manky announced with finality, meeting D-Down's eyes for a few seconds, as if searching for an unheard answer. D-Down rubbed his chin in deep thought, stuck his chrome .45 in his waistband and took off his OR scrubs to to examine his wounds. Three long, pink scars ran across his right shoulder, forearm and neck. He walked over to the shop's office where his safe was and sat down in front of his desk. He stared at the row of flat screens surrounding him which surveilled the area.

He picked up a picture of a family member and him, set it back down then opened his safe with one hand. He pulled out the .45 from his waistband, released the expended clip and replaced it with a full one. He then put it back in his waistband. He quickly walked over to a filing cabinet, opened it and grabbed

a first aid kit.

"My nigga, you still haven't answered my question," Manky demanded as he leaned against the threshold of the door.

He spun around and tossed him the medical kit. "We are going to do this my way."

Peaches checked her text message after ending her shift. *"Wegot dat doe 4 u cum 2 shp!"* With anxiety she bit her lip. *"O.k. on my wy."* She texted, tossing her cellphone back in her purse. *What's the hold up?* she thought. *Are they saying that they got money for me or they actually got Dorian?* She grabbed her cellphone, scrolled through her numbers and pressed send.

"Yeah, what's good?"

"You got my message lil' mama?"

"I got it but--"

"Look I'm not trying to talk on this horn like this but ahh, come to the shop. I also need for you to do something for me involving a simple little phone call."

Manky met Peaches out front and avoided bringing her directly inside the paint shop. *The less she know or sees, the better*, he thought to himself. He glanced at her pink Jaguar coupe. "Cute," Manky said jokingly.

"Well it's the closest color to money daddy."

"Oh yeah, how so?"

"It's the color of the inside of every woman's pussy, which pays them. It yells the femininity of all females trying to get it."

"Well, ahh nigga can't argue about that. Come on." He guided her towards the trunk of her car. "Pop your trunk."

She hit the release button on her keys, raising her trunk slowly. Manky looked around, then dropped two wrapped packages in her trunk. "That's your cut for giving up that info. I appreciate it," he said, giving her an affectionate hug, squeezing her ass and smelling her channel perfume on her neck.

"Ahh how much is this and ahh, who exactly did you want me to call?"

He ignored her first question. "I want you to report my truck stolen."

"What, why? Why you can't do it?"

"Because it would be more believable coming from a woman's voice instead of mine. Put it this way, I'm going to keep it one hunned. My shits sprayed up, aight. There isn't no telling what nosey ass grandma might of caught a glimpse of it." Manky looked at his watch. "This is perfect timing because you just got off of your shift, and ahh that's when you noticed that your boyfriend's whip disappeared. You feel me?"

He handed her a piece of paper written with the year, make and model, license plate number and vin numbers on it. "What's this e-mail for?"

"Yeah ahh have them e-mail the report to that." He pointed at the piece of paper. "It's for in1urance purposes." She gave him awkward look. "Come on lil' mama. You think I'm not going to get a new whip out of all of this? Shhhhiitt, I need mines."

Peaches snatched it, sat in the confines of her car and began making calls. Manky spun around and headed back into the shop.

"What she say?"D-Down asked.

"Yeah, she's handling it right now."

"Look, take Ms. Lee out of the Suburban and put her back in her trunk because we're taking a trip to the wine country folks," D-Down said as he grabbed a gas can and put it in the back of the Suburban. He watched Manky put her in the trunk, zip-tie her ankles and wrists behind her back, gag her mouth with a greasy rag and duct tape her mouth before he quickly closed the trunk. D-Down tossed him a towel. "Wipe the prints," he instructed as he quickly wiped down the outside of the bullet riddled SUV. *I got to do something about these holes*, he thought.

He walked over to his office, opened the filing cabinet, grabbed something, walked back, unrolled a magnetic sign and positioned it on both doors.

Rolling hills disappeared and reappeared like a heartbeat. D-Down followed the caravan of cars through winding roads and well-manicured vineyards. Peaches glanced in her rearview as she watched D-Down's BMW closely following her. *Where are we going and whose car am I driving?* she thought to herself.

Manky activated his turn signal then veered onto a dirt road with fields of grapes on both sides of them. Gravel kicked up hitting the windshield like pellets as they drove for a few miles into the darkness. They all slid to a stop. D-Down stepped out and walked to Manky's driver side door. Peaches impatiently waited as she tapped her nails on the woodgrain steering wheel and watched them exchange some words.

D-Down pointed to the left past some trees then quickly walked to her side and opened the door. "I'll take it from here." He looked at his BMW. "Go wait in my whip. It will be about ahhhh, 15 minutes. We'11 be walking back on foot."

"Why don't I just follow—"

"Nawh just do what the fuck I ask, damn baby girl."

She snatched her purse and quickly stepped out. "Fifteen minutes huh?"

"Yeah."

"Well where's the keys negro?"

"They're in the car."

She watched them speed off in the darkness as she got in the car and reached for the ignition to start it up. "No fucking keys!" She checked her cellphone. "And no signal!"

Manky winced as he stepped out of the Suburban, walked to the back and grabbed a gas can. He began splashing the interior and saturating the new carpet. "Get the engine too folks."

He reached under the dashboard, popped the hood, opened it and drenched the engine. "Aight, aight, give me that shit man. I would just put a cloth wick in the gas tank and blow these mothafuckas up, but ahh we don't need no explosions, no attention. You feel?"

Suam kicked the trunk with both of her zip-tied feet as she laid flat on her back. All she heard was a voice say "no attention and explosion." The smell of gas hit her nostrils as the car doors opened and closed. "Let me out of heeeerrrre!"

D-Down heard the muffled sounds of kicking and screaming after he poured the last few drops of the gasoline over the trunk. He wiped his prints off the gas can then dried his hands. The trunk vibrated as Suam continued kicking. D-Down quickly snatched his chrome .45 from his waistband and fired five shots into the trunk. One round shattered the locking mechanism.

Orange flames began to blaze, caused by the sparks from the expended rounds, ignited by the gas. The intense heat licked the license plate like a thirsty animal in a dry desert. No movement. No sound. He picked up the expended shells out of the muddy dirt and glanced at the jagged, chipped paint surrounding the bullet holes. *Woooooooossssssh!* Flames danced in the black curtain of the sky as Manky tossed a lit match.

"Back up, nigga!" he said tossing another match.

D-Down stood there for a few seconds, tucked his weapon and they both trotted back to the other waiting car.

Detective Melville's nostrils caught the charred smell of burnt metal and exposed electrical wires as he stepped out of his white Ford Crown Victorian. He loosened his tie, took out his badge from his inside coat pocket and clipped it on his waistband. He then took off his dress coat and tossed it onto his front seat.

While walking to the crime scene, he put on some blue latex gloves and pulled out a small leather writing pad. Two uniformed officers were first at the scene. One was questioning two witnesses as the other secured the scene.

"Detective sir!" They both exchanged handshakes as Melville looked over his shoulder at the fresh tire tracks. They both ducked under the police tape. Melville began circling the two charred heaps of twisted metal, then tightened the perimeter. Each car was burned down to the engine block, frame and rims. Stepping back, he took several pictures of the scene from different angles.

"Detective."

"Officer." He eyed him for a few seconds.

"Sir, this here is the owner of the vineyard estates and this is one of his laborers."

"How do you do, ahh and you were the one who discovered this?" he asked, waving his hand behind him.

"Si,si!" he responded, looking down at the scorched dirt beneath his worn steel toe boots, slightly kicking a dirt claw.

"You speak English?"

"Oh yes ehh ey do."

"Okay, so explain to me what happened."

"Well ehh Detective, me was out here doing me rounds, you know, checking irrigation, fencing and ey wos jest ebout son rise then me seen smoke. A lot of smoke."

"What time was it about Mr..."

"Dionisio. Call me Dion but ehhit wos ebout 5:45, 6:00 am. I-I directed the water pressure from the nearby well, detached the watering mechanism and drenched both of thees corz."

"Did you see anyone leaving the scene?"

"No, no."

Melville stepped over the footprints, knelt down and examined them. He then walked over to the smaller smoldering heap of metal and looked at the open trunk with bullet holes in it. He leaned closer and wrote down the car's vin numbers out of inside of the trunk.

"Looks like a large caliber, Detective. Maybe .45 or a .50 caliber." Melville nodded his head as he was in deep thought and continued his inspection.

"I heard something."

"Oh yeah, and why didn't you conveniently tell me this five minutes ago?"

Dionisio took off his straw hat, wiped his sweat with dirty towel and gave him a toothy yellow smile. "Señor you only asked what me 'seen' not 'heard.'"

"Sir, either you're a terrible comedian or you're intentionally obstructing a police investigation." Ravens cawed in the distance as silence fell upon them.

"Dionisio you got to be cooperative. I mean, if you know something you have to tell them." The owner's concerned look spelled out, you better cooperate.

"Listen Mr. Dionisio, was the gunshots close together or spread out?" He stared at him blankly. "Translate to this fucker what I said."

As he did Melville walked along the row grape vines ten yards away and saw the morning sun reflect off of something. He pulled out an ink pen, clicked it, knelt down, dug around some soft soil and pulled up a copper .45 shell casing. "If you vaccuum the whole house and leave a speck of lint on the carpet, it's considered dirty my friend." He pulled out a clear evidence bag, dropped it in, sealed it and put it in his shirt breast pocket.

"Detective do you want this dusted for prints also?" one of the officers asked, holding up a half melted plastic gas can. He shook his head.

"Depends if we're pulling your prints or the perp's."

A two-way mirror casted a warped reflection of Deltrice. She stared blankly through the two detectives in front of her as she watched their lips move, but their words where incomprehensible.

"Hey Ms. Glaude!" one of the detectives said snapping his fingers several times. "Are you with us?"

She looked straight into his gray eye. "Get your hands out of my mothafucken face cop! The question you asked me was 'am I here. Yes!But my man isn't. He died in my arms and you know what he told me before he died, huh? He told me our love is eternal." She started sobbing. "Can you bring him back, huh?!"

Detective Melville listened intently, studying her Haitian features, shoulder length hair and her swollen eyes which showed that she was in no condition to be questioned. A knock on the door broke his concentration. "Excuse me."

His chair squeeked as it slid across the glossy linoleum floor. He adjusted his leather shoulder holster, walked over to the door and opened it.

"Melville, it's our sketch artist," Godfrey mentioned, looking over his shoulder.

"Look, I've told you. I didn't see no faces. There was nothing but gunfire and glass. Then the man panicked and pulled me out the window by my hair with one hand." She felt the small missing patch around her temple. "He-he had on a black ski mask and stepped out of a white Chevy Suburban on rims."

"Well we won't be needing your services," Godfrey told the sketch artist, closing the door. Deltrice shook her head and scoffed at both of the detectives. "You know you're lucky to even be alive and breathing Ms. Glaude. Your lack of cooperation is allowing those killers to roam the streets—"

"You're free to go," Melville interrupted. "We're not charging you for anything Ms. Glaude, but ahh let me ask you this one question." Melville watched her run her manicured hands through her hair and stand up. "Do you know a Suam Lee?"

She was afraid to answer his question. "Well why? Yeah I know Suam."

"Well she's missing."

"What do you mean she's mis1ing?"

"Well let me clarify this." He cleared his throat. "A vineyard laborer found a car registered to her, burned up beyond recognition. There was bullet holes in the trunk, no body, no remains. It's slim to none if anyone could survive that. Ms. Glaude, you mentioned that she was in the white SUV, on rims."

"Yeah, yeah," she responded quickly.

"It was also burned up, but we did receive a report about it being stolen. We have our theories and conjecture but no solid evidence to support this."

Deltrice was impassive and emotionless as she got up. She walked to the door and began walking out. Melville stood up. "If you walk out of that door Ms. Glaude we can't guarantee your safety." The door slammed shut and both detectives were left standing.

Wind blew north across the golf course's sand bunkers and greenruffs as Clamenta prepared to tee off. The caddy handed him a nine iron titanium club. He grabbed a wooden tee and golf ball, staged the drive and hit it. Clumps of grass and dirt sprayed across the manicured green as the ball glided high above the tree line. He tilted the visor of his sky blue and gray Puma hat. He watched it bounce along a dark patch and roll up the face of the grain. He looked at his caddy as he pulled off his golf gloves and put them in his back pocket.

"Well Mr. Barbosa given the 715 yards of course and 37 holes, I would suggest accuracy and our goal is save par 7 under. We got to be modest."

He knocked the grass off of his golf cleats and unbuttoned the collar of his dark blue Puma Polo shirt, "Modest my ass. I'm swinging for a back to back birdie, four under."

The caddy shook his head, grabbed the golf bag and slung it over his shoulder. They both climbed into a golf cart and drove the winding path of the huge golf course. A Caribbean music ringtone lightly played and vibrated Clemente's cellphone. He looked at the private number and pondered on answering it. He then pressed a button on the side of his Bluetooth earpiece. "Hoist!" he barked.

"Ahh Mr. Barboza, what a pleasant surprise!"

He waved the caddy to stop the golf cart, then he quickly stepped off. He instantly recognized the heavily accented voice on the other end. "I'll be damn, Mr. Trigger man himself. Your little war out there is costing my operation mucho dinero-"

"Our roads are not free to use. It cost," he said, reffering to his militia ambushing armed shipments which caused resistance and little room for negotiation.

"A strip of dirt surrounded by thick jungle is not what I call a road Gatillo. Trying to rule by fear only makes more enemies."

"Clamenta, Clamenta, you sound like a politician. Look I'm not calling you to discuss foreign affairs or matters."

Hoist looked across the lush green golf course and watched the caddy patiently wait and stare at his watch. "Oh yah, and what is this about?"

"Your nephew Dorian Jackson got gunned down by unknown assailants last night."

The silence stiffened his body and his mood all at once. "What the fuck? My nephew got shot? Is-is he alive?"

"Nawh he didn't make it.He expired at the scene."

He bit the inside of his cheek as grief pulled at his chest and his eyes burned with shock. "Look Gatillo, I know you had something to do with this. I know it!"

"How so Mr. Barbosa? How so?"

"How else would you know this, and you're fucking like 1,500 miles south from here?"

"If I had any involvement in this, then why would I tell you this information?" He paused for a moment. "Our tentacles stretch to many places Mr. Barbosa. Whether it be the corporate world or the underworld. I have deep pockets and I have plenty of corporate sources to fill them."

"So which one of your sources—"

"Now you know I can't tell you that. Just like you can't tell me your specific sources in the DOJ... ummm ahh, did I just say that?"

Hoist rubbed his neatly trimmed salt and pepper goatee and chose his words wisely. "If I find out you ordered this hit Gatillo, I'll personally slice and peel your skin from around your skull, pull it over your face and take pleasure in watching you suffocate. Then I'll baptize you in the nearest ocean and. allow the sharks to greet you with smiles."

"Very creative Mr. Barbosa. I'm taking notes, but comrade please do your homework before you make these promises to yourself. Like you said 'fear only makes enemies.' Yes!"

"Well anger is the salt to a cold meal."

"What I will tell you, comrade, is that those Americanas who touched and stretched out your nephew, they were amature, sloppy, young, and most important of all, it was someone close to him."

Faces of unknown people passed through his memory within seconds, like a menu screen. "Oh and one more thing. Thank you for exterminating the rat, but ahh I still haven't found its nest."

The Hoist smiled with a devilish grin. "Your guess is as good as mine Mr. Gatillo. Your guess is as good as mine."

Clemente drove up in a Mercedes Benz and parked next to Deltrice as she walked up the cobblestone walkway to her house. His window quietly rolled down as she approached.

"Yeah, we need to talk!" She got in closing the car door. "Tell me everything," he demanded as he locked the car doors.

"Well Dorian got a call from Suam out the blue for a package of cream and fruits. She texted a picture of a purse full of cash, saying she wanted to spend ten racks. She told us the time and place—"

"Oh yeah, where?"

"The waterfront pier."

"Go on!"

"Well she pulls up in a pearl white Chevy Suburban on rims. I was wondering why she wasn't driving her own car."

"Was she alone? Did you see anyone?"

"Not from where I was sitting but ahh someone with a gauge and ski mask walked around the side, pointed the barrel at me and made me get out to open up a tackle box."

"A tackle box?"

"Yeah they thought the dope was in it, but when it was empty he hit Dorian in the stomach with the butt of the gauge. He demanded the shit and he knew that there was a safe spot."

"Is that right?" he said listening and remembering what Gatillo was telling him.

"So-so I got it and as soon as he reached for it, Dorian shot him in the leg." Deltrice watched his razor wire tattoo on the thick cords of his muscular neck as he laughed for a few seconds. "What's so damn funny nigga?"

"I taught him that!"

"Taught him what?"

"To always meet aggression with aggression. He was patient and took his shot."

"Well ahh..." He waved her on to continue. "Then all I heard was gunshots and I felt glass fall all over me and next thing I know I'm being pulled through the fucking driver's side window by somebody. Once I seen Dorian laying there bleeding, and seen the shooter getting away, I grabbed his gun and got off on him."

"You think you hit him?"

"I don't know but I hope his mothafucken ass felt the same pain I was feeling when I put holes through his doors and windows."

Clamente started his car, reached in the side door compartment and sat a chrome Smith and Wesson .357 on his lap before pulling off. Deltrice's heart began to race.

"Where are we going?"

He looked directly in her eyes and sucked his teeth. "To go see my nephew's body."

The morgue technician's starched white lab coat, wire-rim glasses and exceptionally tight ponytail took several years off of her appearance. "Mr. Barboza. Ms. Glaude." She stretched her hand out to greet them both, then quickly retracted it back to her front coat pockets. Deltrice could only imagine how many bodies she'd cut open with those hands. "Please follow me."

162

She turned on her toes like a ballerina and gracefully glided down the descending, glossy hallway. They stopped in front of steel double doors which read "morgue" above it. Clamente walked through its threshold as Deltrice hesitated then walked in behind him. Footlocker sized refrigerator doors were positioned parallel on the thick reinforced walls of the morgue. The technician's shoes squeeked across the red, glossy brick floor as the lights buzzed and hummed above like a giant insect.

She put on white latex gloves, opened up a compartment with one hand, then pulled out the retractable table with a body underneath a white sheet. Small blood spots soaked through parts of the sheet.

"He was brought in as a D.O.A. earlier this afternoon. An autopsy is scheduled after proper identification can be made." She pulled the sheet down to the base of his shoulder blades.

Clamente's face was impassive as Deltrice began crying hysterically. He embraced her. "That's him. That's my nephew, that's Dorian." He laid there with a peaceful look on his face.

CHAPTER TWELVE:

WHERE IS THE REST

ANYONE CAN STOP A MAN'S LIFE,
BUT NO ONE HIS DEATH.
A THOUSAND DOORS OPEN ON TO IT.

Suam stood in a rural gas station bathroom studying her appearance in a cracked and smeared mirror. Her matted brunette hair fell over her shoulders. She wrapped a leopard print, silk scarf around her head, then put on some dark sunglasses. Dirt and grime decorated the tiled floor as she looked at her exposed thigh, dressed in gauze and bandages. She pulled up her sweat pants, tied up her shoes and trashed the used boxes of cheap hair dye. She then stepped out into the dirt parking lot and caught site of a pay phone.

I haven't seen one of those in a while. But thank the enlightened one that I found one, she thought to herself, She limped slightly, dragging her leg towards it.

Brick-B followed Chase in his dark, candy teal-colored Pontiac Bonneville as his Dodge Magnum turned into the paint shop's parking lot. They both stopped and got out simultaneously. "You ready to get back to work lil' bruh?" Chase asked.

"Well I'm here," he said, smiling and slapping himself on his chest. He ran his fingers through his thick, shoulder length dreadlocs and tied them into a ponytail. He knocked the dust off of his cre8tive rex tennis shoes and grabbed his bottled water from his back pocket.

As he took a swig he wiped the beads of water off of his crisp white t-shirt. "Doctor said for me to stay hydrated during my recovery," he announced, proudly holding up the plastic bottle towards him as if toasting.

Chase shook his head. "As long as you stay drinking water and not smoking it, you'll be aight," he said walking past him towards the garage. He unlocked it and pulled a heavy chain. Light flooded the shop as D-Down came out of his office. Chase took one look and knew something wasn't right. *Call it a thug intuition*, he thought to himself.

"What's good Chase, Bricks?" They both tilted up their heads to say what's up. There was an awkward silence for a few seconds. "Wassup with y'all two niggas? Y'all got a problem?"

Bricks took another swallow of his water, wiped his lips with the back of his hand and noticed that he still had on his medical wrist band.

"Nawh folks," Chase responded. "It's you that has the problem and since I fucks with you on getting money. Your problem is my problem."

D-Down watched him as he pulled out a newspaper and handed it to him. He snatched it, fanned it open and began reading the headlines.

"Nurse abducted, car found burned up riddled with bullets. Vineyard laborer alerts authorities after uncovering a possible crime scene. Two vehicles were found fully engulfed in flames. Homicide Detective Melville believes the incinerated Chevy Suburban belonged to a suspect that desperately attempted to try to destroy evidence. The second burned vehicle belonged to a missing nurse who apparently was abducted in the parking lot of her job and forced into the trunk at gunpoint by an unidentified person dressed in OR scrubs. Detectives disclosed no further information in the investigation."

D-Down looked at the journalist's name at the bottom left hand corner. "Jess Schmit," he said under his breath. *Was the bitch dead or alive?* he thought to himself.

As he tried to hand the newspaper back to Chase, he walked past him to the rear of the shop, then snatched a light gray car cover off. He stood there and looked closely at the quarter sized bullet holes which peppered the entire car. He then threw the cover back over the car and stepped out to the back of the shop. He reached into the breast pocket of his crisp Dickie coveralls, pulled out a crinkled Newport and lit it. Chase took a long pull and felt the nicotine calm his nerves.

D-Down stepped outside as Chase met his penetrating eyes. "My nigga you is crazy as fuck—"

"I covered my tracks man—"

"Oh yeah? Then why in the fuck you still got that nigga's whip in our establishment?"

"Waiting on you."

"On me for what— Ahh hell nawh man. There isn't nothing salvageable on that whip!" he said looking towards the corner of the shop at the covered car.

"SSShhhiiit give me a floor jack and a Phillips head screw driver and I'll snatch the shoes and beat in ten minutes," Brick-B announced while pulling the cover back off. "I got to make up for lost time anyway because ahh, my pockets is touching my thigh," he said patting his pockets.

D-Down shrugged his shoulders. "Well there you have it. As soon as he do his thing, then we will put it on a flatbed and dump it."

Chase took another pull and blew it out of his nostrils like a wild steer. "Man D-Down, let's get this shit together."

A mother walking her five-year-old son to school along Leonard Street came across Kemper Street and glanced at an abandoned car in an alley. The sight of bullet holes made her grip her son's little hand even tighter. A tire iron laid next to the custom rims as the driver's side door was half open. Its candy paint still shimmered despite the bullet holes.

A police cruiser pulled up behind it and looked at the paper plates. Officer Rumsfield didn't bother getting out, but instead he made a call. "Detective Melville, yeah I think you should be the first to know before I decide to call this into dispatch."

"Oh yeah, and what is that?"

"Well your little mystery Buick which belonged to a vic that was allegedly involved in a murder robbery—"

"Yeah, yeah where are you?"

"Well I'm parked behind it in a alley off of Kemper and Leonard Street," he said staring at the empty syringes, plastic baggies and graffiti spray painted on a brick wall.

"The Crest huh? The perp wanted it to be found and they changed their method of disposing of the evidence," he said to himself.

"How is that Detective?"

"Well officer Rumsfield ahh, it's not burned to a fucking crisp."

The forensic specialist studied the trajectory and pulled a slug out of the floor board with long tweezers. She dropped it in a clear plastic evidence bag, sealed it and directed her attention to the streaked blood splatters on the driver's seat.

"Hit the lights!" she said to a technician. She grabbed a hand-held black light wand, turned it on and waved the glowing purple hue across the car's tan leather upholstery. The splatters glowed like specimen under a high-powered microscope. With one hand she swabbed a small contaminated area and secured it in a plastic cylinder case.

"Here. Get this to the lab and run a full toxicology and also find out if there is a DNA match in the system. This may be the vic's blood but I would like to be for certain and rule this theory out."

The intern turned back on the lights, walked towards forensic specialist Puentez and grabbed the container. "Right away!"

Melville took the department's police utility elevator directly down to the forensic lab located at the basement. It jerked to a stop and as the doors opened. A young female forensic intern of middle-eastern descent stepped on. "Detective," she greeted him with a slight accent and smiled.

He smiled back. "Hold that door. I'm getting off here." The doors flung back open as she stepped off. "Is Officer Puentez in her lab?" he asked looking at the plastic cylinder with the DNA sample.

"Oh yes, she is there."

"Any new findings?"

"Well I'm running this to the lab right now," she said waving it like a magical stick. The driver's side seat appears to have a self-inflicting gunshot wound splatter. But this is entirely my own theory from my own observation Detective. We still have to rule out if this may be the vic's."

"Yes and if that is the case, then you need to let me or my associate in homicide know."

"Alright, but sir ahh should I let Officer Puentez know that-"

"Don't worry, I'll deal with them both."

"Both!"

He smiled. "Both, meaning her alter egos and anal retentiveness."

She put her hand to her mouth and giggled as the elevator doors closed in front of her.

As Melville walked into the lab's warehouse, he noticed Officer Puentez sitting on a stool hunched over a microsope. Beakers, flasks and tubes spiraled around shiny countertops as blue flames heated different colorful liquids. He glanced at the Buick on the hydraulic lift and its scattered interior parts all over the floor.

"Are you waiting to be briefed Detective Melville?"

"Now how did you know it was me, honestly?"

She spun around in her stool, lifted up her goggles and set the slides she was holding down next to her. "It was your cologne Detective and ahh non-filters." She said, snapping her fingers, "Camels right?"

"You know Ms. Puentez, your detail can be a blessing or it can be a curse." He thrusted his hands in his pockets and walked closer. "So what we got?"

"Well given the time you just arrived, I'm sure you ran into my intern in the hallway."

"Well yes but-"

"Might be the vic's DNA. I ordered a toxicology report and to run the specimen through the system for any matches."

He wanted to comment on the intern's theory but decided not to. "So do you have a ballistics report?"

She folded her arms as she stood up, then walked to a countertop that had a small pan on top. "Well there were three different calibers of weapons expended. Small metal ball bearings, hollow point tip .40 caliber and .45 caliber slugs." She picked up the mushroomed slug of the .45 and held it up like a South African blood diamond. "Well, what I do know is that this shooter likes to keep it simple. High velocity packed casings, accurate grouping and the ejection markings from the barrel are consistent with a double action Colt automatic handgun and that is a match with the slugs we pulled from that burned vehicle."

"Excellent Officer Puentez. Make sure I have a full report on my desk." As he turned around she cleared her throat.

"Ahh Detective, my work is done on this vehicle. I've conducted a complete investigation, prints, ballistics and DNA. There is really no specific need to waste tax payer's money by storing this vehicle on the department's premises," she said waving her hand.

"Well what do you suggest?"

"Does the vic have any immediate family members?"

"I'm sure he does."

"Well I got a call from the C.M.E. and I was informed that there was a positive ID made by a Clemente Barbosa who claimed to be the victim's uncle."

The Hoist, he thought to himself.

"Are you okay detective?"

"Sure, yeah. I was just putting the pieces together, that's all."

"Well I had the morgue technician fax me over the death certificate and identification acknowledgement affidavit with his contact info." She grabbed it out of the fax machine tray slot and quickly handed it to him. He wiped the corner of his eyes and blinked a few times, while reading the small print. "Need your glasses old timer?" she said sarcastically, watching him pat his breast pocket.

He ignored her and placed a quick call and listened to it ring a few times. Clemente picked up on the second ring. He adjusted his

Bluetooth earpiece and set his smart phone on the car's armrest. "Mr. Barboza speaking."

"This is Detective Melville homicide V.P.D. sir, no need to be alarmed."

"That's why I have attorneys on retainer Detective, which eases my mind for calls like this."

"I see, well then fair enough."

"How can I help you?" Deltrice looked at him from his passenger seat as he talked.

"Well Mr. Barboza I was given some documents from our senior forensic technician who received them from the medical examiner's office confirming a positive ID on Mr. Jackson. Dorian Jackson. Your nephew. Correct?"

"Sounds about right."

"We have property that our department has of his, and we need an immediate family member to release it to."

"Oh yeah and that is?"

"His car. An '06 Buick Lacrosse—"

"I don't want that car." Deltrice set her hand on his wrist as he looked into her eyes, then nodded his head slowly.

"Alright Detective, tell me when and where I can pick it up."

A mechanic directed a flatbed truck as it backed up into the Vallejo Buick Dealership's service area. Steve Fowler stood up from behind his desk after viewing his surveillance monitor. He then walked out of his office towards the dealership's garage. A small crowd of employees surrounded the bullet riddled Buick LaCross sedan as he approached.

"Mr. Fowler is this the LaCross sir?"one of the mechanics asked as he wiped grease off of his fingertips with a paper towel.

"Yes gentlemen, this is it!" The sound of the flatbed truck pulling off muffled the laughter.

"This has to be a joke."

"No this is no joke people. This car belonged to a good friend of mine and it can and will be brought back to showroom floor quality, and ahh to up the stakes, I'll add a bonus for all of you guys," he hinted, patting the hood of the car and pointing at each one of the staff members.

"Mr. Fowler, why doesn't the owner's insurance just total it out as a theft recovery and replace it?"

"Two words people, 'sentimental mothafucken value.' You got it?" Some of the employees glanced around at the fleet of cars being serviced. "Don't worry, we will make time and manage it. It's not like were running a charity around here."

He turned around, quickly walked out an emergency exit, walked around a maze of cars and got in his black Audi-RS. He took a glass cylinder tube out of his ashtray, squeezed out a crack rock from a small plastic baggy. Then he lit the tip. The brillo glowed like lava behind the car's tint as he took a long pull, exhaling a chest full of white smoke.

He grabbed his cellphone from his inside dress coat pocket, punched in a number and listened as someone answered. "Yes Mr. Barbosa, the transaction to my account was confirmed and the work is being done as we speak. I'm not sure of the extent of the damage but we have a good team of people."

"Alright Mr. Fowler, I texted you the address to where the car will be delivered."

Steve took the phone from his ear and looked at his inbox. "Alright, not a problem."

The driver looked at the GPS screen as he pulled up to the address. "This is the place."

He grabbed his touch pad in the passenger seat to get a digital signature. He walked up the cobblestone walkway leading up to the entrance. Deltrice opened the door, instantly noticing the driver's GMC insignia on his blue coveralls and easily put two and two together.

"Ms. Glaude?"

"Yes."

"I work for Mr. Fowler at the Buick dealership—"

"Are you sure that's the same car?"

He looked over his shoulder as he handed her the touch pad for her signature. "I know it's hard to believe but, ahh our body shop guys replaced a lot of the parts and switched out the interior. There was really no serious electrical damage, so the mechanical parts were intact."

She looked at the new 24-inch rims, chrome pipes and factory paint. She signed it, handed it back and walked past him to inspect the car. "You need a ride back to the dealership?" Deltrice asked.

"No, I'm being picked up Ms. Glaude. It's okay." He glanced at his watch as a van pulled up. He got in and they drove off.

She tightened her robe's waist belt as she walked around to the driver's side door. *Different style*, she thought to herself, noticing the glossy black paint. The leather seats hugged her as she sat in the driver's seat. Her fingertips ran across the mahogany woodgrain steering wheel, then she turned the keys. The Buick's dashboard, speedometer and navigational screen lit up with a blemish glow. "I-I can't keep this. It-it's too much!"

Tears streaked down Deltrice's soft cheeks as she angrily pounded the steering wheel. "Baby don't cry/Keep your head up/I know the road is long /But never let up/Baby don't cry."

She listened to Tupac's passionate, raspy voice rap his verse as if he was talking directly to her. She wiped her tears with the back of her sleeve then reached in her robe's pocket. She pulled out her cellphone and called Marcellos.

"Come get this car Cellos. It-it just gives me too many memories."

"Trice...Trice I understand baby, I understand."

The sterile smell of the medical examiner's office filled the doctor's nostrils as she pushed a gurney down the long hallway, towards the examination room. The wheels rattled, bounced left and right as the double doors opened up automatically. Technicians dressed in full body jumpsuits stood around a variety of tools to conduct their autopsy. One of them picked up the investigator's report and began reading it.

"So what do we have? What's the cause of death?"

The other technician announced, "Gunshot wound."

"Well if we already knew the cause of death, then what's the use of this autopsy?"

She pushed her clear, plastic visor over her face and grabbed the clipboard. "Because it's the law."

She pulled the white sheet exposing the body. Dime size holes pocked Dorian's chest and waist. She cleared her throat before speaking into her digital recorder. "Black male, between the age of 25-30. No abrasions. No lacerations or contusions. Muscular extremities. Visible gunshot wounds to the upper right chest and lower abdomen." She lifted up his right arm. "Gunshot wound to right bicep, apparent fracture." She put down the recorder and felt around the body's scalp. "No blunt trauma to skull."

One of the technicians scribbled on a notepad as she picked up a scalpel and made a "Y" incision on the corpse and peeled back the skin, like dried latex paint, exposing colorful organs. She picked up a tool resembling large branch cutters that was used to open up the chest cavity. The sound of splintering bone filled the examination room. She probed the damaged organs with forceps in search of the slugs, yet to her surprise there were none.

"We never confirmed if there were exit wounds." The other technicians helped her tilt the corpse so she could examine the back. "Hmmm this is strange. Very, very strange," she said as she set the body back down on the shiny steel table. "Looking at the caliber of the weapon, the distance... Imean, there is no way this man's body could absorb those bullets without exit wounds. It's impossible. It's almost as if the ballistics literally disappeared in the anatomy."

"Like it swallowed it up." The doctor gave the technician a blank look which science couldn't explain, then stared at the lifeless body for a few seconds, walked closer and peered into the exposed chest cavity. "Take a blood sample as I examine the left and right ventricle of lite major aorta. Hmmm it appears to be torn and wrapped around the spine."

As she picked up the bloodied scalpel, the body grabbed her wrist with super human strength and opened its glazed eyes, revealing white pupils. His heart began to slowly beat in a pool of slimy liquid. He raised to an upright sitting position and cracked his neck, then stared at each person with a repulsive look, fell back on the table like dead weight, releasing his deathly grip.

His heart beat twice then stopped as his eyes slowly closed. At that same exact moment the headlights on the Buick in Marcellos' garage flickered.

A black Cadillac hearse bounced across the entrance as it entered through the twisted iron gates of Rolling Hills Cemetery. A motorcade of Harley Davidson choppers rumbled closely behind as a black Lincoln Continental stretch limousine stealthily followed through the bends and turns of the small roads of the well-kept cemetery landscape.

Tombstones, statues and colorful flowers decorated the cemetery for several square miles as one car was parked in the distance. A gold canopy in black trim hung over the grave site. Images of blurred tombstones reflected off of the black hearse as it pulled to a complete stop. The driver quickly stepped out, dressed in a tailored black-on-black suit. He walked to the rear and stood at attention.

Hundreds upon hundreds of people dressed in black, wearing dark shades stepped out of their limos. They walked towards the grave site and took seats. Clamente stepped out of his limo alone and walked toward the hearse. The driver gave him a compassionate nod and stepped aside. Clamente reached in his inside pocket, put on his black leather gloves, opened the back, took out the flower wreath and handed it to the driver.

He then began pulling out the polished gold casket. Tran, Marcellos, Strings and two other close friends grabbed the metal handles, turned and walked to the grave site. Everyone moved to the side to let the pallbearers walk by. The wind carried the cries from mourners through the rough, serrated leaves of the elm trees that surrounded them. They set the casket over the open grave.

"Ladies and gentlemen." A preacher dressed in a black robe with a large gold, embroidered cross stood at a glass podium and flipped through pages of his Bible. "Ezekiel 7:23-27 says 'Make a chain for the land is filled with crimes of blood, and the city is full of violence, therefore I will bring the worst of Gentiles, and they will possess their houses; I will cause the pomp of the strong to cease. And their holy places shall be defiled, Destruction does: They will seek peace, but there shall be none. Disaster will come upon disaster, and rumor will be upon rumor. Then they will perish from the priest. And counsel from the elders. The king will mourn, the prince will be clothed with desolation, and the hands of the common people will tremble. I will do to them according to their way. And according to what they deserve. I will judge them. Then they shall know that I am Lord.' All of us here are links to a large chain and this man here, Mr. Dorian Jackson, is the lock," he said waving one hand across the crowd pointing his bible at the casket.

"When we think of chains, the first thing that comes to mind is bondage. No, what the Lord is saying is secure your land and everything in it." He paused for a moment then cleared his throat. "We have to secure our young people and encourage them to be keys to help unlock these community's minds who gave up on the youth and be bond servants for Christ. To be examples, mediators or hood ambassadors."

He watched the head nods throughout the crowd before continuing. "If we all here was given everything we needed to live, food, medical and whatever else, then what use would this be?" He held up a crisp one hundred dollar bill. "What use would this be?" He paused for a moment for his question to have effect. "Yeah, no value no value whatsoever. This is the reason why our young men die over this, because we give it value. We value what it will purchase, how it makes us feel. The reward we need to value this," he said, holding up the Bible. "Not this." He fanned the money like a flag. "Eternal life or death."

The Buick quietly started its engine and slowly drove off in the distance.

CHAPTER THIRTEEN:

CLOSEST TO YOU

WHAT WE CALL EVIL IS SIMPLY IGNORANCE BUMPING ITS HEAD IN THE DARK.

Marcellos opened up the car door and its new car smell permeated through his nostrils as he sat in the plush leather seats of the luxury sedan. The door closed automatically and locked. At the same time the console emitted a blueish eerie glow.

"What the fuck. I sure don't remember this in the car manual," he spoke out loud as if there was another occupant in the car. The glove compartment popped open revealing a brand-new Buick Lacrosse 2006 owner's manual with a black glossy cover and platinum lettering. He stared at it for several seconds as he held the laser cut keys in hand, inches away from the ignition. The driver's seat shot forward with lightning speed sending his skull directly into the hard woodgrain steering wheel. The keys he held slowly dropped to the plush carpet. Blood trickled from his mouth and nose as he laid there motionless. Unconscious.

All four windows simultaneously rolled down a quarter of an inch. As if it was programmed or if someone tapped all four buttons. Its V-8, super charged engine quietly started and idled in the closed garage as he laid still. Marcellos blinked a few times and slowly wiped his face as tracers psychedelically followed his hand movements. Extreme pain ripped through his upper abdomen as if it was sharp, hyperdermic needles abstracting tissue.

He gripped his chest, grimaced and dug his fingers deep into his skin, as if literally trying to pull out his own heart. Coughing non-stop, phlegm and mucus mixed with his blood as he looked for an escape. He desperately fumbled around all of the levers, switches, knobs and door handles. Nothing. *The open window*, he thought, grabbing it and pulling himself up. The window smoothly ascends and crushes the bones, severing the tendons.

"AHHHHH my hand!"

Marcellos had no strength or breath to even contest as he watched his own smeared blood and severed fingertips slide down the other side of the Buick's window.

Detective Melville stepped out of his air-conditioned, unmarked car and lit a non-filter Camel. His lungs embraced the nicotine like a baby to Similac. He took a visual picture of the whole scene and made a calculation of the perimeter. Ash from his cigarette fell off on to his pants leg. He knocked it off his wrinkled Docker slacks. He positioned his shiny detective badge on his belt then began weaving through crowds of nosey spectators that gathered around the crime scene. A black woman cried hysterically at the front of the crowd, while being consoled by a middle aged male.

"Must be a family member," he said under his breath as he lifted up the yellow "Do Not Cross Police Line" tape. When he originally got the call, it was a possible suicide, but after forensics analyzed the amount of blood, all hell broke loose.

"Detective, over here." He looked up, eyes following the source of the voice coming from the threshold of the one-car garage. He saw a woman dressed down in a button-up jumpsuit, wearing latex gloves and goggles. Her hair was pulled back into a tight ponytail, displaying deep, healthy waves. "Detective right here!" she yelled, revealing her Central American accent in her speech.

He dropped his cigarette, crushed it under his heel and quickly walked up the long drive way. So what cha got Officer Puentez?" he asked as if she was a rookie.

She looked him up and down then sucked her ivory white teeth with sheer disgust. She cleared her throat. "Well Detective, there was excessive blood loss and signs of struggle. There were also several prints around the driver's side door, passenger side door, trunk and hood."

As she was talking, he glanced down at the small igloo ice chest she had grasped in her right hand. "Isn't it a little early for lunch Officer Puentez?" He gestured, tapping on his imitation Movado wrist watch.

She stopped in mid-sentence as she was briefing him, smiled with crafty wit, knelt down and opened the cooler. "Well Detective, I did bring extra to go around. Here, catch." She quickly tossed the severed bloody fingertips at him that were previously on ice.

He jumped back at the sight of its contents and caught the heavy Ziploc bag. Other forensic interns that were conducting menial tasks nudged their partner and laughed to themselves. Handing the evidence back to her, he asked, "What was the time of death?"

"It's unknown at this time until an autopsy is done," she said putting the evidence back in the cooler, snapping it closed and standing up. "Our guess is that it was early evening."

He looked over her shoulder and side-stepped to take a closer look at the vehicle's sleek contours. Its shiny custom paint and dealersh1p plates read Vallejo Buick Dealership. The custom chrome duel exhaust protruded symmetrically from underneath the rear bumper. Melville blinked as a photographer snapped a picture from the front. "Who the hell let the fucking press in here? Hey you. Yeah you. Get the fuck out of my crime scene buddy because you're contaminating it with your presence."

The young journalist pushed up his wire-rim glasses and clutched his digital camera as uniformed officers escorted him away. "You know what, Ms. Puentez inform your team that the game is over. Alright everyone let's wrap it up, move it, move it."

Detective Melville had a better assessment of the crime scene after they all left. With writing pad and pen in hand, he put on his gloves, circled the luxury sedan and began to take notes. He noticed the blood stains which streaked off of the car's window seal and on to the garage's cement floor. He stepped over it and opened the driver's side door. What was before him didn't add up in his logical thinking of a homicide detective.

Throughout my thirty years of experience I've only encountered this cause of death when called upon suspected arson calls. Dried blood, vomit and mucus was caked on the victim's face as the corpse laid stiff in the fetal position. The eyes were glazed over and staring blankly. He slowly shut them then continued to the mouh which he opened up, examining the tongue, which was as black as coal.

"What the fuck!" he mumbled to himself as he picked the car keys up off of the floor board. How could the cause of death be carbon monoxide poisoning but the vic severs his own fingers, when his keys are in plain fucking reach. He took out a small manila envelope, dropped the laser cut keys into it, closed it and marked it exhibit (A).

Compression marks of the woodgrain steering wheel arched around the front part of the victim's skull. "Forensic bastards must have missed that one," he said out loud, but not loud enough for the spectators to hear him nor the uniformed officers to notice. "Now there must have been a perpetrator. How else is the victim going to crush his own skull on the steering wheel? Well I'm not going to find out until I get the prints ran through N.C.I.C. and find a match."

He stepped back, scribbled some more notes then walked around to the front windshield in order to take down the vin number. Another large manila envelope sat on top of the hood. He quickly opened it and dumped out its contents. A cellphone, Newport cigarettes, lighter, gold chain and pendant. California car titles and identification.

As he examined the titles, he matched the vin numbers and compared the name to the driver's license. Flipping the title over, he noticed that it was signed over to the victim a week before. He flipped the car title back over and whispered the name to himself but it didn't ring a bell. Stuffing the contents back into the envelope, he took off one of his latex gloves and touched the screen on his iPhone.

"Yeah this is Melville, go ahead dispatch, the coroner transport unit, ohh and towing. Yeah-yeah ok."

He disconnected the call, walked out the garage and lit up another non-filter Camel as he scanned the small crowd. Out of nowhere, a loud bang sounded from inside the garage. Everyone ducked in the crowd as the detective drew his police issued Glock

.22 nine millimeter and quickly reholstered once noticing that it was the car's door that closed by itself.

A large flatbed tow truck with the name 'Alverez Towing' on the side was parked across from the crime scene. The driver rubbed the stubble on his chin and glanced into the rearview mirror. "I need a shave and I need some sleep."

There were deep black marks and circles under his eyes. He picked up an empty styrofoam cup and spit his chewing tobacco into it. "Why don't this darn meat wagon over yawnder hurry the fuck up." Two men, with no expression dressed in blue jumpsuits wheeled a body bag on a gurney to the waiting doors of a coroner truck. "About time!"

He backed up into the narrow driveway and stopped. He then switched a lever which made the hydraulics lift to a forty-five degree angle. He jumped out, went to work attaching chains and adjusting the hydraulics until finally it was on the flatbed. I-80 was bumper to bumper during the evening commute, so the back roads to the yard was more reasonable.

A country song of Rascal Flats poured through the small speakers in the truck's cab. The industrial tow lane roads were dark and there were no cars for miles. Squabble on the driver's c.b. radio distracted him a car's high beams flicked like strobe lights. He looked in his rearview to confirm that there were no cars.

He was temporarily blinded from the light, hitting the air brakes. The truck fishtailed as he fought to keep the large truck on the narrow road.

"What in hell's damnation is going on here? I know good darn well I detached the car battery before I pulled it up on this here lift," he said blinking a few times. He rubbed away the shadow spots from his eyes. "Whoa, we're finally here." He pulled into the chalky gravel which crackled beneath the tires as if it was alive. He drove down rows and rows of cars until he found a vacant space. He backed in, lowered the lift and watched as the Buick slowly rolled back in its spot.

Two large Bull Mastiffs padded up to the tow truck driver as he was securing the gate to the yard. "Hey boys how are you doing? How you doing?" He playfully rubbed them on their ears, petting them. They barked and licked his hand in response. "You guys keep a eye on things, got it?" He stepped in the truck, spit some tobacco in his cup and drove off.

A car horn instantly started sounding off in the distance. Both of the dogs' ears stood up like antennas and they both took off at top speed to go investigate. The trained guard dogs made their rounds by circling the perimeter and tightening the circle as they isolated the source of the noise. The honking stopped as the curious animals slowly approached. One suspiciously sniffed the air like a lion during hunting. The other sniffed the ground, working its way around the tires of the car. The engine quietly purred to life as the animals paid no attention.

They continued to sniff around the car and gradually made their way to the front. They sat on their huge paws and whimpered as if confused. A dome light came on inside the Buick and both dogs instantly started barking and one hurled its body onto the hood. Spittle flew from its jaws as he barked menacingly at who they thought was there.

The Buick lurched forward sending the dog tumbling. It jumped back up on the hood and kept barking. The other dog bit at the tires over and over. Dirt shot up from behind the car like a shotgun blast as it pealed forward, targeting the animals in its wake. The muzzle of the dog was crushed under the tires as the other flew off the hood of the car. The Buick's front grill crushed its ribs from the momentum, running over its hind legs, breaking and splintering its bones like twigs.

It slowly drove over each paralyzed dog as they laid helpless, bleeding. Backing up, again and again, until they were just bloody, hairy pulps of mangled flesh. Dust kicked up from behind the Buick's rear tires as it accelerated towards the locked fence, busting a huge hole through it. Its brake lights flickered in the distance as the headlights turned on.

Detective Melville stepped out of his unmarked Crown Victorian. He took one deep drag from his Camel non-filter, tossed it on the gravel and angrily stepped on it. Something told me to authorize that vehicle to be kept in the department's evidence garage until further notice. He pulled out his iPhone as he quickly approached the damaged fence to the entrance of the tow yard. He observed the tire tracks and took pictures, forwarding them to the department's secure computer server.

The fence was peeled back with great force. Couplings that secured the post were completely snapped off. There were no signs of debris. No fiberglass. No flakes of paint from the initial impact, which was strange.

"Are you going to catch this fucker? He broke into my tow yard, stole a car and killed both of my dogs. That son of a bitch should-should-"

"Now calm down, calm down mister…"

"It's Evans."

"Okay Mr. Evans, I take it you're the driver right?"

"Yup and I'm part owner with my wife who handles dispatch."

"Okay, was she here at the time of the break in?"

"No she clocked out early to beat the evening commute."

"Did you see anything suspicious when you arrived or when you left?"

"No, no, not at all, just locked up and left."

Melville paused for a moment, sucked his tobacco stained teeth and loosened his tie. He tapped his writing pen on the pad he was using. "And the dogs?"

Mr. Evans' lips curled up as his eyes began to water. "Over yawnder." He pointed between the long row of cars in the distance and Melville saw two mangled objects.

He began following the deep imprints of the tire tracks to the location. Seeing dead bodies was common. He was used to the human anatomy. The organs and the intricate damage a bullet could do to them. But animals. That was different. Entrails, bone fragments and pulverized flesh laid scattered and blotched around the animals' bodies. Their eyeballs protruded out of their crushed skulls like miniature jack-in-the boxes as their spongy lungs flowered out of their mouths like underwater sea urchins. The smell of burnt rubber rose off of their matted short hair coats from the black tire tracks.

"You see what I mean Officer?"

"It's Detective," Melville corrected him.

"Oh, um Detective."

He took more photos of the tire tracks and noticed how they symmetrically zig-zagged perfectly. Calculated. No mistakes. Vexed, he rubbed his stubby chin in deep thought. This person is definitely not an animal lover, and why would the perpetrator target this particular vehicle? A 2006 Buick Lacrosse. Why would he overly and excessively slaughter these animals with a car he definitely was not going to be able to keep?

"Precinct Dispatch," Melville spoke into his iPhone. After giving dispatch the description of the car, its vin numbers, and that it had dealership plates, they put that particular vehicle down on the top of the hot list.

"Mr. Melville, what a pleasant surprise," a voice called in the distance before he approached his car.

"Ahh yeah, that's me but ahh, who in the hell are you?"

"Schmit, Jess Schmit."

Melville tillted up his face and then relaxed. "Ahh yes Mr. Shit. Oh excuse me, Mr. Schmitt." He snapped his fingers and pointed at him. "*Vallejo Herald Times* journalist right?"

"Yes that is I, in the flesh."

"Well I can finally put a face to a name. What can I do for you?"

"Well I'm working on a story and I just want to ask you a few questions."

"Okay, in regards to what?"

He took out a digital voice recorder out, while simultaneously asking, "Sir, is it true that the vehicle that fits the same description of a car that was involved in a homicide was stolen from this tow yard?"

"Well that's inconclusive-"

"Are you speculating that the perpetrator targeted that specific car in order to destroy overlooked evidence, that may connect them to the crime?"

"Well ahh, it's still under investigation and we're determining whether there was foul play, suicide or if in fact it was a homicide."

"Well detective if that was the case and the investigation was ongoing, then why wasn't the vehicle stored in the department's evidence garage?"

"Look Mr. Schmitt, I'm not going to answer that question. You journalists always forget which side you're on-"

"Hey, hey Detective."

Melville turned around and saw the tow driver approaching quickly. "Mr. Evans, yeah I was just leaving. What the hell is it?"

"Well do you remember asking me if I seen anything suspicious when I arrived? Well when I was in route to this here yard, that car that I had hitched did the darndest thing I've ever seen. Well, or ummm, I know this is going to sound crazy but I specifically disconnected the battery to that damn car and I know that for a fact... It ahh flicked its lights, its high beams. Like a strobe light, which blinded me and I almost ran my damn truck in that there ditch. Ohh I was madder than a Puff Ader being stuck with a stick."

Melville waved him off, gave him his business card and drove off leaving the journalist recording his experience.

Binary code of zeros and ones displayed across the Buick's 12.3-inch high resolution screen multimedia display as it hacked the OnStar system. A satellite orbiting 240 miles above the earth repositioned itself and beamed the global positioning data directly to the Buick's built-in computer processor. It drove close behind a CTS Cadillac V-coupe.

The driver glanced in his rearview mirror at the approaching sedan. "Hello, hello!" Manky glanced at his cellphone. "Dropped call," he said to himself. He tossed it in the passenger seat and switched lanes to allow the car to pass him, but it didn't. "What the fuck is up with this nigga?"

He watched the car speed up and turn its lights off, matched his speed, accelerated, got in front of him, switched lanes then decreased its speed. It then got inches behind him, flickering its high beams like a strobe light. It repeated this several times as Manky swerved wildly and punched the gas.

A cargo truck carrying plumbing supplies turned on its blinker and began slowly switching lanes as he saw the erratic driving in his rearview. The Buick rammed the back of the CTS crushing the trunk and sending it fishtailing directly into the back of the truck.

Manky attempted to cover his face but the quarter-inch copper piping impaled the windshield, went through his hands, entered his frontal lobe and exited out of the back of his skull. The driver of the truck hit the brakes, jumped out holding his neck, and began staggering towards the wreckage. The carnage that he saw made him wretch and vomit as the ghostly reflection of the scene reflected off of the glossy paint of the Buick as it drove by.

Chase leaned back in the leather office chair, tied a thick rubber band around his arm, slapped it to find a vein then injected himself. Quickly untying it, the potent drug entered his bloodstream as he relaxed. "VVVVHHHHHH!" Chase looked at the text message on his cellphone screen as the inbox from Manky's number read, "Customer dropd off whip, run diag blk scrape." He quickly called him back but it went straight to his voicemail.

"FFFFFFFUUUUCCCCKKK!" He threw his head back as he stared at the spinning ceiling above him. "Honk, honk, honk!!" Chase looked at the clock on the surveillance monitor which read 1:25 am, yet the Buick was out of view. Pushing himself up, he walked out front to see who it was. *Where is the driver*, he thought to himself.

He circled the black sedan, took a few steps back then quickly looked around him. No one. No footprints or anything. Chase tried to open the door. "Locked!" He tried once more and to his surprise, it opened. The car's dome 1ight stayed off but the dashboard lights emitted an angelic radiance. "Must have a blown fuse somewhere."

He reached under the steering wheel column, pulled out the fuse box and checked the connections under the moon lit night. "Perfect!" The dome light blinked to life. "What is this under my feet?" He looked at his boots and they were covered with motor oil. "I'll be a mothafucka. Now this car is fucking up my high."

Standing up, he braced himself on the driver's side floor board, looked, then pushed himself back up. He knocked the dust off of his hands and pulled small, jagged rocks from his palms. "I can't see shit!"

He sat in the passenger seat, turned the key and tried to start it. Nothing. He then got out, walked to the garage, pulled on the heavy chain to fully open it, then walked back. The gear was already in the neutral position as he reached for it. *That's strange*, he thought to himself as he began to push it into the shop. He closed the roll up garage and stood there. The overhead lights reflected a pool of oil underneath as he stepped around it and got a better look.

"No leak, but where is this oil coming from?"

He flashed a small pin light at the engine block then ran it down the torque shaft and stopped at the transmission casing. He shook his head, stood up, walked over to get a floor jack and guided it back to where he was. He positioned it under the car then started pumping the metal bar attached to it.

"Alright let's see what's going on," Chase said out loud as he laid on his back and scooted his body quickly underneath it. He checked the brake line but he needed both hands, so he put the pin light between his teeth.

The Buick instantly dropped on him as if the floor jack was kicked from under it. The back of the pin light forced its way through his esophagus and severed his spine from his skull which was crushed by the weight of the car. His legs shook in the pool of oil as it mixed with his blood.

Brick-B noticed the dried oil as he pulled his Pontiac Bonneville up to the shop. He got out and followed the trail of oil into the garage. He noticed Chase under a car which was lifted up on a floor jack. Its sound system pounded as the trunk rattled and vibrated from the music.

"Damn!"

He held his ears as he walked towards the car and got in. As soon as he reached for the volume, the music instantly cut off. Bricks looked at the screen and saw that there was a track still playing. He pushed eject but nothing came out. He leaned forward to get a closer look then he grabbed his throat to stop the intense bleeding.

Bricks pulled his hand away as blood sprayed across the glossy woodgrain. Shards of a CD were embedded in his jugular as he gasped for air. He rolled out of the leather seat and fell onto the paint shop's chalky, dirty floor. From the position he was in, he saw Chase's flattened skull which was lit like a translucent, pink jellyfish. The car's engine started, revved and throbbed the dual exhaust. Again and again.

Black smoke poured out as if it was releasing its wrath. The rear tires backed up then spun forward wildly as it rocked back and forth, teetering, finally dropping. It stopped then slowly followed Brick-B as he crawled away in his own blood.

"AHHHHHHH!" The car drove up his legs, snapping and crushing him. He fumbled with his cellphone then put it on speaker as the Buick slowly drove over him, pulverizing his rib cage and pushing his entrails through his closed mouth.

"Where are you going baby? It's like 3:30 in the morning."

D-Down ignored her as he got dressed then glanced at her caramel plump breast as she pulled the light purple silk sheets down to her waist.

"None of these niggas is answering their phones," he said out loud. "I got a call from Bricks' number and all I heard was a revving engine. I call back. Voicemail. I call Chase. Voicemail. Manky. Voicemail."

"Maybe they cupcaking," she suggested, pulling the sheets off of her, and began playing with her clit.

"Nawh the only thing those niggas is cupcaking with is a bitch named 'gutta' you feel me?" He gripped the black handle of his chrome .45 cocked it and stuffed it into his waistband.

After about ten minutes on the freeway. He pulled up next to Bricks' car, stepped out, then felt the cold morning air against his face. "Man these niggas is catting off," he said to himself as he walked towards the shop, reached for the side exit door, hesitated, grabbed the knob then pushed it open. He fumbled at his waistband as he saw a black sedan turn on its high beams and accelerate, running over what was left of Chase and Bricks' lifeless bodies.

It smeared their entrails into the floor as it tried to find traction. D-Down's .45 recoiled in his hand as hot shells and sparks bounced off his flesh. The slugs deflected off of the hood, ricoc,heting and lodged into the ceiling's insulation above. He dove outside, crab crawled to his trunk and quickly opened it. The car dented the garage door, knocking it off its tracks. The heavy chain rattled like a tambourine as it rammed it over and over. Strings of spit flew from D-Down's mouth as he pulled up the spare tire, grabbed the wooden stock of a black AK-47, attached a magazine and cocked it.

His ears rung as the shots kicked the barrel up to the top of the garage. He aimed lower as the Buick smashed through the twisted metal, and he began firing, sending up clouds of dirt and dust. It crushed him against the side of the BMW 7-451 as chunks of blood poured from between his lips. His eyes stared blankly into the night's sky, slowly rolling back to the whites. The assault rifle dropped from his fingertips as the Buick slowly backed up and began to drive away. Suddenly it stopped, set its brakes then spun its rear tires sending dirt and rocks over D-Down's body until it was fully covered, and then drove off.

Orange and yellow rays of the sun crested over the hills outlining I-80 as Detective Melville and Officer Godfrey drove through the gauntlet of flares, heavy traffic and C.H.P. officers working double shifts to direct it. A fire truck and two ambulances parked westbound on the freeway's dirt shoulder as they waited for officers to finish measuring skid marks.

"They sure don't make Cadillacs like they used to," he said pointing the cherry of his lit cigarette at the CRS coupe impaled by a large copper pipe through the windshield. A woman approached wearing a dark blue wind breaker with the word forensics in large yellow letters on the back. She side-stepped the broken glass on the freeway and approached them.

"Detectives."

"Officer Puentez."

She folded her arms and leaned back on her Nike running shoes. The passing traffic on the opposite side of the freeway blew her collar around her neck making her look mysterious like a woman Sherlock Holmes. "I put a rush on the toxicology and guess what? Aside from the victim's alcohol tolerance of his B.A.C. being three times over the legal limit, he's our waterfront shooter from that murder robbery case." She paused for a second before continuing. "Positive DNA match off the vic's passenger seat. It was a forensic intuition and it was a long shot, but lucky or not a hit is a hit."

A person was wheeled on a gurney wearing a neck brace. "Hold up." He flashed his badge at the E.M.T.

"Sir, all due respect. This man is heavily medicated and disorientated." The man squeezed the E.M.T.'s arm.

"I think he's trying to say something," he said pointing his badge at him, folding it and putting it in his breast pocket. He walked forward and put his ear close to his lips, shaking his head a few times as he listened intently. He stood back and motioned the E.M.T. to put him on the ambulance. Melville stood their baffled, scratching his head.

"What's the matter?" Officer Godfrey asked. He pulled him to the side. Out of ear shot. Away from all of the other C.H.P. officers.

"Black sedan, but get this. No driver." Godfrey laughed for a few seconds. "Didn't I just hear the emergency medical technician say that he was disorientated and heavily medicated?"

"Yeah, but we have to follow it up and investigate. There's cameras all over this freeway." He pointed at a cylinder-shaped camera attached to a huge sign.

CHAPTER FOURTEEN:

REVERSAL

TWILIGHT IS THE CRACK BETWEEN THE WORLDS.
IT IS THE DOOR TO THE UNKNOWN.

A woman looked nervously around her before approaching the cobblestone walkway leading to a two-story house. Her movements were hypervigilant as she took each step. Deltrice watched this unknown woman from behind her curtains. This woman stood in front of her door and waited as if deciding whether to knock or not.

Deltrice tightened her grip on her chrome .38 caliber revolver in her right hand and held on to the doorknob with the other.

There were two light knocks, then one loud kick. Deltrice snatched the door open and put the barrel next to the back of the woman's head as she sat at the door step crying. "Suam, is that you?" She turned around, took off her designer shades and gradually stood up. "It is you, come in." She lowered the weapon and gave her an affectionate hug, then held her away at arm's length to take a good look at her.

"Someone killed Marcellos and I think I'm next."

"Cellos? How?"

"They found him in-in that fucking car and he died from monoxide poisoning. I think someone did it to him."

"I thought you were…"

"What, dead!"

"Yeah. Well I'm glad you're alive."

"Oh, really? By the looks of that gun, you don't seem too happy to see me."

"I didn't know who you were and I still don't because Dorian is dead because of you, and now Marcellos," she said now holding the gun back at her.

"Get that shit out of my face girl before we start wrinkling this carpet."

The cylinder moved as she pulled the hammer back. She quickly stepped forward then slapped her with the pistol. A trickle of blood formed at the corner of her mouth.

"Bitch you better just shoot me because I don't give a fuck no more okay. You want to know why Trice, huh? You really want to know why? I've been kidnapped, put in a trunk, tied to a chair, forced to call Dorian at gunpoint, pistol whipped then I was shot in my hip," she said showing her the wound as she pulled her sweat pants down to the side. "Then they set my fucking car on fire with me in the trunk."

Deltrice lowered the weapon. "Who did this to you?"

"How in the fuck am I suppose to know? I never seen their faces. I just heard their voices Trice."

"How did they know where you worked?"

"The only person that really knew where I worked was Patricia and of course Marcellos!" Deltrice uncocked the .38, sat down and her body went limp as tears streamed down her cheeks. Suam squeezed her shoulder and hugged her from behind, pressing her breast against her back. "It's just us now Trice. You and me."

She cupped her face and kissed her on the lips affectionately. She kissed her back, dropping the gun on the floor, and she began to probe her tongue in and out of her peppermint tasting mouth. They both touched each other in ways they had never been touched before.

Suam pulled the waist belt to her quarter-length robe and gently guided her back on the couch, kissing her between her cleavage and working her way past her navel to her tight, wet, pink folds.

She brushed Suam's cheeks with the back of her hand as she watched her suck, probe and pull on her wet clitoris. "OOOOHHH girl suck my pussy," she said grabbing a hand full of her brunette hair. Deltrice snatched her sweats down.

"Hey girl, be careful. I am wounded."

She ignored her. "Pain before pleasure bitch." She reached from in between the couch's cushions, pulled out a twelve-inch rectangular case, opened it and pulled out a black dildo. Suam opened her small mouth as Deltrice wiped it across her wet, glossy lips then stuck it halfway in her throat, then pulled it out. "Turn around!" she demanded as she slapped her hard on her ass.

She ran her fingernail between her wet opening then separated her lips, inserting the rigid sex toy. She backed up to it every time she entered and exited. "You like that huh- huh?" Suam said nothing. She just bit her lip and tightly closed her eyes concentrating. "You need some help?"

Before Suam could respond, Deltrice spit a long string of saliva in between her parted, thick ass cheeks, messaged her anus then inserted her thumb. "OOOOOHHH!" She arched her back, flexed her body and shook uncontrollably.

"Yes girl get that nut girl get that." She collapsed on the floor and Deltrice gently laid next to her and embraced her.

Suam stepped out of the bathroom drying her hair, walked to Trice's bedroom and put her ear to her door. "Girl are you aight?" She heard no response except her constant heaving. "I'm coming in!" she announced. Deltrice flushed the toilet, gargled and walked out, managing to crease her lips and smile.

"What's wrong?"

"It might of been something I ate."

Suam puckered her small lips to the side as if to say yeah right. "Seriously. I'm a nurse bitch. I know the symptoms."

"I-I don't want to—"

"What, you can't accept that fact that your ass is pregnant? How many weeks has it been since you had your-"

"Six weeks, but my cycle always comes late."

Suam walked past her to the bathroom and started opening up cupboards and medicine cabinets. "Come here bitch." She slowly stepped back in and saw Suam holding a pregnancy test. "You know the routine. You pee on this and it changes colors," she said pointing at the box.

"Aight, aight," she said, snatching the box out of her hand.

"I'll give you your privacy."

A few minutes passed by. "You going to be a auntie gggirrrll!!" she said running out, and they both embraced each other for a few seconds.

"What's wrong Trice?" she asked, wiping the tears from her face.

"I got to get answers. So I can explain to this baby why its father is not in its life," she said rubbing her womb.

"Well we are not going to get no real answers from the police because they want answers from us and we have none."

"Yeah I know girl. But I'11 tell you this. We will get answers from that bitch Peaches after we pay her a visit."

"Come on. You think she's going to sit down over coffee and discuss how she set Dorian up?"

"Nawh, the bitch is going to have to speak into the mic," she said waving the chrome .38 at the mirror.

Clamente laid back in his jacuzzi as its built-in jets created a heated, relaxing oasis. He saw his Bluetooth earpiece blinking, so he picked it up, positioned it into his ear and hit the button. "Yeah!"

"Hey you!"

He recognized Deltrice's voice. "How is my little soldier girl doing?"

"I'm getting through it." She looked at Suam passedout asleep in the passenger seat.

"How is the Chryslor?"

"It drives very good but ahh, out of respect, you had to be the first person, to know and you're like the only family--"

"What is it?"

"I'm pregnant with Dorian's baby." There was silence for a moment except for the bubbling water.

"That's a good thing. I'm happy. It was a gift he left to us." A blonde female in a bikini came out of the water holding his shorts. "Hey I didn't say you could come up for air yet." She stroked his manhood, took a breath, then resubmerged as he put his hand on her head and gently guided her back under.

"Did I catch you at a bad time? Because it sounds like you got company."

"Look, don't worry about that. Just understand that trust is earned not given, and you've earned it. As a matter of fact, where you at?"

She took the phone from her ear to look at the freeway sign. "I'm passing West Grand Avenue on 880."

"You're in downtown Oakland. Where you headed?"

"The city."

"Well look, call me when you get back to the 'V,' aight. And one more thing."

"What is that?"

"Your crazy Haitian ass better be safe!"

She smiled. "And I love you too Uncle Hoist." The line went dead.

"We got to get some gas." Suam stretched, rubbed her eyes and yawned. "Who was that?" she asked smacking her lips.

"Our ear to the streets." Switching lanes, she got off on 29th avenue and pulled into a gas station. "You want anything?"

"Could you get me one of those energy drinks?"

"Sure love, just pump the gas since you need some motivation."

The glass doors beeped as she walked through the motion sensor. "Can I have forty on pump five please?"She walked past the newspaper stand to grab a few drinks. She stopped in her tracks in front of it and read the headlines to herself.

"Man killed in hit and run accident who was a suspect in alleged murder robbery. DNA evidence linked Maurice Alvin Yates, also known as 'Manky,' to the robbery murder of Dorian "Doe Getta" Jackson. An unknown black sedan with dealership plates rear-ended Mr. Yates' Cadillac CTS V-coupe on I-80 sending him fatally crashing into the back of a cargo truck. Witnesses at the scene stated that the driver of the car never stopped but freeway surveillance cameras managed to obtain a picture of the perpetrator's vehicle."

Deltrice looked closely at the grainy photo. "They can't be fucking serious. There isn't no driver." She threw a few dollars on the counter and walked out to the car. Suam flipped the lever on the gas pump then set the gas hose in it. "Get in, we got to make a stop before we hit the city."

"You coming?" Deltrice asked as she grabbed her purse. Suam scanned the block on International Blvd and 84th Avenue. A woman wearing a head wrap and carrying a plastic bag of groceries waited on the corner with her kid who was eating icys. On the opposite end, a group of hustlers shot dice as an old man in a wheelchair watched the game. He took sips from a crumpled brown paper bag and laid down side bets.

"Yeah girl, I think that would be a good idea but ahh, how do you even know this lady?"

"She migrated out here to the west coast, after the ousting of the Haitian prime minister," she explained while putting change in the parking meter.

"And she is-is--"

"Yes, a voo-doo doctor."

"A witch."

"Girl you can put whatever label you want on it. But I guarantee this, bitch. We will get some answers."

They both stepped into the African bookstore and inhaled the sweet smell of incense and coffee. A woman in a matching Kent Dashiki and head dress gracefully walked up to them, smiled, and lightly two-stepped in her leather sandals. "Are you two ladies looking for any particular books?"

Suam listened as they exchanged some words in creole, hugged and the woman locked the doors to the store front, and flipped around the sign. "Wait here!" Deltrice told Suam.

They both walked up some rickety wooden stairs, stepped into a spacious room filled with rows and rows of shelves containing glass jars of herbs.

"Have a seat," she said as she walked over to a table and snatched a cover off of a glass aquarium. A coiled Albino Boa constrictor laid motionless in the corner and watched with its black eyes, flipping its forked tongue. She leaned down, opened a cabinet and grabbed a large rat by its tail. It squirmed and gyrated in mid-air as if contesting its fate.

Sensing food, the snake whipped its fork tongue as if licking its lips. As she lifted the top and dropped it in the snake's coiled body, it tightened on its prey and devoured his remains in minutes. "Now what is your concern?"

"Well I-I just don't know where to begin--"

"Honey, just start from the beginning."

"Well I casted a spell and I believe something went wrong, because people are dying."

She lifted her eyebrow and blinked a few times while listening. "What objective was the spell?"

"Love."

"What personal item did you use from the other half?"

"It was a picture of him."

"Just of him?"

She paused for a moment, scrunching up her face in deep thought. "There was a car and money. Lots of money." She watched as the witch doctor smiled, steepled her wrinkly fingers, then grabbed a large hardcover book from behind her. *The Book of Shadows*, she thought to herself as her skin literally crawled off of her.

"When you spelled the vessels with all the four elements and let the light rise out of the darkness, you released a ancient demon of greed." She opened the book, flipped a few pages and turned the book around towards Deltrice. She studied the mythical drawing of a creature with red horns eating at a table with human bones as forks and knives. She turned the book back towards her.

"So what does this mean?"

"Well in the demonic realm there's specific assignments or orders given by high-ranking forces. Their mission is to contaminate the human race with wickedness and continue their warfare against good. Period. You opened a portal for this legion to travel through."

"Legion!"

"Yes Legion." Her heart raced as she forced herself to calmly breathe. "The demon of greed used your vessel as a host to spread evil and so conveniently you provided a idol, riches and a live sacrifice. It's not allowing its soul to cross over because it's intertwined with it like a parasite feeding off the soul's unforgiveness and fueling its revenge."

"How do I stop it?"

She stood up, walked over to the window and watched the heavy foot traffic. "Everything that can endure fire, you shall put through the fire and it shall be clean; and it shall be purified with the water." She turned around walked towards Deltrice, put her hand on her shoulder and looked directly into her eyes. "Money as we both know is a problem, but love…" She pointed at Deltrice's heart. "Love of money will drive a person into all types of evil!"

"So how are we going to do this?" Suam asked as she watched the city traffic pass by them. Customers walked in and out of the entrance of The Pink Palace strip club across the street.

Deltrice spun the cylinder of the chrome .38 and flicked it closed as if in deep thought. "Well we can't just smash in there and pull her out at gun point.

"Says who?"

"Girl we need a plan."

"Well aight ahh, I say wait until the bitch shift is over, follow her when she drives off, then pull up behind her where there is no cameras, and rear end her. You know, kind of like bump her."

"Bump her!"

"Yeah, bump her. And what happens when someone gets bumped?"

"They want to see what happened," they both said at the same time.

"When that high maintenance ass bitch steps out we show her how her goons did me--"

"And put her in her fucking trunk."

"Yuuuuppp." Suam watched as Deltrice fumbled through her purse and pulled out a taser. "Here, remote control her red bone ass with this."

She took it into her hands, flipped it over a few times then listened to the snapping and popping of the voltage. "Where did you get this shit from?"

"It was Dorian's. Yeah he gave it to me and told me to use it in case of emergencies."

"Well if she doesn't-"

"Doesn't my ass. When she--"

"I know, I know." "Aight then, we have a understanding."

"Of course."

"Well look the fact of the matter is that we need answers and this is the only logical way."

Suam zapped the taser again. "You got a point but point that gun in the other direction because ahh, I don't want to get shot prematurely in my other hip."

"If you're so concerned then you take it bitch." She hesitated, set the taser down then tried to grab it. "Bitch, not a chance. You'll fuck around and shoot me and I'm not trying to be no victim of no friendly fire."

They both took turns as one briefly napped as the other watched the entrance. "Wake up, wake up, there that bitch go!"

They both watched her step out and begin walking down Mission Blvd.

CHAPTER FIFTEEN:

PEACHES WITH CREAM

PLEASURE IS NOTHING ELSE BUT THE INTERMISSION OF PAIN.

Peaches patiently waited for the light to change before realizing that at 5 am there was little to no traffic on Mission Blvd. She walked across the street towards where her car was parked. Her Jimmy Choo high heels clicked across the asphalt as she rummaged in her purse for her keys.

The Buick's supercharged V-8 engine quietly started, put itself in drive, and pulled out of the darkness like a venomous Goliath Scorpion from its nest. It followed her. Studied her. It felt her rhythmic pulse raise as it stalked her, gradually approaching her like she was a delicate Monarch butterfly.

Mist came from Peaches' nostrils as she breathed the cold city air. Her keys fell from her fingertips, bounced across the ground and rested underneath her car. After bending down, reaching for them and standing up, she felt as if something was behind her, so she turned and looked. The Buick was inches away from her, blocking her entrance to her car.

"What the fuck!" She squinted, yet seeing no driver, no passenger. "Is this some type of joke?!" she yelled to no one in particular. "Well if it is then this shit isn't funny!"

The car lurched forward and pressed her torso onto her driver's side door. "Ahhhh, what the fuck are you—" She began stabbing and scratching the hood of the Buick as it pressed her even more. It quickly backed up, burning rubber, revving its engine as she fell forward onto her hands and knees.

Peaches began to weep. Blood dripped from her mouth like strings of peeled fabric. Salty tears ran down her swollen cheeks as the Buick pressed its brake and hit the gas, then gradually released the brake.

The tires spun wildly sending white smoke everywhere as the rear end of the Buick fishtailed closer and closer. She forced herself to stand but couldn't. It released the brake and Peaches rolled out of the way before it viciously slammed inher car, T-boning it.

She managed to pull herself up by grabbing onto a chain-link fence, desperately looking for some type of refuge. It backed up quickly and drove towards her.

"Ahh oh my God! You're fucking crazy!"She winced from the pain of her broken knee and twisted ankle. Kicking off her heels, she hobbled and the Buick slowly approached her. "Fuck you. Whatever you are."

She threw her purse and all of her contents spilled across the windshield and onto the ground. She hobbled faster, ignoring the pain, then to a brisk power walk trying to get away. It jumped the curb and accelerated with its high beams on.

A narrow opening between buildings gave her the safety she needed, but the pain of crushed bone sickened her. She held on to the nearest light pole gasping for air and wiping the blood from her mouth on her sleeve. Before she came to her senses, there was no feeling in her body. In her last split seconds of life, the Buick violently crushed her rib cage which tore into her organs like a powerful food processor as clumps of blood spilled out of her smeared lipstick. Her skull smashed from the weight of the car. Fragments of her brain smeared onto one of the headlights which cast a pinkish glow onto her lifeless body, as it slowly backed up and sped off.

Deltrice's throat burned as vomit spewed out her mouth. High traffic passed by as she held locs of her hair to keep it from being splashed. She leaned back in, grabbed a bottle water from the back seat, gargled and spit a stream into the dirt shoulder.

"You okay girl?"

"What do you think? I mean we just seen Peaches get killed!"

There was silence for a few minutes after Suam merged into traffic and switched lanes. "Who-who do you think it was?"

"There's no telling. I mean it almost seemed like that car had a mind of its own."

"Come on Trice, there was obviously someone driving it because she was yelling at them--"

"That bitch was completely delusional. She didn't know shit. She was just worried about breaking a heel."

Suam giggled. "So what did Ms. Cleo the fortune teller witch doctor say?"

"It-it's complicated, Suam, really."

Suam twisted her lips to the side and glanced at her. "Try me bitch, so I can make some type of sense of this shit, because right now it's not making none."

Deltrice exhaled and looked back at her. "I casted a Haitian love spell and..."

"And what!"

"Well I sort of released legions of demons, of greed."

"Sort of, bitch--"

"Ok, ok, I released. I released a demon and it intertwined with Dorian's--"

"Dorian's!"

She ignored her and continued. "Dorian's soul and it's not allowing him to cross over, and it's feeding its unforgiveness."

"Like it's seeking revenge."

She nodded her head. Suam took the palm of her hand and started feeling Deltrice's forehead and the side of her neck.

"Girl, what the hell are you doing?"

"Checking to see if you got a fever."

"Fever, bitch I'm not sick," she said slapping her hand away. "I'm serious!"

"Well then how do we destroy this...this greed demon thing?"

"Well from how she explained it, there is three ways to purify a unclean spirit. Fire, water and allowing it to fulfill its mission and it will depart."

"Okay I understand the first two, but how do we know that we're not its mission's itinerary?"

"Well if we were, then don't you think it would of tried to kill us already?"

"Well ahh Marcellos is dead and he's connected to me. I mean he is connected to us Trice. Us!"

"I know but you got to understand—"

"Look Trice, all I understand is that you're telling me that this thing is on the loose and it has killed and it will keep on killing until we stop it."

Rain drops began falling on the windshield.

Detective Melville walked around the two cars in front of the paint shop, wiped the dust off of the windshield then wrote the vin numbers and license plate numbers off of each one. He knelt down and brushed dirt and gravel away from D-Down's buried body.

He grabbed hia wallet, opened it and wrote the victim's name down. Stepping back, his eyes followed the trail of motor oil through the expended shell casings into the garage. Yellow triangular plaques marked each expended shell scattered around the crime scene. *It was literally a war going on out here as if the victim was taking his last stand or something*, he thought to himself.

He scribbled some more notes and took some digital pictures from different angles, saved them, created a file and e-mailed them to his office computer. "The garage door looked like someone threw a boulder through tin foil," he said to himself as he walked up to it and touched the serrated edges of steel. "These markings are similar to the markings at the tow yard."

As he stepped into the garage, he instantly noticed uniformed officers and technicians with their faces covered with surgical masks, discussing their theories, and they had secured the scene until homicide arrived. From a distance, it appeared to be brown rice sprinkled over both of the mutilated bodies. But as he got closer, he noticed the squirming maggots devouring the rotting flesh.

He studied the dried blood and tire tracks spread across the dirty, chalky floor of the paint shop. The tracks zig-zagged over the vics as if they were erasing a problem on a chalkboard. Most of the officers and technicians gave him a quizzical look as he conducted his investigation and examined the mutilated corpses. He inhaled the stench, licked his dry lips and cleared his throat.

"Come on people, this is the smell of work. Get used to it!"

They shook their heads and continued with their conversations. Melville pulled the broken pin light from the victim's throat and secured it in a plastic evidence bag. The other victim was face down as if trying to desperately crawl away. Something reflected from his palm, shaped like a small, quarter size triangle. He pulled back the waxy flesh with tweezers, grabbed the arrowhead-shaped object and held it close to him.

"A piece of a compact disc," he said to himself. "It seems to have been embedded in the vic's throat and he attempted to pull it out."

He looked at the long, 180-degree arch of blood splatters around the body. "*Whatcha gonna do, whatcha gonna do when they come for you. Bad boys.*" Melville stood up and answered his iPhone.

"Detective this is--"

"I know who it is. Private numbers always show up regardless if the caller chooses to or not--"

"Alrighty look, I got a dead stripper--"

"Yeah, well why didn't you call another detective Mr. Anderson? Besides, what is the jurisdiction?"

"San Francisco."

"That's my point."

"Does Patricia Mitchell get your neurons firing detective?"

"No!"

"She is directly related to a vic in a case you're working."

"Yeah, who?"

"Marcellos Mitchell."

"Yeah, yeah, I remember--"

"Well good Detective. Well ahh she was found ran over in front of a seedy strip club called The Pink Palace. My sources briefed me and we have reason to believe that the Guiteraz Cartel family was behind the hit in order to send a message to the other employees."

"What for exactly?"

"Well I'll answer that. For them to give up info on Alexio Guieteraz's disappearance."

"Look, I'll look into it--"

"Check your inbox so you can!"

CHAPTER SIXTEEN:

SCOPE

YOU CAN'T SAY CIVILIZATION DON'T ADVANCE; HOWEVER, FOR IN EVERY WAR THEY KILL YOU IN A NEW WAY.

A caltrans worker wearing a yellow hard hat and vest stood by a railroad crossing. He set orange cones and signs which read "Keep clear 20 feet." He looked into the sky above him and saw the dark clouds from miles away. He could smell the moisture of rain in the air.

"We11 gentlemen, this is the luxury of working out in the elements. It's quitting time!" the foreman said to his co-workers.

Rain drops pelted the dry asphalt and brought oil to the surface, which created a thick slick. Cargo trains and Amtrak carrying travelers shared the same tracks at one hour intervals.

"So which park was this?" Officer Rumsfield asked Officer Staggs.

"You see, you're not even listening to my damn story. I said Wilson Park."

"Oh okay."

"Yeah, well I knew one of them in the group had a weapon because as we pulled up he clutched at his waist and I observed some suspicious behavior. He then broke away from the group as if he was looking for a place to stash something."

"The deer in the headlights tactic huh."

"It works every time," they said in unison.

"So you hooked him and booked him?"

"No, not yet. I wanted to see what type ^{of} cat and mouse game this nigger was going to play, because I really wanted some paid time off leave."

"That's risky business--"

"Yeah but it's all part of the job--"

"Yeah well, tell that to Internal Affairs."

Their black and white police cruiser passed by Railroad Avenue as they traveled north on Sunset. The Buick waited as the cruiser passed them, activated its blinker, made a right turn and drove directly behind them.

"Why is this asshole riding our fucking bumper?" Officer Staggs said as he stopped in front of the railroad crossing.

A whistle blew in the distance as a train quickly approached. Yellow and red lights flashed back and forth as the railroad arms lowered on the side of the tracks. The police cruiser's windshield wipers whipped back and forth like a race horse's tail in a starting gate. Rumsfield hit the touch screen and began to run the car's plates but there was none present. At that moment high beams flooded the inside of their car with blinding light.

"Fuck, that does it," Rumsfield said activating his overhead lights for a routine traffic stop.

He grabbed his night stick and attempted to step out when all he heard was a revving engine, screeching tires and the sound of an approaching car. He jumped back in as they were rammed from behind, smashing their trunk and lurching their police car forward.

He hit the brakes but it was useless as the car easily slid across the oily asphalt. The automatic door locks malfunctioned, locking both officers in their crypt. The large spotlight of the train approached as their car continued to slide forward. Officer Staggs quickly pulled out his weapon and rolled down the window which stopped halfway. He contorted his body, switched hands and began firing his weapon. The slugs hit the Buick's windshield but bounced off.

"One of those bullets had to have hit him!" he yelled, dropping an empty clip on the floor board and replacing it with another one.

The sound of twisted metal was heard for miles as the train collided with the car, splitting it and its occupants in half. Ripping through each officer like a human meat grinder. The police car was totally engulfed in flames as the scene reflected off of the Buick's windshield. It slowly reversed, turned around and drove away.

Beating blades of a news helicopter bent the branches of trees and fluttered the yellow 'Do Not Cross Police Line' tape as it circled around the crime scene at a low altitude. Its spotlight lit up the railroad tracks like pillars of fire. Compartments of the train zig-zagged across the burned field. Uniformed officers searched the area and knocked on doors of nearby residents trying to find leads or potential witnesses.

"I just talked to Rumsfield. He located a vic's car for me. I-I just don't understand."

"Detective, let's face it, they had a lot of enemies in the streets and that officer involved shooting was the straw that broke the camel's back."

"I just can't accept that. I mean in this field of work there's a term we use--"

"What, collateral damage?"

"This is a prime example of collateral damage," he said waving his hand at the carnage and twisted metal.

They both stepped out and walked towards the railroad crossing. Melville stopped, knelt down and looked at the expended shells circled with chalk. He pulled out an ink pin and picked up the shells with the tip.

"Police issued," Godfrey said patting him on his shoulder.

He set it back within the circle marking then touched the moistened ground and caked oil with skid marks leading across the tracks.

"Either they were forced into the moving train, which explains the shells, or they fired shots out of anger because their brakes went out."

Godfrey gave him a look of yeah right. The helicopter arched around the scene as its spotlight probed through trees, road blocks and alleys. Ambulances, fire trucks and a command post decorated the charred field. Melville lit a Camel non-filter and inhaled. He then looked at the extinguished, charred brush fire that occurred after the explosion.

"How can you smoke in a time like this?" Detective Godfrey asked as he walked past him down the railroad tracks towards the train's engine compartment.

"I have a prescription from-"

"Yeah from who? Doctor fucking death!"

Melville smiled with his tobacco stained teeth. "You know what, the reality of it all is that death is inevitable and everybody has vices, and mine happens to be--"

"Nicotine, shittt if nicotine was a suspect that I could take into custody then Iwould have a magazine rolled up with its name on it," he said tapping his side arm.

"I appreciate the empathy. Really. But ahhh, let's conduct this investigation so we can catch the bastards that did this," he said as he exhaled a cloud of smoke, then followed him.

"How could the train derail from an impact of a vehicle?" Godfrey questioned as he walked up to the disabled train engine.

"Were there any civilian casualties?" Melville asked Officer Puentez as she took pictures and made detailed notes of her observation.

"Minor injuries. Nothing life threatening. The engineer is pretty banged up but he is coherent."

He stooped under the yellow tape and viewed the destruction first-hand. The police cruiser was burned to the frame and its wiring harness and plastic melted over it. A smoldering shoe of one of the officers laid next to the tracks.

"Where are the remains?" Officer Puentez pointed at two body bags behind them and they quickly turned around and unzipped the bags. "Once you have seen one burned body"—he zipped both bags up—"you seen them all." Melville put out his cigarette, unwrapped a stick of gum and began chewing it. "Want one?"

"No thanks. Ahhh when did you all of sudden start chewing gum?"

"When I decided to stop smoking humps."

"All of a sudden."

"After seeing this," he said pointing at the body bag. "It's time to stop."

Godfrey shook his head as Melville noticed a man and woman dressed in black business suits and white button-down shirts.

215

"Detective." They both flashed their badges and he ignored their names and stared at them in disgust.

He leaned over to his partner and whispered, "They're like Jehovah's witnesses with fucking badges." Melville smiled. "The feds, what an unfortunate surprise. What can I do you for?" he said looking at the woman's shapely hips in her black dress slacks.

"I'm right here Detective!" she said pointing at her eyes. "Look, as much as you, your partner and your whole department don't want to hear this, the Federal Bureau of Investigation has jurisdiction over this now," she said giving an arched Nazi wave salute across the crime scene. "Detective. Two officers have been killed--"

"Obviously inspector--"

"Well their hasn't been an arrest. I mean we may have a possible vehicular serial killer on the loose."

"Inspector, on behalf of the department, I'm the senior homicide detective on this case. I'm leading this investigation and I'm fully competent as a thirty-year veteran to do so. I'm sure the chief of police will contest any of your guys' involvement in this investigation."

"Sir, your superiors are the ones who approved it."

Dressed like a janitor, Clemente wheeled a plastic trashcan through a hallway of an abandoned building. He looked out the store front window towards an auditorium with a parking lot full of cars, then grabbed a small suitcase out of the trashcan and quickly ran up five flights of stairs to the roof of the building. He slowly walked over to the edge and peered over.

"Perfect, nothing is obstructing my view." He knelt down, set the case on the gravel and opened it. The black carbine sniper rifle was sectioned in pieces and he stealthily assembled them and then glanced at his watch. He rotated the silencer on the tip, pulled the bolt action back, locked and loaded. He took the scope out, snapped it in place and began adjusting it. The barrel rested over the building's edge and he waited. The night sky gave him plenty of cover and the wind stood still as if he was in the eye of a storm.

Blinking a few times, he scanned the parking lot with the crosshairs and measured his kill zone around an emergency exit. A car alarm went off as he watched as one of the valet attendants leave to go investigate. He came back, grabbed some keys, disappeared for a moment then pointed at the entrance as he began to walk towards it.

"Where is this fool going?" he said to himself. He figured it out immediately after he noticed his target step out an emergency exit on the opposite side of the building. He swung his barrel at the valet booth, aimed at his head and fired a silent round. A wet red dot appeared on his forehead, his scalp flapped up in the back of his skull and he fell limply onto the valet booth's floor.

"Thank you, thank you everyone." John Anderson waited for the applauding crowd to stop before he continued. He adjusted his tie and cleared his throat. "Ladies and gentlemen, thank you for your generous contributions and endorsements in order to make this campaign a reality. You see, I believe success is measured in how much effort is put forth, but being elected for mayor is not for status, or power, or even having the exclusive membership to the finest country clubs so I can test my best titanium golf clubs," he said, making a swinging motion, stepping back to the podium.

He readjusted the microphone and looked at the crowd. "There is a saying by career criminals and that is 'don't get caught doing crimes during election year' because if you do, the judicial system will make an example out of you." A roar of laughter came across the large crowd.

"Even criminals know the mechanics of politics. Fighting crime is like an art. A craft. It's like a captain studying the wind. Its currents and weather. But the question is, how can you study something that is unpredictable? The answer is that everything from a mathematical approach has a pattern. Now in physics, there is a cause for every effect. When you eliminate the cause then an affect doesn't exist. I specialize in the craft of eliminating the cause."

The crowd stood up and applauded as District Attorney John Anderson walked off the stage, waved and moments later appeared at his table with his wife who was dressed in an ocean blue evening dress. She smiled, squeezed his arm and took a sip of her wine. "Wonderful speech darling."

"Let's just hope that they all feel satisfied after paying ten grand a plate."

"Mr. Anderson, sir, your car alarm is going off and valet is unable to deactivate it."

His wife attempted to get up but he stopped her. "Don't even think about it honey. I'll take care of it." He straightened his tie, stood up, unbuttoned his suit coat and walked out the nearest exit. "Where in the hell is valet?"He heard the alarm blaring louder as he began walking towards it through rows and rows of luxury cars. Pointing his spare key, he pressed it and the alarm deactivated instantaneously. "Valet is definitely not getting a tip from me for this shit."

He spun around, began walking back and across a black Buick sedan with its hood completely open. He suspiciously looked around and he continued to walk away until the engine turned over. It stopped then tried to start again.

"Hey buddy, do you need a jump or something?" he suggested as he walked towards the front of the car and peered over. Clemente lined up his shot, squeezed the trigger and at the same he saw the car's hood close on top of his target.

"What the fuck!"

He lifted up the barrel, leveled it and then peered through the scope again. The Buick started its engine and revved it, as he tried to pry himself loose. His neck tie flapped around and caught on to the fan belt, pulling his face directly into the spinning blades. It sliced his face and neck like freshly minced meat. The engine was sprinkled with blood as he shook and stopped struggling. It pulled out of the parking place half dragging his lifeless body underneath.

The hood slowly lifted up, drove forward and quickly hit its brakes sending Anderson's body falling to the asphalt and running over his legs as it peeled off.

Mist covered the top of the Central American tropical jungle as El Gatillo's army was in a tactical wedge formation and quickly marching through it. A bright orange and black lizard drunk the moisture off a large leaf as El Gatillo adjusted his R.P.G. strap from around his shoulder. He felt his cellphone vibrating in his army uniform's breast pocket and he instantly thrust up his fist. His left and right flanks threw up their fist and everyone quietly took a knee.

"Hello." He slapped a mosquito off of his neck and wiped sweat from his eyebrow.

"Now you've got creative Gatillo."

"Ahhhh my amigo 'Hoist' what a pleasant surprise but I'm sort of in the middle of a war and-"

"A assassin driver, that's very creative!"

He chuckled for a few seconds and glanced at the mud between his boots. "Ah I see. Well ahh, one of my sources told me about District Attorney Anderson, which got the information from one of his constituents and ahh, one of my loyal soldiers briefed me about a candlelight vigil for a whore being killed at the rat's nest."

"So you do have eyes out here huh?"

He laughed for a moment. "Hoist I have eyes everywhere. But look, I don't have interest in Americana propaganda and menial issues of so-called assassin drivers. Come on. That is not my— How do you Americans say, 'my motus operado, my friend."

"So who do you think is behind this?"

He adjusted his sleek rocket propelled grenade launcher. "The whore may have pissed off one of her tricks and Anderson simply should of tipped his valet driver."

Hoist shook his head and actually believed him.

A federal agent special operations team member kicked open an exit leading to the abandoned building's roof. He swung his modified

AR-15 bushmaster assault rifle around the corner as his team ran around him pointing their weapons.

"Clear!" the mechanical voice said over the hand-held two-way radio in the agent's hand.

He looked at the top of the building with camouflage field binoculars. "Come to the northeast side of the building alpha-1 over."

He watched the squad leader appear at the edge and wave his antenna in the air. "Affirmative alpha-2, I have a visual. Hold position alpha-2."

He turned around and walked towards the valet booth where a body laid motionless. He instantly noticed that there was no exit wound. The bullet actually imploded in this man's skull. "Hmmmm now the only rounds that can administer this type of damage is mercury-filled hard jackets. If the round doesn't fill you, the poison from the mercury will," he said to himself.

He spoke into the two-way radio, "Alpha-2 fall back from position."

"Roger that alpha-1."

Melville shook his head, folded his arms and watched the federal agents conduct their investigation. "This is bullshit," he said to himself.

The agent stood over Anderson's body for a moment then leaned closer, rubbing his chin, obviously in deep thought. He turned and glanced at Detective Melville leaning against his white Ford Crown Victorian. He stood up and walked towards him. "Detective."

"Inspector."

He looked into his eyes and studied the deep creases in his face. "Look Detective, I'm just a rung on a fancy retractable ladder and honestly"—he cleared his throat—"we started on the wrong foot here and we are both pursuing the same thing here. Closure and finding this sociopathic killer who enjoys using his car as a murder weapon. But ahh, we have a dead valet driver with a gunshot wound to the head with no exit and my crime scene intuition tells me that we're dealing with two perps, focused on one target. The first perp is a professional. He's clean. No shells, no gunshot residue, no witnesses."

He pointed at the valet booth and they both looked in that direction. "Our ballistics expert found the bullet hole five yards away and forty-five degrees from that direction, indicating that our shooter was there on the northeast side of that building. During my time in the Marine Corp and also doing a shit load of recon missions, I learned that trained snipers don't miss, and at 250 yards away that's like stepping on an ant hill in mid-summer."

Melville unfolded his arms and dropped them to the side. "And!"

"Well this other perp is impatient, full of rage and wants to make a point. He or possibly she. I mean we can't rule out a woman here now but this person knows cars. I mean this person knows the intricate parts of them to the point where he can manipulate electrical devices as if functioning artificially. We have a department in the Bureau that investigates unexplained phenomenon such as this--"

"Wait, wait, wait, are you trying to tell me what I think you're telling me, because I mean we have a person whose major artery is severed. His neck is broken along with both his legs and he has so many lacerations all over his face that he resembles a blossomed sunflower, and you're indirectly telling me that we're dealing with some type of artificial intelligence.

I mean we're talking about a car here. Not a non-fiction character from a Steven King movie. Look, the media is going to be nipping at our department's heels for a solid explanation here and frankly what you're telling me is not acceptable. Come on inspector, you even said it yourself. Closure. Now you think the DA's wife is going to accept--

"Alright Detective enough with the oratory. I get it. I get it." He looked over his shoulder at the victim's wife in an expensive, emerald ocean blue evening dress, crying while being being consoled by someone. He rubbed his temples. "So what do you suggest Detective?"

"Wait, wait, you're asking for my opinion? My help--"

"Yes Detective, I'm asking for your professional opinion since you have extensive knowledge on this case. It's completely ideal that your professional opinion is seriously considered."

"My professional opinion is seriously considered,"he sarcastically mocked him. "You fed guys have all of these resources and then shit on these smaller agencies who are this close. This fucking close"— he made a pinching gesture with his thumb and index finger—"to solving a case."

He paused for a few seconds. "Look inspector, first off we need to get the community involved if we want to catch this killer. Saturate the northern Bay Area and east bay with 8x12 flyers of the alleged perp's vehicle and offer a handsome reward for any information leading to an arrest and conviction. The second thing is that the perp's vehicle has dealership plates. A Buick I believe. I'm sure a dealership can identify what make and model this car is from the grainy footage the freeway cameras captured in a case I was working.

Now after the identity of the car is confirmed of the car is confirmed, then we need a list of owners who the dealership sold that particular car to--"

"I can do even better. After we obtain these owners then we will access their GPS records for the past six months to determine if they were in that proximity when these crimes occurred."

"Excellent," Melville responded as he snapped his fingers from an adrenaline rush.

Steve Fowler sat behind his desk at the Vallejo Buick Dealership reading the cover story of District Attorney Anderson being murdered. He bent the corner of the newspaper and glanced at the surveillance monitor as two black, government issued, luxury Lincoln Continentals drove up. A man in his early forties stepped out, buttoned his suit coat and straightened his black tie. A woman in a dark suit and white silk blouse took off her shades after getting out of the car, and approached him. He zoomed in and adjusted the camera angle to make out their conversation. One of them pointed to the sales floor.

"What the fuck are the feds doing here?" he said to himself as he met the agent in the hallway.

"Mr. Steve Fowler?"

"Yes."

The agent flipped open his badge. "Special Agent Duncan. I'm conducting an intense investigation--"

"Step into my office." They walked in as he closed the heavy door behind them. "Have a seat."

"I'd rather stand sir."

"Suit yourself--"

He glanced at the newspaper's heading and began pacing the floor in the spacious office, then stood at parade rest. "Our agency contacted your chief execs in Detroit, Michigan and they sent out a memo to all of the certified dealerships on the west coast to release all records in regards to all owners of this particular sedan." He reached in his inside pocket, took out a 4x6 black and white photo and tossed it on his desk.

Steve spun it around and looked at the grainy picture, leaned back and steepled his fingers. "That's funny inspector. Our company has a policy for releasing clients' personal information. Now it's not that I'm being uncooperative but ahh, I haven't received no memorandum or no court order."

He threw his badge on his desk. "That's my order and I need to find out what's the make and model of this car," he demanded, tapping the glossy photo. "And I need a compiled list of clients you have sold or leased this particular car to. If not, you can then add obstruction of a federal investigation on your resume when you're looking for another regional management position."

Steve took off his reading glasses and clearedhis throat. "Well in that case I guess I don't have no choice!"

The agent sat down, put both his hands on the arm rest and planted a small listening device under it. "Everyone has choices Mr. Fowler and some results reap better results than others. But let's start with that photo."

"Newest Buick La Crosse, fully loaded '06!"

"How can you tell?"

"How can I tell? I'm a car salesman for Christ sake." He spun around in his chair in front of his computer, typed a few keys then a moment later a color printer clicked and buzzed next to him. "Grab that for me will yah."

The agent snatched it up and quickly inspected it. "Buicks must be a hot seller."

"Yeah well, the bailout did GMC alright I guess."

Bail out my ass. It was a political campaign maneuver, he thought. "Does your business have service drivers who deliver customer vehicles?"

"Well yeah, of course--"

"I need a delivery log for the past six months Mr. Fowler."

"Well I think-"

"Sir please, just execute please." A few moments passed and he reviewed the list and compared the dates. "I think that will be all for now but my agency will be in touch and I mean in touch." He stood up thrusted his hand out and they both shook hands. "Ohby the way if you have any questions, here goes my card since I'm in the field."

"Actually, I do have a question. There was some mention of a sixty thousand dollar reward leading up to the arrest and conviction of the district attorney's killer."

"Yes, ahhh that's correct."

He rubbed his chin in deep thought as he watched the agent step out of his office. Steve quickly came back to his office, looked around and flipped over the chair the agent was sitting in. Then he peeled the bug from under the arm rest, dropped it in his ashtray on his desk then lit it. He set back down, set his feet on his desk and placed a call.

Clemente took the exit off of 880 to the Oakland inner harbor. Cranes outlined the docks like colorful praying mantises waiting for a ship carrying precious cargo. He noticed an incoming call and touched the button on the side of his Bluetooth earpiece.

"Yeah this is Hoist." After recognizing the voice he flexed his forearms on his steering wheel then relaxed.

"Mr.Barboza I got to give you a heads up on something."

"Oh yeah, what might that be?"

"I got a visit from the alphabet boys--"

"Who, the federals?"

"Yeah."

"Well what was the purpose?"

"They wanted the business records of all of my previous and current owners of Buicks, their service records and delivery locations. They must be reaching their long arm of the law to catch this killer because ahh, they're not cutting the red tape—"

"They're ducking under the red tape."

"Exactly! Even to the point of planting a listening device in my fucking office." He looked at the burned up ashtray then leaned back.

"Well ahhh Mr. Fowler, I appreciate your courteous token of pulling my coattail about all of this. But ahh, I shouldn't be expecting no visit from the feds, because I'm not on their radar."

"No but your nephew Dorian is and his girlfriend."

"Deltrice."

"Yeah, that's her name but ahh once they connect the dots they're going to be-"

"Knocking on my door," they both said at the same time.

"Well from my experience dealing with these people, when the feds got you, they got you, and they're not going to get you right away. Nawh they're going to allow their evidence to stack up first. All I can do is be prepared when they eventually come knocking and have my script on point, so fleeing or remaining silent is a admittance of guilt in their eyes. So I'm just going to continue on with my daily activities and make myself readily available."

"You're a smart man Mr. Barboza."

"Steve, I didn't live this long for making a poor decision twice."

"My agents and I combed through this list with a fine tooth comb detective," he said handing the paperwork over to Detective Melville.

"Whats your conclusion?"

"Our logistics department crunched the numbers and ah, we were able to access each and every GPS record. We also compared it to where all of the murders occurred, except this car owner in particular."

Melville looked at the highlighted name and pronounced it to himself. "The service record shows that the car was refurbished and delivered to a Ms. Glaude but this refurbishment doesn't account for any loss of sensitive data. I mean, it's tucked away safe somewhere on an encrypted server's hardrive controlled solely by OnStar systems, which has a contract with GMC."

Melville picked up a nearby landline phone in his office and handed it to him. "Call and get it."

An I.T. specialist sat in front of a high resolution flat screen monitor, reviewing the source of the breach but there was no trail. The file that was accessed by the intruder was now inaccessible and the only way to access it was to reformat the entire system. He hit a few keys and took a screenshot of his findings then picked up the business card which was given to him by Agent Duncan. He typed in the e-mail address, attached the file and sent it.

A few seconds passed and a return message stated that the Department of Justice of Federal Bureau of Investigation received e-mail with attached document, size of one gigabyte. "You got an incoming call on line one," the voice informed the employee through the intercom.

"Yes this is the I.T. department. How may I help you?"

"This is Agent Duncan with the F.B.I.I received the file and opened it and ah, try to explain to me what I'm seeing here."

"I'm going to put it to you like this. Whoever hacked our system was very clever because for one, there are no tracks to the source, and for two, the file which was viewed is inaccessible unless we format our system and that is like disabling 911."

"Speaking of disable. Can you disable the car and track its position so our team can secure it?"

He pulled up a three-dimensional map of California, hit a few keys and it displayed a small blinking red sphere. He punched in a few keys and the system required his access code for authorization. He quickly punched it in and clicked enter and instantly the blinking stopped. "Done!"

"What's its location?"

"Check your e-mail."

On 73rd Avenue and San Leandro Street in the city of Oakland, an employee working the cash register at a U-Pull-It tow yard threw his hands up in surrender as he stared down the barrel of a U.S. Marshall's assault rifle.

"Don't you fucking move pal!"

He looked over the agent's shoulder as a team of them spread out and covered each other as they moved forward. Agent Duncan slung his weapon over his shoulder, pulled out a touch pad, touched the screen then zoomed in on the signal. He walked into the junkyard, stared at the rows of dismantled vehicles, then back at the screen.

As he watched, the signal got stronger so he grabbed his side arm, crouched down and gave a signal to one of his team members. He leaned his back against a car and told the team to circle around. He took one last look at his touch pad, drew his weapon and came from behind his cover, then reholstered it. "Clear!"

Everyone lowered their assault weapons and stepped forward as Agent Duncan picked up a dash riddled with bullet holes.

"Agent Duncan, we have a serious dilemma here!" his supervisor announced as he tapped an ink pen on his desk. He dropped it, interlocked his fingers and leaned back in his leather chair. "This investigation has expanded to eight months and those tight wads who cut our checks in D.C. are squirming in their seats like they're prairie-dogging. The variable in this equation is simple. A car. Now our exponent is nine, meaning nine bodies and my law enforcement intuition tells me they're all connected."

He slammed his fist on the dark stained oakwood table then thrusted himself out of his chair. "But we don't have no suspect in custody to interrogate in order to confirm this theory."

He walked around his desk, looked down at the bullet riddled dashboard and kicked it clear across his office like an NFL punter. "You listen here Agent Duncan, I expect an arrest of a potential suspect soon or else you'll have a fucking desk job in Juneau, Alaska doing logistics on endangered penguins."

He fidgeted at the thought. "Yes sir." He turned and stared at the city skyline through his office window.

"Oh yeah one more thing, remove that fucking dashboard from my office. It doesn't match my carpet and by the way, our latent print technician will handle it. In the meantime you get back in the field and produce."

CHAPTER SEVENTEEN:

TAKE A DIP

WHEN WE BUILD,
LET US THINK THAT WE BUILD,
FOREVER.

The San Francisco skyline lit up like an engineer's soundboard in a recording studio against the darkness. Winding steel girders outlined the Pacific Coast Highway that was cut into the cliff's walls of rocks. Judge Collins drove his red 1965 Mustang as it climbed the incline with ease. He tapped his finger and hummed to his favorite oldies station.

Steel belting on his left front tire suddenly frayed and blew open as he drove around a turn. He muscled the steering wheel to keep it steady as it skidded, fishtailed and slammed into a steel girder. He continued driving and stayed in his lane until he was able to find a safe place to park. His headlights flashed upon a small open lot of dirt as he pulled up to the cliff's edge, set the brake and quickly stepped out. He unbuttoned his Polo shirt and wiped his sweat as he walked around the car.

"Damn it, not my baby. For the love of god!"

"I think my water broke," Deltrice said holding her bulging stomach.

Suam's lips moved like a fish that flipped out of an aquarium and landed in a cat's food bowl. "Girl you're three weeks late."

She snatched her arm. "Bitch if you don't get my travel bag and help me to the car, ooooohhhh so help me!" She gave her an evil look.

"Ok, ok, satan!"

A four-inch gash peeled back the left side of his car, knocking off the door handle and side mirror, denting the fender and quarter panel. The tire was shredded to pieces, so he grabbed a spare tire and bumper jack out of the trunk. He positioned the jack under the car and began to loosen up the lug nuts before attempting to lift the car.

Let me call my wife and let her know of my accident, he thought to himself. He walked back around and reached for his briefcase. Suddenly headlights from a car came on lighting up the inside of his '65 Mustang. His leather bucket seats shined like glossy fists as if they were attempting to strangle him. He quickly opened the briefcase, then closed it after realizing that he had left his cellphone at his office.

"What good is that going to do?" he said under his breath as he stepped out. He covered his eyes and squinted.

Suam pulled up in front of Kaiser Permanente Hospital.

"Ma'am, ma'am, you can't park here--"

"This woman is going into labor!"

The woman in OR scrubs sprinted into the building and came back with a wheelchair.

"Thank you, thank you." Suam looked at her nametag. "Doctor?"

"Yeah, I guess that's what the nametag says." She smiled, then helped her as she waddled towards the wheelchair and slowly sat in it. "Look, you have to tell me how far apart the contractions are okay? Here, take my watch." She took off her watch and handed it to Suam. "Now do you know where delivery is?"

"Yes, yes I do."

"Well I'11 meet you two there and let the doctor know who's on right now to be expecting aaaaaa..."

"Oh, Ms. Glaude. Deltrice Glaude."

"Okay." She smiled warmly and took off in a full sprint.

"Hey ahhh, I may need some help buddy. I seem to have a blown tire." He felt something wet drip down the side of his face. He touched it, looked at it and realized that it was blood. "I also may have suffered a head injury."

He heard a car door open and close, so he staggered forward into the blinding pulsing light. The sedan's rear tires spun wildly as the rear end squatted and dug into the loose dirt. The car bared down on him like a panther on a wild boar. He held his breath as if his brain gave his body commands but it didn't respond fast enough. At the last millisecond he dove out of the way. The car clipped his heel with its spinning front tires.

A nurse dressed in a cotton jumpsuit, surgical mask and a cotton hair net stepped forward as they came in. "I'll take it from here— Suam? Giiiirrrrlll is that you?" She shook her head. "Girl we need to talk because we thought you were... You know."

"I know. It's a long story but we will talk. In the meantime let's take care of my girl!"

Judge Collins' '65 Mustang shook from the impact with extreme force as glass rained down on him cutting his face. He blinked a few times to make sure this was really actually happening.

The Buick backed up and peeled out towards him. He rolled out of the car's way, crawled under his Mustang to the passenger side and pulled himself up by the door handle. He wrestled with the handle to get the jammed door open, as he was rammed again and pushed closer to the cliff's edge. With a hard yank, the door squeaked open. He quickly crawled over the seats and reached for the keys.

The sedan backed up then rammed the left rear quarter panel, spinning the car half off the cliff.

A receptionist handed Suam a medical wristband which she took and secured around Deltrice's wrist. Pain overtook her as she clutched her fist and grinded her teeth. Suam looked at her watch and made a mental note to give it back to that doctor. They walked through some double doors and quickly entered the delivery room with a medical team waiting. They instantaneously went back to work changing her into a hospital gown, attaching, poking, prodding and they placed her legs in stirrups. Suam came in the delivery room also dressed like the rest of the medical team.

"Good lord people. Is she being prepped for surgery or is she going to deliver a baby?"

"Ms. Lee, I'm glad you could join us." She walked to Deltrice's side, grabbed her hand in attempt to comfort her and she instantly squeezed it with inhumane strength.

"Ahhhh my hand. Did you guys give her an epidural?"

The doctor moved in front of her, flipped up her gown and slightly opened up her thighs. "You're dilating at twelve centimeters, now push!"

She grinded her teeth and gripped the other side of her hospital bed to do just that.Puhh!" Pain ripped through her body like a strong jolt of electricity as she pushed again and again and again.

He started the engine and hit the gas trying to get traction. After realizing that his efforts were futile, he opened the driver's side door and took a hard swallow as he looked at the 400-foot drop towards jagged rocks and crashing black waves beneath him.

The car jerked back and he looked up into the darkness mixed with dust. He listed to the revving of the sedan's engine as if it was a fisherman waiting with a harpoon for a whale to surface.

I have no choice, he thought to himself. "FEAR IS THE ENEMY OF WILL!" he yelled out to no one in particular, as he climbed up his Mustang that was suspended in air. He gripped the inside of the wheel well and pulled himself up then stood on the bumper. It was twisted around the steel girder bent from the weight.

The Buick pinned him to the steel girder, crushing his shins and knees. He fell forward after it backed up again, then slowly drove inches away from him as he threw his hands up in defense. Its radiator fan blew hot air on his face as he smelled its antifreeze and fluids. The heat from the high beams singed his hair and burned his eyes.

"My eyes, my eyes!"

The sedan backed up, revved its powerful engine. The shifter moved to drive and it fishtailed, swerving wildly at Judge Collins, knocking him over the cliff's edge and sending his burning car close behind him. Flames licked the cliff walls from the explosion as the Buick was parked at the top of the cliff. It backed up and drove off.

The sound of a screaming baby boy filled the delivery room as Clamenta walked in with balloons that read "It's a Boy," red roses, and See's candies.

"Sir--"

"No, no it's okay. He's family!" Deltrice said holding the baby and waving him over. They all looked at the newborn baby and were mesmerized by the resemblance to Dorian.

"You're live in five-four-three-two-one," the camera man announced as he pointed to the news anchor.

"We have breaking news ladies and gentlemen. A Vallejo Superior Court Judge by the name of Robert Collins'"—the engineer working the boards punched in a digital high resolution picture of the Judge—"red 1965 Mustang was found at the bottom of a cliff, off the historic, scenic Pacific Coast Highway. He apparently was on his way to his beachfront estates in Half Moon Bay when a blown tire may have caused his car to veer off the highway, wreck into a steel girder and plunge to his death in the Pacific Ocean."

He touched his earpiece and bowed his head at if in prayer. "We have our news helicopter on the scene right now."

The producer linked the signal with a slight delay, monitored the feedback and increased the volume. "I'm circling the scene. As you can see this has gone from a rescue mission to a recovery mission."

The camera panned left and right then gradually moved back showing a panoramic view of scorched cliff, twisted, charred red metal and tire tracks leading directly over the cliff. "As you can see, forensic technicians are in climbing gear and harnesses and are rappelling on ropes to get to the wreckage before the high tide destroys the evidence before they can recover it."

The camera refocused on the top of the cliff and showed the news van parked a distance from the scene. "We have our reporter on the scene right now."

"Thank you ahh, I'm at the scene and behind this yellow tape and past that stee1 girder is a 400-foot drop onto jagged, solid rock and bone-crushing waves. Its undertow can pull you miles out into the Pacific Ocean. Mr. Collins has been a superior court judge for the last two decades overseeing court dockets ranging from minor infractions to capital murder cases. I see detectives inspecting the scene at this point and ah, let me see if I can get a statement."

The cameraman hustled behind the reporter as he got a detective's attention. Melville straightened his tie and ran his fingers through his straight salt and pepper hair. "Sir, Detective."

"Melville. My name is Detective Melville."

"Alright Detective Melville, from what you have discovered, do you think there may be any type of foul play in this?"

"Well that is too early to tell right now because we have to finish conducting our investigation. What I can tell you is that these steel girders are designed to withstand a head on collision."

"Are you implying that this could be the cause of an engineering defect?"

"I'm not implying anything sir. I'm simply assessing the damage and drawing several conclusions. There's actually three crime scenes if you want to get specific. We have the skid marks on the road. Then we have the evidence of paint as if the driver side-swiped the steel girder then got out. There is a tire iron and car jack covered in dirt and last, we have the car, which you already reported."

"Alright Detective, thank you."

Adjusting the overhead light, the Chief Medical Examiner unzipped the body bag and immediately pulled down her plastic protective visor. She grabbed her digital recorder.

"CSE#A1878 Robert Joseph Collins. Let the record reflect. Victim's extremities appear to have excessive abscesses or inflamed, pus-filled swelling." She squeezed one and lime green, milky liquid excreted from it.

"Take a sample of that!" she barked at her assistant. The entire body was charred badly, to the point that muscles and tissue were exposed in various patches. "Left heel tendon damaged." She lifted up the corpse's hands and noticed red paint under its nails.

"Victim appears to have a red substance under his nail. Possible sign of struggle."

She looked at the assistant and she was already taking samples. She nodded and smiled before continuing with her external examination. She set down the digital voice recorder and looked closer at the body's pupils.

"Wait a minute, this can't be accurate!"

The assistant looked confused as she watched her quickly walk to a drawer, grab an optic hand-held light and adjust it. "What-what is it doctor--"

"SSSSHHHH." She grabbed a scalpel, inserted it around the exposed, bloody eye socket, sliced the tissue and carefully pulled out the egg shaped eye. Veins and optic nerves hung like a stolen car stereo. "Victim's cornea are completely destroyed from excessive heat."

She spun the bloodshot eye around on the scalpel and noticed the thick, white membrane covering the pupil. "Take this, I got to make a call to our forensics department and the lead homicide detective who's handling this case.

"Listen Detective, either Judge Collins was legally blind before he was allegedly murdered or someone intentionally blinded him with something with the heating capacity of an industrial spotlight. This injury is not consistent with blunt trauma, whiplash, lesions to organs or even lacerations. Yes there are small compression marks to the frontal lobe but-"

"Ms. Puentez I dont mean to interrupt but"-he looked at the skid marks leading form the curve on Pacific Coast Highway and followed it through the soft dirt and over the cliff-"we have to rule out our rationality right now. I mean we have to step out of our common fundamental reasoning and logical basis on this one and say anything is possible at this point."

"OOOOOOOOOOOOOKKKKKKAAAAAYYYYY!" she responded superciliously.

"Look Ms. Puentez-"

"Call me Anna."

"Alright Anna ahh…" He glanced at his watch. "This scene is secure right now, until daylight. Let's say we meet at Duffy's and discuss this over a few drinks."

"You know what?" She thought for a moment. "I might just take you up on that offer."

Melville stirred his drink, watching the ice clink the sides of the glass as condensation built up and dripped down the side. He tilted up the bottom, drained it and motioned the bartender, who was cleaning glasses, for another drink.

"Easy, easy Detective."

He turned towards the velvet sounding voice and slid off the stool at the bar. "Ms. missiles and fire upon helpless villagers remotely, like it's a fucking PS3 video game, then I'm sure a vehicle can be developed the same way. I mean look at those geeks at MIT. And they already have cars parking themselves-" She stopped in mid-sentence as she watched him move her half-finished drink away. Puentez, or I mean Anna."

Her curly, wavy, brunette hair was flowing over her shoulders as her make-up accentuated her Central American features. She wore wedge toe platform sandals and a silk open collar shirt under a designer cardigan sweater with matching, tight fitting denim jeans which showed off her curves in all the right places. She slid into a stool next to him, dropped her purse in her lap, looked into his glazed eyes and smiled.

"So Anna--"

"Bartender, start me off with a double shot of tequila, Patron please."

He poured the gold liquid, set a coaster onto the polished bar and she winked at him before he walked away. She took two deep swallows, licked her glossy, full lips then set her glass back down then folded her arms.

"So rule out our rationality. Explain?"

"Well when I was observing Agent Duncan conduct his investigation, he approached me and we buried the hatchet. He started profiling the perps and went on to--"

"What was his analysis?"

"Well one was professional, clean, but the other perp, who was hunting the same exact target, interfered due to his impatience, rage and eagerness to make a serious point. He also didn't rule out a woman perp either."

They both smiled as he casually squeezed her thigh, cupped his glass and took another swig.

"He went on to describe a secret department in the Bureau that investigates unexplainable phenomenal events. The conclusion that I came up with, from his dialogue, is that we could be dealing with some type of artificial intelligence of some sorts."

She stared at him blankly, then turned towards the bartender. "Another double for me and the gentleman please."

"So what is your input Anna? I mean come on now. I've never been a guy to base anything unless I have solid facts."

The bartender set the drinks in front of them and they both simultaneously gulped down their drinks. "Well if the government can develop a drone equipped with hellfire

"Anna everything you just explained is just that. Explainable. What the Bureau is dealing with is unexplained and a phenomenal event at that."

"We need to get that agent to let us see those files."

"What you need is some rest chica."He slapped a twenty on the bar, put his arm around her and walked her out to the parking lot were a waiting yellow cab was. He opened the door and guided her into the back seat. As he closed it she put her leg out to stop it. "No, no, no, you're going to keep me company," she demanded biting her bottom lip with delight.

Melville's manhood stirred in his boxers as he looked into her hungry brown eyes then got in next to her.

She pulled off her cardigan sweater, kicked off her wedge toe platform sandals, unbuttoned her shirt then pulled off her denim jeans.

"No panties huh?" Melville said surprised as he laid naked on her queen size bed, stroking himself.

She flung her hair back, climbed on her bed towards him and straddled him. She quickly reached behind her back, unsnapped her bra and gently tossed it on the floor. He reached up and lightly squeezed her soft, plump brown breast which hung like taut lemon drops. He leaned up and sucked her hard nipples as if he was being nursed.

She playfully pushed him back on the pillows. "I know you want this kitty cat don't you?" He shook his head like a stray dog begging for a treat. "How long has it been?" she asked between kisses. He parted his lips to speak but she stopped him short with her index finger. "SSSSHHHH! Don't speak Papi, you'll just ruin the moment!"

He gripped her thighs and rotated his large hands to her ass as she opened up, extended them and allowed his pulsing flesh to enter her tight, wet folds of Latina pleasure. She gyrated and grinded her hips as if she was dancing, slipping him in and out every time. As the minutes turned into hours, she sped up and slowed down between her climax. He felt her muscles tighten and loosen with every spasm. She slowed as he stiffened then swung her thigh over him, got off then stroked him until he came all over her plump breast...

"The killer's psychological profile just doesn't add up Ms. Puentez. I mean it's almost as if he or she is a phantom. Its moves are calculated, precise and personal. The wounds inflicted by the killer are serial in nature but yet accidental to an extent--"

"Precisely Detective. The intent is as if it's a state of retribution."

"Like court is being held in the streets."

"Literally," they both said at the same time.

Melville looked at her for a few seconds then directed his attention back on the freeway. He noticed an abandoned, dark-colored sedan with multiple tickets, smothered with dirt and bird shit. "Why would someone just leave a perfectly good automobile on the side of the highway like this?"

"Dealership plates," Melville grunted as he pulled behind it and stepped out on the graveled shoulder, walked around the vehicle and leaned closer to view the vin numbers on the dashboard.

"What is it?"

"I can't get a good look. I may have to—"

"Why are we doing C.H.P.'s job?"

"There is a possibility…" Melville said as he walked to his trunk, opened it, grabbed a flat, long piece of metal with a hook on one end and a handle on the other. He then side-stepped to the passenger side of the car and slid it between the window and door.

"A possibility of what?"

The door lock popped up and he grabbed the door handle to open it. "That this could be our suspect's car."

What are the odds of that? she thought to herself.

Melville leaned over and unlocked the driver's side door for her to get in. The new leather squeaked from his movement. Wind rushed in from passing traffic as Puentez began to climb in. She adjusted her side arm holster then gripped the steering wheel to steady herself. Melville flipped through documents in the glove compartment when the dashboard console lit up.

The driver's side door slammed shut with so much force that it was as if someone broadsided or side-swiped the car. "AHHHH oh my god my leg!"

The door continued to open and shut several more times as she struggled to get out, but the car door pinned her in between the opening. Finally wiggling free, she hobbled into oncoming traffic.

"Anna nooooo!"

The door shut and locked as an eighteen wheeler exploded her like a bag of blood and slices of flesh. Her lower extremities separated from her torso and decorated the diesel truck's front wheels. Brain matter and skull fragments were embedded in the truck's vented gri11 as it jackknifed and skidded one hundred yards to a long stop.

Melville looked in shock at the horrific scene, not noticing the sedan's engine start and the shifter switch to drive. It peeled out, fishtailing into heavy traffic, cutting drivers off and sending cars crashing into the center divider. He quickly tried to unlock the door. *Nothing*, he thought to himself.

He then jumped into the driver's seat, pushed the brake pedal to the floor and pulled the emergency brake. "Nothing!"

Cars passed by in a blur as he gripped the steering wheel, but it slid through his palms like he was on the losing end of tug-of-war for his life. The freeway curved as he saw the bridge quickly approaching and he felt the car increase its speed.

Gears shifted and the speedometer needle moved past one hundred like a second-hand on a stop watch. Cars hit their blinkers and switched lanes. He fumbled for his seat belt, buckling himself in as it swerved left then a hard right. There was silence as the car barrel rolled over the bridge, sending pieces of cement and steel girders splashing into the Pacific Ocean below.

The Buick gyrated in mid-air like a top spun at its axis. Melville knew his chances of surviving the impact were slim and he was expecting his death within seconds, which seemed like an eternity. The whiplash of the impact was absorbed by the deployed air bag, knocking him unconscious. Sea water filled the car slowly as the ocean current made it drift to the middle of the bridge.

Melville blinked a few timed to refocus but he didn't realize why he was in the car full of ice cold water, up to his neck. Blood from his head wound turned the water to a crimson red as he tried to release the seat belt, but it wouldn't.

I got to shoot my way out of here, he thought to himself. Grabbing his .40 caliber Sig Sauer from his shoulder holster, he cocked it, held his breath and went under. He aimed at the lock and fired a shot, releasing it instantly. The car was fully submerged and dropping quickly in darkness. Melville crouched on the seat, aimed at the windshield and released the whole clip.

Every bullet only spiderwebbed the reinforced glass as the guns explosion echoed. He kicked the front windshield several times until it folded and snapped. He inhaled one last deep breath and went under water as the car descended deep to the ocean's floor. With his lungs burning, he dropped his gun and looked at the crystal oasis above him as he swam towards it kicking off his shoes.

Sea water spewed out of his mouth. Coughing, streams of blood mixed with mucus ran down his chin as he treaded water. Finally catching his breath, he gathered enough strength and looked up towards the bridge hundreds of feet above him and saw specks of people pointing down at him as if saying he's alive.

He contorted his body, slicked back his gray hair which stuck to his face, swam to the nearest shore and laid on his stomach covered in pieces of kelp, caked sand and soaked clothes. Foam from the waves lapped at his body as he listened to them. The Buick's high beams flickered several times as it rested on the ocean floor.

ABOUT THE AUTHOR

Henry "Moufpeez" Williams is an accomplished recording artist and songwriter (www.Amazon.com/Moufpeez). He owned and managed Moufpeez Graphic Design in the Northern Bay Area. Now he is an aspiring literary writer of Crime Drama Urban Fiction novels, poems, short stories and self-help books for prisoners.

Born in Vallejo California, Henry grew up in Fairfield California and the Bay Area streets became his Ivy League University. A few run-ins with the law as a juvenile landed him in the gladiator school of the California Youth Authority where he evolved into a writer and educated himself.

Moufpeez is now planting his pen in the fertile soil of the Urban Crime Drama market. *The Scraper: "Where Evil Meets the Road"* is a successful, lucrative attempt to wake readers' game up on his creative writing talent. Self-taught with the ink pen and paper, he developed his craft with a charismatic, believable style, bringing his vivid storytelling to readers from a different point of view.

Moufpeez has also created a Non-profit 5O1(c)(3) called: Moufpeez Book Project. Their mission is to invest everything in providing readers in prison with free literature and educational material.

Thank you. God bless and everything comes to those who hustle while they wait. Be expecting a new book and music featured on Moufpeez Publishing L.L.C.

Contact Information
e•mail: therealmoufpeez@gmail.com
www.facebook.com/Moufpeez
twitter:@Koufpeez

Stamps For Champs L.L.C.
Attn: ABOOKYOUWANT c/o H. Williams
P.O. Box 16141 Rumford, R.I. 02916
www.facebook.com/Stampsforchamps
twitter: @Stampsforchamps
e•mail: Stampsforchamps@gmail.com

Stamps for Champs is an ongoing fundraiser for kids who are separated from their parents. Kid's whose military parents are deployed overseas. Kid's with parents who are recovering addicts or even possibly incarcerated for whatever reason.

These kids did not volunteer for the position they are currently in. A letter can brighten their day with a smile, and get them through the next day knowing that someone actually cares. You will not only be helping young 4-year-old Samuel, but you will also be helping thousands of other kids whose parents are displaced.

Please donate stamps to "Stamps For Champs."

THERE IS A LITTLE CHAMPION IN ALL OF US

Made in the USA
San Bernardino, CA
08 June 2020

72990475R00156